The Prince of Keegan Bay

VERONICA HELEN HART

CHAMPAGNE BOOK GROUP

The Prince of Keegan Bay

This is a work of fiction. The characters, incidents and dialogues in this book are of the author's imagination and are not to be construed as real. Any resemblance to actual events or persons, living or dead, is completely coincidental.

Published by Champagne Book Group
2373 NE Evergreen Avenue, Albany OR 97321 U.S.A.

~ ~ ~

Third Edition 2020

ISBN: 978-1-653801-14-5

Cover Art by Chris Holmes

www.champagnebooks.com

Version_1

Thank you, Bob— "At times our own light goes out and is rekindled by a spark from another person. Each of us has cause to think with deep gratitude of those who have lighted the flame within us." —Albert Schweitzer

Chapter One

"Give me those." I reached for the opera glasses Violet gripped as she peered at Jessica's house.

"She's getting out of the car."

"I can see that without the glasses. I want to know what's in those grocery bags."

Violet lowered the glasses and glared at me. "How do you know she's carrying grocery bags?"

I pointed out the window. "If you'll take a look you'll see those white objects in her hands. She goes out every third day and comes back with at least three of them. Nobody who lives alone needs that much food. She's up to something."

Violet leaned her chubby elbows on the windowsill and peered once more through the glasses. "Wal-Mart. Right around the corner. She used to ride her bicycle to the store. Wonder why she takes the car now?"

"For the very reason I just said. She's up to something. Harboring somebody in that house. And I checked the register in the office—no guests registered at her place." That is one of the many park rules, we must register any overnight guests and they aren't permitted to stay more than thirty days.

This whole adventure never would have happened if I hadn't lost my husband, Barclay. Honestly, I lost him on a trip to the Galapagos Islands four years ago. We were scuba diving off a small boat with a large group of tourists. For a while it seemed like the whole world was looking for him, even though it was only the other divers, professional and amateur. Personally, I suspected he climbed into a different boat and didn't even notice he wound up with a group of Finnish research scientists, or maybe they were Norwegians. I never learned which. Anyway, ever since I've been living alone, I've taken to having afternoon refreshments with my neighbor, Violet Hathaway.

My life had degenerated to this, an old woman with nothing more to do than spy on my neighbors. It wasn't always like this. For years Barclay and I worked together on his research papers and books. When he retired officially, I began my own attempts at writing. After we moved into Keegan Bay Park, an "age qualified" community south of Daytona Beach, I found a writing group. We took turns meeting at each other's homes. Barclay, on the other hand, was content to write his memoirs in our second bedroom-turned-office. Occasionally we took trips to far off parts of the world. He would investigate the flora and fauna; I would take notes and then sell travel articles.

Unlike our former home, a seventeen room Victorian house in New England, this house is a large doublewide. Residents in Keegan Bay Park are asked to refer to them as manufactured homes, but they are trailers arranged in a well landscaped park-like setting with meandering streets lined with live oaks and palm trees. Lovely as the house is, it is still a two bedroom, one story home that could be blown away by a strong wind. The fact that it hasn't disappeared in any of the hurricanes these past eight years is more a testament to the engineers who arranged it on the lot rather than to sound construction.

Here on Keegan Bay Central Court it is my assigned task to keep an eye on the neighborhood, a task Violet helps me to take seriously.

Violet is a few years older than I, several inches shorter and many pounds heavier, though to be truthful, ever since Barclay's disappearance and my new habit of afternoon "tea", I have been adding a few pounds to my own usually slender figure. She lives immediately next door and likes to come over to my house to chat and share a spot of tea in the afternoons. She'll often pick up an object from a shelf in my living room and ask where we had brought it from. I could then spend quality time explaining the artifact, when and where we'd discovered it, whether in a shop or on a beach or poking up from the ground on a remote jungle path.

Two weeks ago, on a Monday, I observed that Jessica Robbins, a slight woman several years older than Violet had changed her routine. Normally she walks to the swimming pool at eleven in the morning and then returns home for lunch to watch her soaps at one. By her own accounting, she then naps from three until four, checks her email and then communicates with her daughter and northern friends on her computer until it is time to make supper. Three evenings each week she plays cards or bingo at the clubhouse, and on Saturdays she attends the Elks' Club for Bingo. Sundays she goes to church. When necessary, she rides her bicycle to the grocery store. That had been her routine for the year and a half since she moved into Keegan Bay Park. But, two weeks ago she stopped doing all those things. When I noticed the change in Jessica's schedule, I went to the community manager, Carol, and asked in as off-hand manner I could manage, "Is Jessica Robbins all right?"

"All right? Why are you asking, Doll?" My name is really Doris, but my family called me Doll from the day I was born and the name stuck. I'm the least likely looking Doll you'd ever want to meet, but there it is.

"Just wondering, that's all. She hasn't gone down to the pool for a couple of weeks and she pretty much told me to mind my own business when I questioned her a few days ago." That statement was not entirely truthful. I only asked Jessica when I saw her putting out her garbage three days ago, "Where have you been keeping yourself, Jess?"

She'd replied, rather aloof, I thought, "I'm not going out much these days." After which she scurried as fast as her little body could move back into her house.

Carol raised her eyebrows, which I took as a signal that perhaps I should listen to Jessica.

I shrugged. If they wanted people to be court captains, then they ought to listen to them when they suggest something might be amiss. Like the night old Andrea shot Harry and nearly killed him when she learned he'd been visiting the Purple Onion up on Ridgewood. That's the place in Holly Hill where they have the naked girls serving drinks. I told Carol that she ought to keep an eye on that couple. Ever since Andrea invited Harry to move in with her, I knew there'd be trouble. And I was right. Two eighty year old fools. She shot him in the arm and then had to spend the next six weeks catering to his every whim. Andrea sure taught him a lesson, though. As far as I know he never went back to the Purple Onion. And now the two of them ride around the park in their golf cart each afternoon like a pair of lovebirds.

So, there we were sitting in Keegan Bay Park at my front window, Violet and I, checking up on Jessica. I graciously accepted the opera glasses from her as if I hadn't been nagging her for the past twenty minutes and watched as Jessica disappeared into her house and shut the door behind her. I hadn't been able to see what she'd been hauling in those bags. Nary a hint. I'd have to wait until she went to the store again to see if I could figure out anything.

"Pity the houses next door to her are empty. In a couple of months the snowbirds will be back and maybe they can tell us something," Violet suggested.

"We can't wait that long. What if she has someone living in there who's intimidating her? Threatening her life?" I replied. "She could be dead by then. What if I get Bob to pretend he's from the pest control and say he has to check her house?" Did I mention that I was often accused of being a drama queen?

"Bob? When does a doctor have time for that sort of nonsense? He's your friend; you ought to know that." Violet picked up the glasses from the windowsill and went to refresh our drinks. Scotch for me and gin and tonic for her. Our afternoon 'tea.'

"That's just it, he's my friend."

"Friends don't send friends into danger without fair warning. What will you tell him? That you suspect your seventy-two year old neighbor is housing a desperate criminal and would he please go search the house? He'll tell you to call the police."

"If I really believed that, I would."

Violet sighed. She does that when she's exasperated with me, but this time, I knew I was right and I was determined to learn Jessica's secret. I accepted the drink, took a sip, ready to give up my watch for the day when I caught some movement across the way. Jessica's door opened.

"She's coming out again!" I snatched up the opera glasses and tried to focus before Jessica disappeared behind her house. "Taking out the garbage. She's been doing a lot more of that lately as well."

"So, ask the boys when they come around what's different about her trash." Violet likes to think of herself as bright. The "boys" work full time as the maintenance men. José is in his sixties, a pleasant fellow with a small mustache, dark tan and heavy Spanish accent. George is gray haired, in his forties and works to help pay his own lot rent here in the park. They pick up the trash, keep the pool crystalline, replace light bulbs in the clubhouse and do any odd jobs required around the place. The full timers have been working at Keegan Bay Park forever, certainly since I've been here. There is also one part time position, but that person keeps changing. The newest one, a sullen looking boy in his early thirties, never says a word. He mows, clips hedges and scowls. Amongst the three of them, they're responsible for four hundred lots as well as the grounds.

"They won't tell us anything, you know that," Violet said.

"Want to go to the movies tonight?" I asked, changing the subject. I don't think spying appealed to her today.

"I'll have to check with John." She and her husband had been together for over fifty years, fifteen of them in Keegan Bay.

"Go check with him and I'll find out what's playing."

She left and I sat down, suddenly despondent. These abrupt, overwhelming bouts of depression had been happening more and more since I haven't had Barclay around. Except for the once a week writing meetings, I haven't figured out a productive way to spend my evenings. Though Violet and I spent quite a bit of time together, I was beginning to find her company tedious. The afternoon 'teas' were enough time with her. I mentally slapped myself on the side of my head for suggesting a movie.

"He's gone off to help build another set for the theater," she said upon returning.

"Then we can have an early bird supper at the diner and catch the six thirty showing," I said with a vague attempt at enthusiasm.

"What's playing?"

I hadn't bothered checking. "I don't know, but with six theaters, something is bound to sound good. And they rotate the start times, so we'll find something we both want to see at a time that's convenient."

We saw *Nights in Rodanthe*. "Life changing events set in motion as a woman whose husband strays, seeks solace at an isolated inn." Ho-hum. And the meatloaf had been bland, too. I really ought to make a note to myself that I have seen all the plots about mixed up middle-aged people. They are no longer awe inspiring. Though I have to admit Richard Gere was easy to look at; sadly, if he looked at me all he'd see is an old lady who insists on fooling herself by dying her hair and wearing youthful clothing. I do make some effort to keep myself reasonably slim and fit, but those afternoon Scotches show up in the mid-section, especially when I go to buy new clothes and am forced to look at myself in a full-length mirror.

The next morning, knowing that Violet would sleep late after being out 'until all hours' for the movie, I took the opportunity to watch the house across the way from seven o'clock until hunger sent me in search of breakfast. Then I went on with my day, pushing Jessica and her unusual shopping habits to the back of my mind.

~ * ~

On Thursday I was completely sidetracked by an unexpected visit from my oldest son Ian, his wife Audrey, and their three offspring. He had called from the Orlando Airport. I do love my boys, but surprise visits are unsettling to say the least. They were on their way to Port Canaveral for a cruise and thought they would pop in and take me out to play miniature golf and then to dinner at the Top of Daytona, things they'd promised the children they'd do, never thinking that I might have other plans.

"But, I haven't shopped. There's no food. The least you could do is give me some advance notice!" I scolded when they arrived.

"What? You're so busy? We wanted to cheer you up. Get you out of the house for a change. It's not healthy the way you live here alone waiting for Barclay to come walking through that door."

He knew how to hurt his mother, intentional or not. "I'll have you know I went out to dinner and a movie two nights ago. You think I sit in here three hundred and sixty five days a year waiting for you to fly south and take me out?" My heart raced with anger at his lack of understanding.

"Dinner and a movie?" Audrey said with a twinkle in her eye and, I suspect, hoping to change the subject. I hadn't considered that she'd think I had a date.

After taking a moment to regroup, I smiled my best enigmatic smile. "I don't want to say in case it doesn't come to anything."

"Grandma has a boyfriend!" she chortled gleefully.

Donnie, Robbie and Mike, my grandsons, sat like lumps on the sofa staring at the television, each one of them disappointed that the wireless world hadn't yet reached the interior of my house. I told them if they wanted to text message or speak on their cell phones they'd have to either stand in the southwest corner of the dining room near the window or do it outside. The center of the courtyard provided the best reception. Though they'd come south for the hot weather, not one of them was eager to stand out in the sun to talk on the phone. Not one of them wanted to go to the swimming pool either, with "all those old pod people."

"Pod people?" I asked.

Audrey provided the explanation. "There was a movie years ago called "Cocoon" where the old people stood in the pool and then were sucked up and became young again. Anyway, we called them the pod people and that's how I referred to the folks here when I first came to visit. The kids remembered."

Nice kids, honor roll students, so they tell me, but teenagers just the same.

By the time they left for their ship two days later, I had heaps of linens to wash, blow-up beds to deflate and a refrigerator to replenish. I hardly thought of Jessica the entire time.

If I have to be honest, I didn't think of her at all because I was either busy or exhausted. What triggered the next event happened because I had to get up at three o'clock one morning to use the bathroom. Feeling restless, I wandered around my darkened house, guided by the light from the streetlamp, enjoying the clean quiet of my home when a movement outside caught my eye. I pulled the curtain aside and lifted a slat in the blinds. A car moved in my direction from the house across the way. It turned right onto the main street leading to the highway. I saw Jessica. Why would she be going out at three o'clock in the morning?

I went into the kitchen and made myself a cup of tea, real tea, and brought it back to the window and parked myself for the duration. What could Jessica need so desperately that she had to go out in the middle of the night? My opera glasses rested in the same spot, undamaged by the children when they had used them to study the little lizards in the shrubs out front. I peeked around the neighborhood. All was quiet; houses dark. Of the nine houses in our courtyard, only four were currently occupied. One was for sale, the other four would come alive between late November and January when the snowbirds arrived, in this case, Canadians.

The snowbirds happily maintained two residences, one up north and one here in the park, flitting from one to the other as the weather changed, frequently hopping up and down the coast for weddings, birthdays or other life altering celebrations and ceremonies. These days, it was more often to attend funerals. But, tonight our Keegan Bay Central Court remained tranquil.

I was considering a third cup of tea, not Johnny Walker, when the car returned. I picked up my glasses and waited. First Jessica stepped out of her car, leaving that door open, and looked around as if expecting to be spied upon. I dared not move my glasses lest she see a reflection from the streetlamp. I held my breath as her gaze passed over my house. She appeared satisfied and stepped up to her kitchen door and unlocked it. She opened it so that now there was only a small gap between the car door and her kitchen door for me to view her activity.

She leaned into the back seat of the car and pulled out an enormous bundle. Big enough to carry – a baby? That's exactly what it looked like, a baby's car seat. By her actions, it appeared that the car seat was filled with something. What else would one put in a baby car seat except a baby? Where on earth would Jessica have found a baby? And why was it at her house?

Chapter Two

Should I tell Violet about my discovery? I wondered while lying in bed, heart racing, waiting for a good time to get up. If I arose too early there'd be nobody to talk to. The Today Show began at seven. That would be something to do. Barclay and I used to watch it together, but frankly, the cheerful chatter that early in the morning had become annoying. I could always check the old movie channel and have my granola while watching Bogart or Edward G. Robinson. I opted to remain in bed until nine o'clock and didn't turn on the television at all. Instead I dropped five CD's into the player and let classical music set at "shuffle" take over my day as I lounged and tried to read a Linda Fairstein novel. I couldn't focus. In desperation I called Violet over early for tea.

She arrived on my doorstep at one thirty.

"I'm so glad you called." She bustled in, wearing her lavender floral print dress with the white lace collar. "I was beginning to get worried. Is everything all right? Recovered from your children's visit? How are they? Have you heard from them?"

"One question at time!" I laughed. "Yes, everything is all right. I'm pretty much recovered, just have to clean up the bathrooms and as to how they are, I suspect by now they're somewhere snorkeling along a coral reef, either having the time of their lives or wishing they'd gone to Disneyworld."

"So," Violet said with a shrug of her shoulder and tilt of her fluffy white-haired head. She indicated the direction of Jessica's place. "Anything new?"

You might wonder if Violet is my next door neighbor, why she couldn't see for herself. Let me explain. The houses are set in circles or curlicues, streets and lanes that run off the main Keegan Bay Way. A clever designer packed these four hundred homes in amongst the tropical foliage creating an illusion of privacy. Through an odd configuration of growth, I have a clear view right across to Jessica's house.

"I do have something to report," I replied. There are others who are far more intrepid than I, at learning the gossip and much happier to pass it along. Though since Barclay disappeared, I do tend to watch out the window and inspect our court for discrepancies, I rarely know what's going on. So today, before telling Violet of my discovery I first poured our drinks, arranged some crackers and cheese on a small platter and set us up at the window.

Violet knew I had something juicy by the addition of the afternoon snack that also happened to be leftovers from the kids. Crackers with squirt-on cheese. To my surprise, the healthy food, vegetables, salad and fruit, they demolished. I fixed us each a cracker and teased the moment a bit further by eating one of the atrocities first. I wiped my mouth with a paper napkin, took a deep breath and said, "She has a baby."

Violet's blue eyes widened making them look even more owl-like behind her old-fashioned cataract lenses. I watched as her mind processed the information. Surprise first, followed by disbelief. She pursed her lips. "She's seventy-two. She can't have a baby."

Her expression dared me to contradict her. I happily did. "I saw it. It was in a car carrier thing. She took it out during the night."

She leaned toward me, wide eyed. "Are you going to report her?"

"No. And don't you. I haven't even considered reporting her. After all, unless the infant remains in there beyond a few months, what harm can come?"

"But, it's against the rules to have babies or dogs in the park."

"It's definitely not a dog."

"You do know that old Leona Anderson has a Pekingese that she walks late at night, don't you? Everyone knows it, except Carol. No one complains even though it's against the rules."

"Well, Jessica's neighbors haven't complained either. They're all still in Canada. As far as I know I'm the only person who has seen it. I'm more concerned with her taking it out in the middle of the night."

"And you're sure it's a baby?" Violet wasn't convinced.

I ignored her skepticism. "What if it's sick? Why else take a baby out at that time?"

"Assuming it is a baby, if it's sick you'd take it to an emergency room or to urgent care in the middle of the night." Violet hesitated as she thought it through.

"Right. But, it would have to be suddenly injured or spiking a high fever," I finished for her.

"I agree. We shouldn't tell anyone until we know more. We'll keep this to ourselves for the time being." She wrapped both her hands around her glass and hugged it to her bosom.

"There's plenty of time to notify management if it becomes necessary. Maybe she's only babysitting for a little while. But she did buy an awful lot of groceries." I could feel myself frowning in concentration.

"Maybe the baby's parents are living there, too."

"Impossible," I decided. "Unless they're criminals and can't afford to be seen at all. There's been no evidence of other people living there. No, she bought a lot of food because she plans to have the baby there a long time. Bags of diapers are bulky. I wonder how many of those disposable diapers a baby goes through in a week. Remember smelly diaper pails? Rinsing the stinky ones in the toilet? All they do now is throw them away."

"Does Jessica have any children?" Violet asked.

"I think just the one daughter up north." As I didn't play cards or Bingo, I had never chatted with her other than a polite greeting in passing. "The people she played cards with would know more about her. I'll call Vivian Todd." Vivian is the superior information gatherer for Keegan Bay Park. Generally, if something is going on, she knows about it.

I called. She had been resting in anticipation of this evening's bridge game, but said she wouldn't mind answering a few questions. "Don't mention that woman's name in front of me. She didn't show up three weeks ago and we haven't seen her since! When I called her she told me she had to take a break from everything, cards, bingo. She hasn't even come to a single dinner, not that *you*'d know. When's the last time *you* came to anything at the clubhouse?"

"I was at the last homeowner's meeting," I replied defensively. "What I really wanted to know, Vivian, is did she look ill or had she been behaving strangely prior to quitting everything?"

"Why? What's happened to her?" I could almost see her ears prick up like a horse seeing a carrot.

"Nothing. I've missed seeing her ride her bicycle out to the clubhouse and when I called her, she seemed a little depressed." Mention that someone in the park is depressed and the residents gaggle on about their health problems. If the subject is male, it's his prostate, if it's a woman, there are a myriad of diseases they choose from.

"Ah, depressed." The horse took the carrot. "Now that you mention it, she did say she hadn't heard from her daughter in a long time. She was concerned about her. But, you know Jessica, she's always concerned about someone or something. She's a real worry wart."

That didn't sound like the Jessica I knew, but we each have our own versions of our acquaintances and friends. "A worry wart. Do you know where her daughter lives? Up north?"

"Oh, no. She lives in Port Orange, maybe six miles away. She works as a waitress in one of those new boutique cafes. That's all I know. If you do talk to Jessica, tell her we're not talking to her. She really had some nerve walking out on us without any explanation."

That was the extent of the information I was going to get from Vivian Todd.

"One child," I said to Violet. "A daughter. Hmm."

"What?" Violet stood and stretched her short body, getting the kinks out.

"What, what?"

"You went 'hmm'." She mimicked my facial expression with furrowed brows and pinched lips.

"Maybe it's the daughter hiding out from her husband," I said. "Maybe they're in the middle of a messy divorce and she doesn't want anyone to know where she is. Maybe he threatened to take her child away from her."

"That's a lot of maybe's and none of it makes sense."

"And why not?"

"Her mother's house is the first place anyone would look." Violet pushed the squirter and created little acorns of fake cheese on a row of crackers. "Have one."

"But there's a baby at her house and we know it isn't hers. A seventy-two year-old woman giving birth would be a big deal. It would have been in the papers and all over the news and internet like when that sixty-some year old woman who took hormones."

"I don't take the paper," Violet said dismissively. "I'm going to walk over there and ask her outright where she got a baby from."

I dropped the cracker and held up my hands like a traffic cop. "Don't! You can't be snooping around in other people's lives. If she wanted us to know she has a baby there, she would have told us. I know we're not close, but our houses are."

"She might be in trouble." Violet shook herself free and straightened her dress, tugging it down over her ample hips. "You can wait here or I'll call you when I get back."

"I'll sit right here and watch for you. How long do you want me to give you before I call for help?" I folded my arms across my chest and glared at her.

"Thank you, Doll. That's sweet, but I don't think I'll be in danger from Jessica or an infant."

"But the other one? The person we suspect is in there with her? The reason we've been watching the house?" I stood, towering over her and squinted fiercely.

She hesitated. Her voice quivered a little when she said, "Give me five minutes in the house and then you can come looking for me."

"You could be dead by then, dead and chopped up into little pieces and thrown into the garbage or flushed down the toilet. I've read books where things like that happened."

"Books?" she squeaked, visibly shaken by the statement. "More than one? How do you sleep at night reading that kind of stuff?"

"Not well, to be sure. If I see anyone scramble out the other side of the house when you go in, I'll know something's up."

Violet returned to her seat, hands folded and fumbling in her lap. "Look, you read those murder books, why don't you go over there and I'll watch from here?"

Having just unnerved myself, I tried to put myself in the place of a real detective instead of a bored, snoopy old woman. We believed that Jessica had a baby in her house and though we weren't the closest of friends, I would have thought she'd at least tell us so we wouldn't report her to the office. Now that we knew, before reporting her to the office, I thought it would be better to get the facts first. Subconsciously I had completely disabled Violet. She could never walk over to that house by herself now.

I stood up. "I'll go. You watch. If I'm not out of there in ten minutes, you call the police. "

I left before I could come up with any more reasons to remain uninvolved, secure in my own home.

Sun glistened off the rear window of Jessica's red Taurus. I eased myself around it to the kitchen door and tapped before I could change my mind. What if her daughter was visiting? Jessica was entitled like the rest of us to have a guest up to thirty days, an entire month.

I braced myself for whoever would answer the door.

Chapter Three

Several miles and a whole world away Moira Robbins drove along the roughly paved road through the rundown trailer park toward her latest hideaway, still angry with herself for getting fired and then for the traffic stop. She'd bought the old Honda so she could drive around unnoticed, never realizing it had a burned out taillight. As for the job, it was her first since college more than ten years ago. Early in her shift she'd dumped a tray of beers onto a customer; the last in a series of blunders as far as her boss was concerned. Then, to make matters worse, when she was stopped by the officer, she'd handed him her real identification instead of the fake one she'd paid so much for in New York. When she rolled down the window, the beer soaked t-shirt made him suspicious.

"Step out of the car, ma'am."

She knew she was in trouble as she waited by the back of her car for him to check the computer in his car. Cars sped by the busy interstate, some slowing to ogle the tall brunette in the tight shorts and t-shirt. Perspiration dripped into her eyes, but she was afraid to move.

He sauntered back to her within minutes and handed her the driver's license. "Just do me a favor, ma'am, and get that light fixed." With that, he saluted and returned to his vehicle then waited for her to pull back into traffic.

Puzzled at being let off without even a Breathalyzer test or being made to walk a straight line, she focused on the road ahead, desperate to keep her hands from trembling on the steering wheel.

As she stepped into her single-wide trailer furnished in Early Thrift Shop, an odd odor made her hesitate before entering, but then she realized, in such close quarters, it was probably the beer still damp on her tee shirt. She threw her purse on the divan. Dishes were still in the sink from two nights ago, the last time she'd eaten at home. Ignoring them, she headed for the bathroom at the back of the unit to take a shower. There would be no late night trip to the Wal-Mart parking lot to spend a few moments with her baby tonight. But her heart was breaking every day she couldn't see little Hamid, Hamilton Robbins on his American birth certificate. She didn't think they'd figured that one out, yet.

Tomorrow, she'd go on another job hunt. She could try a dress shop, though as a salesclerk she might overawe women with her size. Being as tall as she was, six feet one inch, and weighing in at one sixty, her friends told her she often came across as pretty intimidating.

Her minuscule shower made her feel claustrophobic, so it was only five minutes before she stood in her tiny bedroom changing into her pajamas. The peculiar odor lingered.

She slid between the six hundred thread count Egyptian cotton sheets, one of the few luxuries she refused to give up, and turned out her light. The German Shepherds next door barked.

Every time any of the neighbor's dogs barked she became alert, waiting for men in black hoods to slide through her windows to slit her throat. Though most of the other neighbors complained about the big shepherds living in such close quarters, she was grateful for their existence. Bruno and Maxwell had become her best friends and the nicest part of their watchfulness was that she didn't have to take care of them. Unfortunately, they not only barked at strangers, they barked at any moving, living thing. Stray raccoons, squirrels, armadillos, or even moles poking their heads up from their burrows set them off in a barking frenzy.

"To sleep; perchance to dream," she sighed. "Hamid, Hamid, Hamid. There is something amiss in Florida. I wish we could go back in time and start over. I miss you."

The dogs settled down. She drifted off to sleep, only to wake again suddenly, sitting bolt upright, her heart racing. The German Shepherds barked right outside her bedroom window. Her closet door creaked. Someone was in the room with her. Moving slowly, she reached under her pillow to pull her Smith and Wesson Model 66 from under her pillow. She slid it down by her side, index finger on the trigger. Perspiration oozed out of every pore of her body. She dared not breathe. In the faint glow of the moonlight, she detected a dark form move toward the door to the hallway.

Her mind raced, seeing black-clad men in every corner of the room, swarming over her, smothering her. Maybe her mother was right, nobody was looking for her; it was her over-active imagination and this phantom in her room was part of another bad dream. In one dream little Ham was being tossed from one villain to the other across her bed just out of her reach.

The dogs' barking turned to low growls. They sounded like

they were almost in her bedroom Tears wet her face. *I can't go on! I can't do this, Hamid. Why did you have to die? Why?* A silent question, a useless cry into the void. Should she shoot the intruder now? Though she'd learned how to use a gun as a young girl, she'd never actually shot at any living thing.

Whoever it was didn't realize she'd awakened. The odor she'd detected earlier permeated her claustrophobic bedroom. The shadow moved on into the hallway. She slowly leaned forward to watch the silhouette advance toward her kitchen.

Sliding quietly from the bed, she eased her way to the hall and stuck her head out far enough to see what the man was doing. Using a small flashlight to guide him, he had reached the desk connected to the end of her kitchen counter and was rummaging through the drawer. He was dressed in black, looking like a paper silhouette against the light. Her heart stopped.

She gasped.

He dropped the papers and turned toward her. "You will be coming with me," he said with a trace of a middle-eastern accent, reminding her of Hamid. "And now I have the evidence of your child, I shall find him and be richly rewarded."

He couldn't possibly have any evidence. There was none to be found in her trailer. It could only mean that he'd been following her and had seen her at the parking lot, then trailed her mother. *He knew where Hamilton was living.* She caught the glint of a gun barrel pointed in her direction. With each portion of a second feeling like a minute, she contemplated her own death, thought of her son as an orphan, and knew she had to surprise this intruder before he became aware that she carried a gun.

She raised the Smith and Wesson and pulled the trigger.

Chapter Four

That same afternoon while Moira was busy getting herself fired, I was approaching her mother's kitchen door to find out what was going on.

Jessica pulled the curtain aside and peeked out. If I hadn't been watching for her I never would have noticed the curtain move. Whatever was going on, the poor dear was behaving awfully paranoid. I smiled in as friendly a manner as I could muster.

She opened the door as far as the security chain would permit. "Hello, Doll," she said in a flat, dull tone. Not exactly the warm welcome I'd envisioned.

"Jessica! I haven't seen you for ages," I sort of lied, after all, observing her wasn't the same as "seeing" her. "Are you all right? Is there anything I can do for you?"

The door slammed. I wondered if I ought to turn around and go home or try again, but before I could make up my mind, the security chain slid free and the door reopened. "I am so tired, Doll. Come in."

I stepped into the dark coolness of her kitchen and waited while she replaced the chain and turned the deadbolt in the door. The blinds were drawn. Baby bottles littered the kitchen counters along with boxes of baby cereal and little jars of fruit. Jessica must have forgotten she'd left them out because she stepped in front of them as if to shield them from view.

"Perhaps there is something you could do. I—I don't know where to begin." Her eyes were red, whether from sleeplessness or crying, I couldn't tell.

"It's all right, Jess. I saw you last night. Not on purpose," I quickly added. "I was up going to the bathroom and happened to look out as you came home. You have a baby. I'm impressed. I didn't think it could happen at our age." My attempt at humor.

"Don't be ridiculous, Doll. Just come inside." The humor ignored, I followed her dutifully into the living room. "Can I get you a drink? A glass of wine? A soda?"

"Nothing for me, but you go ahead."

"No. Can't drink these days. Too much responsibility, you know." She sank into the folds of a large overstuffed chair, nearly disappearing; she was such a tiny woman.

"No, I don't know. So, what's going on? Who's the baby?"

Her body stiffened and she leaned forward in the chair. For a moment I thought she planned to throw me out, having changed her mind about inviting me in. Then her lower lip quivered and she blurted, "He's my grandson." And having said those words, she broke down and sobbed, pulling tissues from a box on a nearby table. Unsure what to say or do, I went into the kitchen and poured a glass of iced tea for her and returned, waiting for her story.

After a few more snuffles she began. "His legal name is Hamilton Robbins. Moira, my daughter, was married in Switzerland, but he was born in upstate New York."

So far, I didn't understand her nightly excursions. I relaxed, trying to be patient until she could compose herself and continue. With a quick glance at my watch, I hoped Violet wasn't keeping too careful track of the time.

"She never took the time to register her marriage here in the United States and never bothered to change her name on her passport and driver's license, so when Hamilton was born, she gave him her own name to protect him."

I listened with some skepticism, having been in a senior park for a few years, I know how old people can ramble and confuse events. "Protect him from what?"

"Her husband's family. Kidnappers. Even terrorists."

She looked so bleak and miserable I wanted to hug her, but she sat so rigidly straight, I was afraid I'd crack her in half. "Then I can assume her husband is wealthy? Um... can you excuse me for a minute? I promised to meet Violet soon and I just want to let her know I'll be a little late," I said as I pulled my cell phone from my pocket and prayed it was charged.

After letting Violet know that Jessica and I were engaged in conversation and assuring her that I'd fill her in later, I slapped the phone closed and looked expectantly at Jessica. "So, terrorists are after her child? Where is her husband?"

"His private jet crashed last year in New Jersey. January twelfth. He never knew he was going to be a father. She'd only learned that day and planned to tell him that night." At this, tears trickled down her cheeks, highlighting the deeply etched wrinkles in her skin.

"Take your time," I said soothingly, the way people do on

television when someone is confronted with great sadness.

"They were married in two thousand."

"How old is the baby?"

"Hamid died earlier this year," she repeated as if she still didn't believe it herself.

Totally confused, I took Jessica's hand and asked, "Hamid? Is that Swiss? And why is the baby living here with you?"

Jessica sighed, a sigh too large for her small size. "He was Middle Eastern," she went on. "Moira met him during her post graduate studies in Kushawa."

"I don't think I've heard of that one. Where is it?"

Jessica smiled weakly. She'd heard the question a thousand times. "It's a little country on the north coast of the Arabian Peninsula, between the United Arab Emirates and Oman. Right on the Persian Gulf, beautiful little country."

I reconsidered that glass of wine she'd offered; this was going to be a doozy of a story, but I said, "Go on."

"He was enormously wealthy, part of the royal family. We had a wonderful life. I traveled with them—at their invitation—to all parts of the world. When I said I really would like to have my own home in Florida to retire to, he immediately hired an architect to build a mansion for me. It would be filled with servants so I'd never have to lift a finger. But I explained that I wanted to be in a small community where I could have friends and still be independent. When I found this park, he bought this house for me. He would have bought the entire park, but I told him that wouldn't be right. I wanted to live my own life here without ten servants rushing to my side every time I lifted a hand to blow my nose." As if to prove a point, she plucked another tissue from the box and blew her nose. No servants appeared to help her.

"Ah." I never considered how inconvenient it could be to be enormously wealthy. Imagine, ten servants rushing to my side at the same time.

"He said he wanted a son but for years she didn't get pregnant. She was having too much fun with all that money. And that was fine with me, too. When she was little, Emmett and I couldn't give her much, but we did adore her. She was a quiet girl, something of a misfit at school. Though Emmett tried to impress on her how beautiful she was, she felt awkward around the other children. You know how small towns can be."

"What made her so awkward?" I was picturing some deformity and was prepared to be angry on her behalf even though I'd never laid eyes on her.

"Tall. She's six feet, one inch tall and beautiful, though she'd never believe it. Look at the photos over there."

I pushed myself out of the soft, cushioned chair and went to the bookcase where several framed photos stood on the tidy, dust free shelves. I picked up a photo of a young woman wearing a graduation cap and gown. She had an oval face with pronounced cheekbones, a lovely smile with beautifully even teeth, and penetrating green eyes surrounded by thick dark lashes. The eyes were framed by neatly arched eyebrows. Her father was right. Moira was a beautiful girl.

"She graduated from Colgate University. Through her own efforts she earned her degree in history and then went on for her Masters in Archeology. She went on a dig in Kushawa. That's when she met Hamid—he was teaching archeology."

"I see." At the moment I didn't care, I was mainly curious about how she came to have the baby living in her house and wondering what an 'enormously wealthy' widow was doing dumping her kid on her elderly mother in a, no matter how you try to dress it up, trailer park.

Jessica sighed. "Emmett and I did everything we could to protect her from the ignorant children. Luckily, she did enjoy learning. She would come home from school anxious to get her homework done and then she'd help me with supper. She rarely played with other kids. So, she went from Daddy's protection to Hamid's protection."

"It's what most women did when we were young."

"It seemed so magical at the time. Our little girl, just like Grace Kelly growing up to be a princess. And Moira was equally as beautiful and elegant as Princess Grace. Except for the red hair. And Hamid was no Prince Rainier."

Leaving the photo on the bookcase, I returned to my chair and tried prompting her to get back to the baby. "Where are her wedding photos?"

"She asked me to hide them for the time being. It was only a simple, civil ceremony. Within weeks of the wedding he dropped his work with the university. No more archaeology. They spent most of their time traveling, skiing, yachting and doing those things you see the so called 'beautiful people' do. I wondered how much fun could a couple have, but she seemed happy enough. Anyway, all her life she felt out of place being such a big girl. Hamid stood well over six feet tall, a handsome devil he was, and he made her feel special and beautiful. I wanted to like him."

I waited silently. What could I say? She wiped a tear and continued.

"According to Moira, even though he was the eldest, he had so many brothers that no one cared whether or not they had children."

Although fascinated by her story, I still wanted to know what it had to do with the child being left in her house. "So, Moira became pregnant and your not-so-princely son-in-law died shortly after." I had to keep pulling her back.

"The NTSB couldn't find any reason for the plane to have crashed. Or not to have crashed. The case is still open." Jessica raised then dropped her hands back into her lap as if to demonstrate the plane going down. "The end of a dream.

"When he died," she continued, "I went to her and together we went to Kushawa. She was crushed; I'd never seen her like that. We went through the funeral ceremonies and grieving together with that large family. Nothing left to bury. She was sick the entire time, even to the point of throwing up on the prince's carpet in the official throne room. Talk about embarrassed! I didn't yet know the cause of her sickness. She hadn't confided in me, her own mother. During the official ceremonies, I stood in the background behind the other women."

Based on my own travels with Barclay, I had no trouble picturing this tiny woman, probably dressed in black, hiding in the shadows of a palatial room behind a line of traditionally garbed women.

"And then?"

"I returned here to my little home. Hamid had bought it the year before. Then Moira called me in February to tell me she was pregnant. But she wouldn't let me know where she was staying. She said she hadn't let anyone else know because she was frightened."

"Of what?"

"The KARP."

I leaned back in my chair and looked at her for a moment. "You're going to have to explain that."

"KARP stands for Kushawan Alliance of Royal Princes. Moira explained it to me before she left." And then, as if fearing she'd been speaking too openly and loudly, Jessica leaned forward and whispered. "She was afraid that they'd found out about the baby. She had to abandon everything."

"Why?" I whispered back at her. "What does she think the royal princes would do?"

"Keep your voice down! She did everything she could to keep her pregnancy and the baby's birth a secret. No one knew. At least, she didn't think so. She'd gone into hiding at a home run by nuns. All very discreet. Then everything changed."

"What happened? How did it change?" I asked becoming more bewildered.

"She calls it her maternal instinct." She saw me roll my eyes and held up her hands as if to ward off an attack. "Let me start from the beginning. Hamilton was born on July 25th. Because Moira didn't plan to give him up for adoption, the sisters allowed her to live in a separate wing of the home with her baby. For a full month she lived in total seclusion to recuperate from the birth. In August she returned to the city thinking she was no longer part of the Kushawan community and no one would be paying any attention to her. But it was only a short while before she sensed that Hamilton was in danger. Little things, like seeing the same person on a street corner three days in a row. You and I know hormones go crazy after you have a baby, so I'm not so sure, but she needed her mother and came here."

"You'd think," I whispered back, recalling my conversation with Violet, "that this would be the first place they'd check."

"Not really. Hamid put this place in my name. Moira has so many homes where she can hide that I imagine they looked at them first. Besides, why would they look for an infant or a princess in a trailer park?"

"Manufactured home park," I automatically corrected.

"She figures they're busy watching the other houses."

"So, she thinks it's her husband's family who's watching her?"

"Let me explain. Tradition has it that royal princes are not named until they enter their sixth month of life. Once they are named, they become part of the official family and entitled to all rights, titles and inheritances. This began centuries ago, the actual story being lost in history. So many infants died during the first few months of life, even royal children, that rather than waste time and energy on a boy child born to one of the reigning prince's wives, it was ignored and left in the harem until it survived a full five months whereupon a holiday would be declared. There would be a huge celebration at the site of the royal palace. Today, the ceremony still takes place at the ruins of the original palace out in the Kushawan desert.

"She is convinced that because of the conflicts in the royal Kushawan family, the nineteen existing princes aren't too keen to be sharing the oil money with yet another prince. Though he wasn't terribly interested in it, Hamid was next in line for the throne, making baby Hamilton heir to the Kushawan throne, provided he lives until December 26th. It's her theory that KARP has sent out an assassination squad to find and kill Hamilton, our little unnamed prince." She sat back, exhausted from this lengthy explanation.

I was, frankly, stunned to hear her story. I waited for her to finish.

"Recently we became suspicious when we saw a new maintenance man on the crew. That's when she moved out and rented a trailer a few miles away in a seedy little park. She's calling herself Myra Gerstein."

"And left the baby behind," I said, knowing my voice sounded judgmental.

"She's still sure that nobody knows about him. She has some cockamamie idea that she can lure them out into the open and confront them without them ever knowing there is a baby. What she'll do with them once there's a confrontation I have no idea, but I do know Hamilton's safety is her first priority."

Exasperated, I said, "Then if she's that wealthy why doesn't she hire bodyguards and be done with it?"

"When Hamid was alive, I know they had something similar to the Secret Service protecting them. But now, with her not knowing who's after her and not wanting to be a part of that life, she's afraid to access her accounts for the large sums of money that would entail."

I heard a baby's cry from somewhere in the house. Not a scream, a soft mewling.

Jessica's face melted into a smile. Grandma. "He'll be awake soon and wanting his food."

"How old is he?"

"Eight weeks. I started him on rice cereal three days ago. He weighs nine pounds already. He's going to be a big fellow. I'll go get his formula ready."

"Wait. If he's been living with you all this time, when do you take him to the doctor?" I asked, still unsure that this arrangement was in the best interest of the infant.

"What would he need a doctor for? He's perfectly healthy; he's not around other children, so there's nothing for him to catch. He can't get sick. I won't let him." She stood and headed for the kitchen.

So there, I thought. She won't let him. I followed her into the kitchen where she began the process of putting his meal together. "Has he had his shots?"

She smiled a sly conspiratorial grin, her thin lips a mere slash in her face. "I have a friend in the profession, but I can't tell you who. If it ever becomes necessary, I'll take him to her." When she saw the look on my face, she laughed for the first time. "When Moira was growing up, I ran a childcare center at our house. I did that for twenty-five years. That's why I was going to the clubhouse regularly. After so many years of only the company of children, I do so enjoy being around adults." She gave a little laugh. "Whom, it turns out, actually aren't that different from the children. What they don't know about each other, they make up. Fill in the gaps with their own imaginings. Whatever would they think of this mess I'm in?"

"I still don't understand the mess you're in. Your daughter, as a widow of one of the world's richest men, has a child who should be equally as wealthy. "

"Once he makes it to December 26th." She tipped the bottle and dripped milk from the nipple on to her wrist. "All ready. I'll go get him."

I waited in the living room to see what an infant potentate looked like. He appeared as chubby and cute as any two-month-old baby. I could see that he would have problems if they tried to raise him as an Arabian prince. His eyes remained blue, his hair fair and his complexion whiter than my best bleached undies.

Jessica looked from the baby to me. "Didn't I tell you? Adorable."

"What do I tell Violet?"

"Nothing!" Her voice squeaked, startling the baby, who paused briefly in his suckling to glare wide-eyed at her. "No one must know. I only told you because I was feeling so overwhelmed when you knocked on the door and I know I can trust you."

"Of course you can," I said as I patted the hand that cradled the baby's head. "You can trust everybody here with something as big as this. I'm sure you can," I said, fully aware of how false I sounded. "Anyway, I've already told Violet that you have a baby here. I can hardly take it back now. So, what do you want me to say?"

She glared at me.

I raised my hands defensively. "I didn't know the whole story or I never would have said a word!"

"Listen to me. Moira thought that her presence in the park would attract attention. She and I brought in the things Hamilton would need for a few months. She doesn't tell me where she's staying but keeps in touch with her cell phone and every few nights we meet in the Wal-Mart parking lot so she can hold him for a little while. It breaks my heart, but she insists this is the way it has to be.

"As for Violet, you'd better tell her as much as you think necessary to keep her from reporting us. If Carol finds out, we'll be out on the street, money or no money. I'll call you in the morning."

"Just one more question. Why wouldn't they kill the baby *after*

December 26th?"

"As I said, tradition, custom. It's evolved into a mystical belief that if you do harm to a named royal heir, you will die a horrible, ugly death and never make it to heaven. A curse will be on your sons and descendants for generations. According to their custom, he must be killed by midnight of December 25th."

Chapter Five

The blast of the weapon deafened Moira, startling her more than the bright flash from the muzzle in the darkened room. She froze, staring at the body, which now slumped across the desk as blood seeped from under his head, creating a black river that crept toward the edge. Any second it would drip onto the floor and soak into the carpeting. She'd never be able to get it out, she thought incongruously.

"Not on your life," she whispered, answering his order to go with him. Her hands began shaking, she couldn't catch her breath. *What do I do now? Oh, my God. What do I do now?* Her mind was in a whirl.

A door slammed nearby sounding like an echo of her shot. The dogs barked. The man next door shouted, "Shut up, stupid dogs. It's a raccoon. Idiots."

"I'm calling the cops, you don't stop that noise!" a woman's voice screeched in the distance. Another door slammed. Regular noises in the night where she'd chosen to live. Even gunshots were normal as neighbors conveniently disposed of nuisance wildlife, not wasting the time of the Animal Control Officers.

Moira fumbled with the knob that turned on the stove light, unable to take her eyes off the intruder. His head had fallen at an awkward angle on the table. There was only a small spot in the middle of his forehead, but the back of his head oozed in sickening globs down the far walls and curtains. Should she call the police? But then, her identity would be discovered. The trailer park owners knew her as Myra Gerstein. The press would show up. She couldn't have that. She had to keep her identity, and that of her son, secret.

"Oh, God. What am I thinking?" she wailed. Clutching the gun to her chest she eased her way around the body, still terrified that he would leap up and attack.

With her eyes on him, she lifted the cushion off the built-in sofa and hauled out her black flight bag kept ready with emergency cash and essential travel items; the only thing left to do was grab her purse from the bedroom.

She was wearing a T-shirt and underpants. She had to dress. Her brain started working again. Forcing herself not to throw up, she searched the intruder's pockets for identification and the evidence he claimed to have about her and Hamilton. Finding nothing, she turned off the light and retreated to the bedroom, focused on getting away from the trailer. She pulled out slacks, slipped her feet into sandals, grabbed a fistful of other necessities from her top drawer, and stuffed them into her bag. Now she had to leave the trailer. Terrified at the thought of having to go near the body again to get to the front door, she used a box cutter to slit the screen from her window so she could slide out into the night.

The dogs growled.

"Hush," she whispered. "Don't bark, and I'll send you a couple of steaks, all right?"

Max whined as he pulled at his chain to reach her. Bruno saw a familiar person and returned to his doghouse, chain rattling.

The outside light went on at the trailer next door, barely lighting the dirt clearing that made up the front yard. The owner stepped out, shotgun in hand, wearing shorts partially hidden by an overhanging beer belly. "Where do you think you're going?"

Her own weapon was tucked inside her duffel bag. "I have to get away," she answered honestly.

"Problems with the old man?" He indicated her place with his gun.

"Right. Old man," she responded, grateful for the convenient excuse he provided. She continued edging her way toward the end of the structure. "He found out where I live."

"Did I hear a gun go off?"

"Gun?" She forced a derisive laugh. "That was him smashing my TV. Good thing the dogs barked. Scared him and he took off like a... a jack rabbit."

"Huh. No accounting for people. Go on. You want me to tell the managers anything?" He scratched at his hairy belly.

"Um. No."

He gave her a little salute and a wink. "Good luck, darlin'."

Within minutes she was headed south on I-95 toward Miami.

She didn't particularly want to go to Miami. She wanted to go to her mother's house and pretend nothing had ever happened. She wanted to be twenty-one years old again and never have met the tall handsome man whose tousled hair blew so charmingly in the desert wind.

~ * ~

She'd been working in the middle of the Kushawan desert, sand clinging to her bare arms and legs as she picked small shards of pottery out of a square grid. Like Persian poetry, he had smiled down at her. He took her hand and helped her up.

"Professor Hamid Al Wafiki. I am the supervisor of this dig. I want to express my appreciation of your hard work, Miss Robbins."

She stood and was delighted to find that she didn't tower over him. Instead she had to look up to meet his gaze. "You're quite welcome, Professor. How is it you know my name?"

"I asked. I have observed you for three days and hesitated to come speak with you."

Could he actually be shy? This gorgeous hunk of humanity? She felt her face break into an idiotic smile. "Why is that?"

He looked down at the ground. She half expected to hear, "Aw, shucks, ma'am," but he said, "In other parts of the world, it is customary for men and women to have intercourse…"

She grinned.

"Have I spoken incorrectly?"

"No. The word is technically correct, but in American English, it might be better to say 'socialize' rather than 'intercourse.'"

He hesitated and she could see his mind working on the words. "I see. Now, I've embarrassed both of us. I'll start again. In my country, it is not customary for a man to speak alone with a woman, much less an infidel woman. Though we are modern by Middle Eastern standards, there are some customs that do not change."

"Infidel?"

"You are not of my religion, therefore you must by default be infidel. Is that not so?"

"Well, I'd hardly say that. Is there something I can do for you, Professor?"

"Will you come to my tent, that is, my office, for a cup of tea? You are surely entitled to a break in work."

She brushed her hands off on her khaki shorts, pushed stray wisps of hair behind her ears and then gladly followed him into the relative coolness of the tent, headquarters for their archeological dig.

Her mind raced with beautifully erotic thoughts as she waited politely for the servant to pour tea for them. She knew her face was beet red from blushing and she could only hope that he would think it was from the heat.

His hands shook slightly as he lifted his glass and saluted her. "To good international relations. My country is pleased to have this partnership with your university."

"Yes." A squeak. She cleared her throat and lifted her own glass. "To international relations." Even now she still blushed when she recalled saying that.

He chuckled.

She fell in love.

Damn! Why did he have to turn out to be a prince of the royal family? A charming prince, no less. Of all the brothers, he was the only one uninterested in the governing of his country. He said he enjoyed his role as a professor, had studied in his own city's university as well as in Switzerland. He'd traveled the world to do research and here he was, sitting across from her in a tent cluttered with ancient bones and pottery pieces, smiling at her.

This would make interesting news for her parents to whom she mostly wrote, "Nothing new today, hot and sticky."

At six-foot-four and two-twenty-five Hamid was huge. He made her feel small and feminine. He adored her. She worshipped him. He was foreign, elegant, handsome, and rich, the heir to the Kushawan throne. Their money came from oil. When they'd married ten years ago things were fine. Her parents and grandparents loved him. She and Hamid kept homes in Brunei, Paris, Monaco, New York, Geneva and Buenos Aires. Having grown up in the small town of Paris, New York, she'd been captivated by the luxurious lifestyle. She took immediately to shopping in the real Paris in France, and in Geneva and on Fifth Avenue in New York. Whatever she wanted, he wanted for her.

The money came in so fast they wouldn't be able to spend it all in a dozen lifetimes. And although they set up trusts to support children in orphanages and contributed millions to medical research, Hamid did draw the line at depriving themselves of any luxury for charity. It started out as such a nice life.

~ * ~

The *1812 Overture* interrupted her thoughts. Her cell phone. Only her mother knew the number. She glanced down at the phone on the center console and then at the speedometer. She was traveling at ninety miles an hour. She didn't dare try to speak on the phone now. She'd have to find a place to stop and return the call.

A sudden onslaught of emotion overwhelmed her and her eyes clouded with tears as her hands trembled causing the car to swerve onto the verge. She hit the brakes and then remembered the broken taillight, praying that whoever was behind her had been alert. A horn honked. Her heart raced.

After wiping her eyes, she saw a sign for a rest area, "Next right." She gratefully pulled off the highway and rolled to a stop in a parking slot.

With trembling fingers she pushed the call-back button while scanning the parking area for any suspicious looking people. Under the streetlights in the early morning chill, a group of adolescents milled around a white church bus eating snacks and drinking soft drinks.

An elderly couple wrapped in heavy sweaters slowly trudged along the walkway pulling a wheeled cooler toward the picnic area while a young mother with two little girls exited the women's rest room.

It seemed forever before her mother picked up the phone. "Is that you, Moira?"

"Mom, what's wrong? Why did you call? Is Hamilton all right? Tell me they haven't found you, too." She squeezed her eyes shut in fear. Perspiration trickled down her forehead and under her arms.

"No!" Jessica answered quickly. "Nothing like that at all. What do you mean 'found' me too?"

Moira couldn't tell her about the man in the trailer. "I—I don't know. I had a bad night. I was fired from the café and then stopped by a policeman for a broken taillight and I smelled like beer." Closing her eyes, she took a deep breath. "Why are you calling so early in the morning?"

"I couldn't sleep knowing that I had to tell you. Don't be mad at me. I had to tell someone about Hamilton. I couldn't stand the pressure of doing this alone anymore." Her voice sounded weepy.

Would she always be living on the brink of panic and fear? But, if *they* had found her mother, Mom wouldn't be calling to tell her. "Who? Who knows about Hamilton?"

"Doll Reynolds. My neighbor. She saw me bringing him home from our visit the other night. I thought it might be useful in case something happens to me. Someone else ought to know what's going on." Her mother's voice went quiet for a moment.

Moira was silent in the early morning light. She heard the roar of tractor-trailers charging down the highway. The kids began climbing into the bus, chattering and laughing amongst themselves, some of them singing. "It's all right, Mom. And nothing's going to happen to you. Keep him safe. I might not be able to call you for a while." She thought about the dead man in her trailer and knew that she'd started something, but they'd be after *her*, not Hamilton. Maybe that was for the best. As long as she was on the run, he'd be safe.

"Where are you, Moira? Is someone with you? I hear voices."

"I'm at a rest stop on the highway. I'll call you when I have a new location. I had to move during the night. I was going to call you later. Take good care of Hamilton. Tell him I love him. Tell him every day." She closed the phone.

Chapter Six

"Hamilton is safe. Hamilton is safe." Drawing comfort from the mantra Moira continued heading south. And then, without warning, another phrase from her past took over. It was in Hamid's voice. "We must be wary of KARP."

She'd asked him to explain. "KARP, Kushawan Alliance of Royal Princes."

"But you're a royal prince, right? So why should we be wary of them?" she asked him idly as they nestled in one another's arms on the king sized bed aboard a palatial yacht at harbor in Monaco.

"If we were to ever have children, it would make them very unhappy."

"Is that why you resist whenever I ask about us having a child? I know I agreed to put it off until we'd had time to travel together and to get to know one another. Don't you think the time has come?" As she spoke she trailed her fingernails lightly down his chest and over his stomach.

Without warning, Hamid flung the light cotton blanket off the bed, shoving her hand away at the same time. The force sent her over the side of the bed. She landed on the plush carpeting.

"That's enough!" he shouted. "My father warned me marrying a Western woman would be wrong. What did I know? Nag. That's what you do. That's what you are! Get dressed! We'll be late for the race."

She grabbed up the blanket from the floor and covered herself, suddenly ashamed of her nakedness. "I don't want to go to the race. You go. You and your friends have a good time."

He rummaged around in his dressing room, slamming drawers and cabinets as he collected his clothing for the day. "You want to know what KARP would do to any child of ours? They'd slaughter it, that's what they'd do! As long as we are married, five years, ten years, fifty years, we shall not be having any children together. I've been considering using my privilege to take another wife."

He might as well have slammed his fist into the back of her head, the shock of his statement was so painful. Sitting still as a statue, she waited until he'd showered and left their stateroom before she could force herself to get up and get dressed. That was three years ago. He never followed through with his threat to seek another wife and even if he had, traditionally, Moira would have had to give her approval. Though they remained together, the polish of their marriage had been tarnished by that one violent action. Moira had never in her life been physically struck by anybody, much less someone who was supposed to love her.

When they returned to New York for an extended period of time, under the pretext of needing to work out, she joined a gym where she could learn martial arts. It gave her some security for her personal safety should he ever become violent again, but it added another level of distance to their relationship.

He took up flying, something she never enjoyed, so their times together became fewer and fewer. Often he went straight to the guest room when he returned from one of his overnight solo flights. At least, she hoped they were solo. Occasionally he came to her room.

~ * ~

The sun emerged from its rest and sent a strobe-like effect across the highway, peeping out between lines of trees in nano-seconds. Her eyes felt gritty and she had trouble focusing on the road. She rummaged around in her bag for her sunglasses.

If they caught her, she'd be dead, dead, dead, but only after they tortured her to learn the whereabouts of her baby, the potential heir to the Al Wafiki titles and wealth. Could the man she'd killed have been with KARP? Of course he could have. And how did he get to her trailer? Her stomach did flip-flops as she realized she hadn't looked for a car. What if his evidence was in a car near her trailer? But she hadn't seen one when she pulled away. Then again, urged on by terror, she hadn't paid any attention to her surroundings.

With trembling hands, Moira sped down the highway. "Dumb! Idiot!" she berated herself as she flew past eighteen-wheelers and SUV's full of families. Families going on normal vacations, living normal lives.

Would the KARP people look for her in Miami? As she traveled further south, away from Hamilton, her first thought had been to hide in the immense population of the city. Though she spoke several languages, she wasn't truly fluent Spanish. She could read and write it, but she knew she had too much of an accent to become lost in the Spanish community.

The exit to Cape Canaveral or points west appeared on her right. If she wanted, she could turn west then head south down the center of the state into areas unknown by most, except for maybe the Seminoles, but she'd stand out like a sore thumb. A vision of herself towering over a band of black haired Native Americans brought a smile to her face. Brief though it was, she felt better. She was taking action to protect Hamid's son. Her child. She cruised beyond the exit that would have taken her inland and headed toward the Palm Beaches. Maybe she'd stop there and find a room, giving herself time to regroup.

It wasn't bad enough that there were so many other terrorist groups in the world to fear, but Hamid had to tell her about KARP. She had to keep Hamilton hidden until December 26th. If only Hamid hadn't died in the plane crash. Died. She had to get used to the idea that he was dead. This past year had been so taken up with the pregnancy and hiding out that she often put him out of mind, as if he were away on a business trip. Now she wondered, did he suspect her pregnancy? Could he have known?

Thoughts whirled as she considered her options. How to keep KARP away from Hamilton. All right, make them follow her, lead them away from the baby. Even if it took every second of the time till he entered his sixth month, each day they were after her would be another day they didn't know of his existence or, if they did, where he was.

A Wendy's sign caught her eye and she pulled off the highway for a bathroom break and a quick bite. She drove for the next two hours undisturbed by the telephone. Traffic moved quickly but steadily along the crowded interstate. An occasional teen hot-rodded through, weaving amongst cars, begging to crash or cause one, but a beneficent God saved the idiots for another day. In a quick flash thought she wondered what kind of a driver Hamilton would be when he grew up. A brief smile formed on her lips at the idea of her infant son being an annoying teenager.

At the Palm Beaches she pulled off the highway again and found a hairdresser, emerging two hours later as a spiky-haired blonde. She'd liked the red hair she'd had for the past few months, a color closest to her own dark auburn. The blonde in the mirror wasn't bad looking. Even the operator said it went well with her green eyes.

When the signs for Miami, Downtown Miami, Beaches, and points south and west cropped up, she was already exhausted. She'd begun her day by killing a total stranger, and now drove toward a highly congested city with no destination in mind. South Beach? The historic Art Deco district. Why would anyone think to look for her there? Why not? What about the Haitian neighborhoods? No. Not that or any other ethnic specific area; as a blonde she'd stand out even more than before. That was a dumb move, changing to a blonde.

Hopefully, the dead man in her trailer would not make the national news. The neighborhood she'd been in was notorious for drunken brawls, drug deals gone bad and domestic disturbances. One more dead man wouldn't excite anyone. Maybe her gun toting neighbor would find the body and get rid of it for her. For the short time she'd lived there, he had become particularly protective of her. Him and his dogs. Maybe he'd feed the dead guy to the dogs then no one would find anything!

Four giant green road signs appeared ahead. The road would split in seconds. Decision time. She pulled left, going for South Beach. With a deep breath, she relaxed against the seat as she moved past the Port of Miami on her right. Two large cruise ships, nose to tail, or bow to stern, waited for several thousand vacationers to embark on a week or month long journey into the Caribbean. No cares. No worries. Eat, swim, gamble, enjoy the shows and spas. She considered making a U-turn at the end of the causeway and seeing if she could check in on one of the ships. Why would anyone think she'd taken a cruise? Not a bad idea. She frowned. Too much ID required.

She moved on. Traffic slowed to a reasonable fifty or so miles an hour. At South Beach, without any design, she turned right onto Washington Avenue, heading south until it dead-ended. She parked next to an old renovated hotel with a Vacancy sign. It would be home for the time being. She'd clean up, have supper and then make her next decision.

Chapter Seven

I set my phone down. Jessica had called me immediately after she spoke with Moira. She was in such a state, I called Violet and between the two of us we provided Jess with a breakfast of homemade biscuits, Violet's own strawberry jam and a plate of bacon and eggs that I cooked.

Jessica stared at her food without eating a bit, but she did sip at the cup of fortified tea. Violet cuddled Hamilton against her ample bosom. The infant cooed contentedly.

"They'll kill her. I know they will. And then they'll come looking for the baby. Do you think they saw me going out at night, taking him to see his mother? What are we going to do?" Jessica wailed again.

She'd been doing that since we arrived. I prayed for the telephone to ring and for Moira to tell her mother that it was a bad dream, a nightmare. But, that didn't happen. And to make matters worse, we turned on *News at Noon* only to learn that a body had been discovered in the trailer park where Moira had been living. Police were looking for Myra Gerstein, the name Moira was using. The reporter stood outside a police tape in front of the shabby trailer and spoke with a grizzly, gap toothed man in his forties.

"Did you know Miss Gerstein well?"

"Nah. She liked my dogs. That's all I know." He grinned nervously at the camera.

"What did you hear last night? Did you hear any gunshots?"

"Nah. The dogs barked at an armadillo once. That was it. She's a nice lady. I hope she's okay," he said as he made a thumbs-up gesture to the camera.

The reporter signed off, promising more information later in the program.

Violet and I remained with Jessica until late that night and left her only after we'd double checked around her house to make sure her screens were secure and the patio doors locked.

The days became two weeks with no further word from Moira. At least that's what Jessica told us. She did say the phone would ring at times but no one would be there and she was afraid to speak in case it was KARP. November arrived and Jessica grew more and more withdrawn with worry over her daughter, but at least Violet and I could help manage her daily life for her.

We shared the baby supply shopping, buying clever toys for infants, things that weren't around when our own kids were babies, like DVD's of colors and sounds to make Hammy brilliant; and colorful musical mobiles that he could swat with his hands and feet in his little crib. Jessica didn't like us calling him Hammy, but we had our own proprietary interest in him and we wanted to give him a nickname.

I learned how to diaper an infant all over again and to prepare already prepared cereals. Things had changed quite a bit in the forty-five years since I had my last baby and even the seventeen years since the youngest grandchild, but nothing changes the stink of a poopy diaper.

Getting rid of the disposable diapers proved a challenge. At first, I took them in a garbage bag to the dumpsters, but one day I caught the maintenance men watching me. After that, I put on my oldest sweatshirt and rode my bicycle to Jess's, stuffed the garbage bag under my shirt, secured it and then pretended to be doing my workout.

I rode around the park until I was sure that the men were working at some distant location, and then I'd peddle as fast as I could over to the dumpsters and unload my trash. Environmentally not sound, as I had the diapers double wrapped in plastic bags, but the system worked for us.

If the maintenance guys found out we were harboring a baby, they could report Jessica to management and that would leave poor Hammy out in the cold—so to speak. The other benefit of being Hammy's personal trashwoman was that I was getting fit.

So far the weather had remained hot enough to keep the air conditioning on and the windows closed. In a short time all that would change. The snowbirds would arrive.

It would be cool enough to open windows at night. The northern visitors would begin their rounds of court parties with tables set out in the street. Afternoon cocktails in someone's carport; a different carport each day. They would wonder why Jessica kept her windows closed and remained withdrawn and aloof from all her friends. We had to think of a plan while we waited to hear from Moira.

There was always the hope that Moira would find a safe place and send for the baby.

The little guy continued to grow, requiring more food. We added spinach, peas, carrots, and fruits to his menu. He devoured it all. Our little prince.

In early November the first of the snowbirds in our court arrived. Sally and Myles Hampton hailed from Ontario, a boisterous couple who, to our great relief, had booked a Caribbean cruise for the first week after their arrival. They drove in on a Thursday night, popped over to let me, as court captain, know they were back, and then apologized.

"We'd love to have our usual party, but we're going on a two week cruise Saturday. It was such a special deal through the Panama Canal that we couldn't resist. You won't mind, will you?" Sally said. "We'll do something for Christmas."

I shook my head solemnly. "That's all right. If I had someone to go with, I'd go on a cruise, too."

"Oh, ho-ho!" Myles bellowed. "You can come along and sleep on the sofa in our stateroom. My little sex-retary here wouldn't mind fixing it up." He elbowed his wife in what some might be consider a playful manner. She winced.

"You're very kind," I murmured. I kept my eyes downcast to avoid letting Myles see my aversion to his manner, "But ever since I lost Barclay..." I didn't finish the sentence. Whenever I spoke of Barclay, I choked up, torn between annoyance and grief at his disappearance. And it surprised me because on a day-to-day basis, I hardly thought about him. Consciously.

Sally was sympathetic and understanding and so we had two week's reprieve.

The following week I went to see Jessica with what I thought might be a good idea.

She didn't answer my knock. I tried again. Then I tapped on the kitchen window and called her name. Eventually, I heard the locks release and the chain slide off its track. She was partially hidden behind the door as I stepped in so I didn't notice the change in her at first. The door clicked shut, the chain rattled, the locks snapped into place and I headed for the bedroom to check on Hammy.

When I returned to the living room, I saw that Jessica was huddled under blankets in the corner of the sofa. A TV tray stood next to her, with half-filled water glasses.

"You're sick!" I cried out with alarm, ashamed that I hadn't paid a bit of attention to her when I entered the house. "You were fine two days ago."

"It hit me like a ton of bricks Monday night. I began to ache, then I felt feverish."

"Sore throat? Sneezing?"

"No. Just aching and hurting all over. First I'm freezing cold and then I'm too hot."

"Why didn't you call one of us? What about Hamilton? Is he all right? He seems to be sleeping peacefully."

"I thought about calling you, but I don't want you or Violet getting sick, too. I'll be okay in a couple of days."

"I can call Bob. I know he'd be happy to come over and check you out. It wouldn't hurt to have the baby examined as well. What about your own friend in the profession? You said you have a friend who would give him his shots. Can't you call her?"

"No, I can't. She's at a conference and then she's going north for the holidays. If I'm not better tomorrow, I'll let you call Bob." I began to suspect that there might not be any "friend."

"We need a plan for Hammy. Myles and Sally will be home in another week. The others will soon be arriving. And it isn't healthy, not taking him out in the fresh air and sunshine."

"I open his bedroom window afternoons while he's napping when the sun is in the right position," she said rather defensively—and weakly.

I paced the room. My eyes fell on photos grouped along the top of the bookshelf and mounted on the wall above. There were also photo albums mixed amongst scrapbooks of her travels with her husband and daughter. While trying to consider what came next, I picked up one of the scrapbooks. It was of Belize in 1990.

Moira was a gangly sixteen years old at the time. Long auburn hair hid her face in most of the photos taken in front of Mayan ruins and rain forest. It reminded me of my own son's trip with his family a few weeks ago and I picked up the photo to study it closer. Everyone looked worn out, much as Jessica did this day.

We had to get Jessica well and a new home outside the senior housing development so she could keep Hamilton. I thought more about my young friend, Bob. He owned a condo on the beach side of Daytona. If I consulted him officially, I thought he wouldn't be able to say anything to anyone about my desire to find a home for an infant. I knew there was something wrong with this idea, but I still had to present it to Jessica. We had to take some action.

"No! I'm not letting him out of my sight for a minute. Moira entrusted his life to me."

She coughed.

I thought of all the soaps I had watched years ago when my

own children were babies. When an actor coughed, he or she usually died within a few days. Praying I was wrong, I ignored Jessica's pleas and dialed Bob's cell phone.

"I have this baby I need to hide from international terrorists," I began when he answered.

"Good story. Who wrote it?" he answered.

"Bob, it's true. I have to hide a baby for a while until his mother can come claim him. Can you help me?"

"Is this an illegal matter?"

"Answer the question. Can you help me hide a baby for a week or two? It's a matter of life and death."

Jessica flapped at me from her cocoon on the sofa.

"Why don't you go to the police? That would be the safest thing to do. Whose baby is it?"

"I can't tell you. And we can't go to the police. I'm not kidding when I say this is a matter of international terrorists trying to kill him and possibly his mother. He's worth several millions of dollars. Maybe hundreds of millions. I don't know for sure."

"Billions," Jessica croaked from the sofa.

"Really, really rich," I added.

"If he's that rich, then hire security. But, wait a minute. You can't have babies in Keegan Bay, can you? What's he doing there?"

"Hiding."

"What did he do, crawl in and tell you all about it?"

"Don't be ridiculous. He's the grandson of my neighbor, Jessica Robbins…"

"Oh, God. Don't use my name," Jessica moaned and fell back onto her pillows.

"Jessica is sick and I need to get this baby to a safe place." Even as I spoke I began to realize that I shouldn't be saying so much over the phone.

"Take her to a hospital and then take the baby home with you. I'll come over after office calls." Bob Stewart was a pediatrician, a handsome devil in his mid-forties, fairly tall, sandy haired and always managing to look well groomed, even in his tropical, casual doctor clothes. He liked to put on an air of detachment with his patients, but I knew his heart was in tune with every single one of them. As soon as he saw Hammy, he'd fall in love with him as I had.

"He wants me to take you to the hospital," I told Jess after hanging up the phone.

"No. I can't leave Hamilton. Moira would never forgive me."

"I'm going to get the car. Violet will sit with the baby until I get back and then I'm packing him up and taking him home with me while you get better. Even if they don't keep you, you need some rest. You can come over to my house to see him once the doctors say you're not contagious."

"I'm not contagious with anything. I'm just tired. Let me rest here for a while and I'll be fine."

"How will you feel if your daughter comes back and you're dead and the baby is lying in there in his own soil, crying…?"

"All right! All right!" She wept. "Take me to a doctor. The walk-in clinic. You'll see. They'll give me some vitamins and a huge bill. Call Violet. I'll go get dressed." She pushed the blankets aside. Her skeletal body shocked me. Had I missed the weight loss in my concern about the baby? Today Jessica wore a short cotton shift that hid nothing. Skin hung in loose folds from her bones. Tiny is one thing; emaciated is quite another.

It occurred to me to check her refrigerator. The topic of money or income had never come up before. With her wealthy daughter and her world travels until recently, I assumed she was well off. Inside the fridge were partially empty baby food jars, bottles of formula, two half-filled jam jars—one grape, one strawberry—a container of eggs, a tub of butter substitute, and a half loaf of whole wheat bread.

I shut that door and opened the freezer. Two old boxes of batter fried fish and a half used bag of frozen raviolis. She'd been spending her food money on baby food and other supplies for Hamilton. If I found Moira first, I'd wring her neck for putting her mother in this position.

With Violet ensconced in Jessica's house, we took off for the clinic. Because the general population used these clinics instead of a family doctor, it looked like the wait would be long. I settled Jessica in an orange plastic chair and went in search of a vending machine.

Chapter Eight

By five in the evening we had Jessica in a cubicle and settled onto a gurney. I'd been plying her with orange juice and peanut butter crackers from the machines. Though she only nibbled at the crackers, at least she had some nourishment in her. During the day, the story had come out about her finances. She and I grew up in an age when people didn't discuss those things; sex, money and religion were considered personal, not open for public discussion. Now it was essential that I know all the details so I could help her.

After considerable prompting she finally, reluctantly, gave me her information. Social Security was her primary source of income. She'd had quite a bit in stocks, but the economic difficulties a few years ago, wiped much of that out. When she had been in Europe and the Middle East with her daughter, Moira's husband paid all her expenses and even kept her in spending money, so while she owned expensive clothes, she didn't have much cash to spare for things like an extra mouth to feed.

"I do have some cash in the bank," she said. "The money I saved while living with Moira. So, if you need anything, I'll arrange for you to have it when we get home. We can go to the bank first thing in the morning. You've already done far too much for us."

"Nonsense," I replied while secretly agreeing with her and enjoying the challenge of hiding a baby from prying eyes—and management. "Just for the record, how much do you have in the bank?" I waited to hear a sum in the range of one or two thousand dollars.

"It's somewhere between one hundred and fifty and two hundred thousand, I think. I haven't checked lately. It only earns a little interest and I haven't been putting anything in since I moved here. I need my monthly checks to live on now."

"What are you doing starving when you have that much money stashed away? Are you crazy?" I felt like slapping her, but of course I didn't.

"I'm saving it for an emergency. You know how the stock

market fluctuates."

"You'll need it. If they keep you in here any longer, they'll get your house, too," I grumbled.

"Don't be silly; I have insurance and they can't take your house away from you in Florida." She tried to make light of her situation, but as soon as she said those words her head lolled to the side.

"Jessica?" I grabbed her bony hand. Cold. "Help! Someone help me!"

"Stop shouting, you'll disturb the other patients. What's the problem?" a fat young woman in a floral scrub shirt and trousers stepped through the curtains.

"We've been here for hours and a doctor still hasn't seen her. Please, get someone right now!"

The woman, a nurse I supposed, picked up Jessica's limp wrist and checked her pulse. Looked at her watch. Pulled the blood pressure cuff from the wall unit and wrapped it around Jessica's arm. She looked bored as she waited for the machine to pump air into the cuff. She then read the monitor, wrote notes on a chart and left the cubicle. Jessica still hadn't moved or spoken.

Within seconds another young woman looking like she might be fresh out of high school, wearing a white lab coat over jeans and a t-shirt, stepped through the opening. "I'm Doctor Huntington. What seems to be the trouble?"

"Mrs. Robbins is gravely ill," I reported.

The girl, I couldn't think of this ponytailed child sporting pink plastic clogs as a professional woman, scowled at me. "I am referring to you. My nurse tells me you need some help."

"Not for myself. For my friend," I replied, startled at her response. I pointed to Jessica, hoping that her pathetic condition might engender some Hippocratic sympathy from the child.

Dr. Huntington lifted an eyelid, pressed a stethoscope to Jessica's chest and said, "I'm sorry. You should have brought her in sooner. She needed medical attention…"

"I brought her in hours ago!" Then it hit me what she said. Dr. H. was pulling a sheet up over Jessica's face. "Aren't you supposed to call a code something?" I whimpered.

Dr. Huntington rushed to my side before I would have fallen to the floor. She eased me on to a chair then pushed a button, pulled an oxygen mask out of the blue and fixed it over my nose and mouth. "Just breathe normally," was the last I heard before I woke up on a gurney in another cubicle.

~ * ~

"She had over a hundred thousand dollars she said I should know about to help care for her grandson," I explained to the fourth "officer" of the bank, yet another self-important young woman, this time dressed in a business suit with neatly coiffed black hair and long red fingernails. I was beginning to wonder what young men are doing for a living now. "I do not know where any other next of kin might be. As far as I know, she only has the one daughter and grandson. Hamilton is too young to sign documents. I don't understand why I can't do it for him. He's in my possession, so to speak."

"You realize if the state learns of this situation, he'll be removed from your home."

I glared at the woman. That was not information I wanted to hear.

She took my meaning and raised a defensive hand. "It's none of my business, but it happened in my family, that's how I know. You need to find a next-of-kin, the quicker the better. In the meantime, we can't do anything about her estate. And thank you for notifying us. We'll put a freeze on her account. And you're so kind to be caring for her grandchild."

Well, shit, I thought, not feeling kind at all. I drove home in despair. How would I explain this to Violet? She had been taking care of Hamilton for the past four days. I pulled up into my carport and before I could get to my front door, there was Judy with a Wal-Mart bag.

She put a finger to her mouth. "Shh. Don't tell anyone, but I heard about the baby and wanted to help. Here's a package of diapers and a little something for food."

She handed me the bag and slipped away before I could say anything. Judy lives three streets away. She's a widow. I eyed Violet's house and marched over there.

"Violet!" I shouted as I pounded on the door.

She appeared at the screen. "Hush!" Had she been hiding behind the door watching me talk with Judy? "What did that busybody want?"

She had.

"Judy? She gave me this." I held up the bag. "Diapers. And some money for food, so don't be acting so mean about her."

"Knows everything. At least thinks she does."

"She was a spy; she ought to know a lot about things. How much is there?" I asked as she pulled an envelope out of the bag.

"Twenty-five dollars. That'll help some. What do you mean she was a spy?"

"She worked for the Canadian government overseas. Very hush-hush. She told me all about it when we first moved here. But still, Violet, how did she know about Hamilton?"

Violet blushed. She really did. "She called and wanted to know why I hadn't been at bingo for a while. Before I could say anything, Hammy cried. Bellowed like someone stuck a pin in him. It was a bubble 'cause as soon as I picked him up and threw him over my shoulder, he let out the biggest belch you ever heard in your life. You'd have laughed."

"And I suppose Judy was listening the entire time."

"She was."

"And you told her everything?"

"No, just that we don't know where his mother is. I also told her that we haven't reported anything to the office yet about Jessica's passing."

I didn't like it, but once the cat is out of the bag... "She'll keep it to herself, I'm sure." Was I?

"So, now we have a little fund for food. But, how long can that last? You and I can't go on forever supporting him."

"Bob is coming tonight for our writers' meeting. Have Hamilton at the house at eight. He can examine him. Maybe we can put him on real milk instead of formula. That'll save some and make moving him from house to house easier. Less costly."

"I think we should keep him at Jessica's house and take turns staying there ourselves."

"Either way it's disruptive. We leave him there and you have to leave John. We have to pack our clothes and then hope Carol doesn't come knocking on the door for any reason. It would be better to have him take turns staying in our homes," I said as Violet handed me a cup of real tea. We had to give up our afternoon version since we assumed our new responsibilities of parenting Hamilton.

"Think what it would be like for Hammy. A different parent and a different home every week won't be any good for him."

"We could move him on Sundays to a new house. No one gets tired of him and he learns an eclectic lifestyle."

"A hobo lifestyle, more likely," Violet said. "And just how many people are you planning to involve in this?"

I ignored her question. "We still have to report Jessica's death to the office."

"Carol never goes house to house. We're good until the end of this month anyway. Now, tell me what happened at the bank. Can you transfer the money to her checking account?"

"No. They froze the account. Now only her next of kin can claim the money. Or maybe the state if they take custody of the baby. And she didn't have her checking account there anyway."

Violet frowned for a moment. Hamilton's voice cooed to us over the intercom. "He's waking up. I'll get his lunch ready. Would you like to feed him today?"

"Me? I'm not that good with babies. I managed to change his diapers a few times at Jessica's." The fact is, I wasn't all that fond of babies. Until my own became walking, talking toddlers, I was always afraid I'd somehow damage them. I never did understand how people related to their babies.

"You're being silly. When it's your turn, you'll have to feed him."

"I'm going over to her house now and see what I can find. Her checkbook must be there someplace because it wasn't in her purse or in the drawer with all her other papers," I said.

"Thoughtful of her to arrange her own funeral like that. A bit creepy though. Well, if you find it, please don't report anything to that bank. Maybe we can forge her signature for a while until we get the other money."

"I'll let you know what I find."

With that, I took the key and headed across the courtyard to Jessica's place. No matter where I looked I didn't find a checkbook. Nor any statements of any ordinary bills. But, there was a computer on a small desk in the corner of her bedroom. It was a tidy bedroom, with shoes carefully stacked in individual cubicles and dresses and blouses separated by color. I'd already searched her bureau so knew that the drawers were tidy and well organized. My mind toyed with ideas of raising money by selling some of her expensive designer items on eBay as I turned on her computer.

I held my breath waiting for it to ask for a password, but it didn't. *Hooray!* Then I skimmed her recently used files, poked around in her history and checked out her selected favorite sites. Both banks she'd mentioned were there. I hit the one that didn't hold the savings account and up came the webpage. And the request for a username and a password. I knew that would happen. Now all I had to do was try to guess how her mind might have worked. A neat, orderly woman. Everything in its place.

Except her daughter, from whom we hadn't heard. The television news never reported the identity of the dead man in Moira's trailer, but had described her as "Myra Gerstein, a six-foot redhead." Fortunately, they didn't have a photo of her. The police apparently had no connection between Moira and Jessica because no one had come by with questions. The newspaper had a small item that said the man was shot during a domestic squabble. None of us dared to go over to Moira's house to learn anything more.

Jessica told me when we were at the hospital that she had spoken to Moira that same morning. She also told me that Moira insisted she not tell us that they'd been talking. That, at least, made me feel a lot better about Moira. But, Moira had never told Jessica where she was hiding now.

Poor old Jessica. I hoped wherever she was, she knew we were taking good care of her grandson and that each and every one of us planned to give that daughter of hers "what for" if we ever saw her again.

I tried versions of Moira's names. Moira Louise. Forward and backward. With numbers and without. Then I tried the name of an old dog whose photo had been in Jessica's wallet. Forward and backward. With numbers and without. One look at my house and no one would refer to me as neat and tidy or organized. In spite of that, I tried to think like such a person.

Jessica Robbins, widow. Retired. Living only on her social security. No pension. First I put her full name in as the username and then said I had forgotten my password. I did that on my own computer each time the companies sent me new passwords, which I then promptly forgot until I had the idea to write them all down and keep them under my keyboard for easy reference.

A new password would be sent to my email address provided I could answer a few security questions. Uh-oh. I hit the okay button and waited. First came the mother's maiden name. That was easy; I had been through all of her papers and knew where to find that information along with the place of her father's birth and the last four digits of her social security number.

Within five minutes I had the password and the bank account. She had a balance of five hundred seventy two dollars and fifty six cents. I looked for her credits and debits. It looked like she never wrote any checks. There were small monthly withdrawals from an ATM, and all her bills were paid automatically, even her maintenance fees at the park came out regularly. Her social security was an electronic deposit.

This account showed no evidence of any large deposits. We'd have to forget the hundred thousand in the other bank.

This could be easier than any of us thought. As long as the government and the bank didn't know she was dead, we'd be able to provide a home for Hamilton until his mother returned to claim him.

Not that we'd let her after what she'd done. Killing a man in the middle of the night and then skipping out on her kid. The girl had an awful lot of explaining to do.

The telephone rang. My heart stopped. Did someone know that Jessica was dead and that I was on her computer illegally? I waited for her answering machine to pick up, but as soon as the message began, the caller disconnected. Could it be Moira looking for her mother? If it was, why didn't she leave a message? It was easy to answer my own question. She was afraid the police might be listening in. Did she know that no one notified her mother or called her to ask any questions about the dead man?

I took the risk, picked up the phone and punched in the call back code.

"Mom?" Moira's voice said.

"No, Moira, it's not your mother. This is Doris, Doll, Reynolds. I'm a friend of your mother's."

"Thank goodness. Are you the one helping her with Hamilton?"

"One of them." *How could I tell her about her mother?*

"Uh, is my mother there?"

"She's not available at the moment," I said, stalling for time. I wished Violet were with me. I wasn't feeling terribly clever.

"Look, I'm calling to apologize. I know it's been a long time, but she knows why I had to leave. If she's there, tell her I'll explain everything on December 26th. It's better if she doesn't know all the details. She's safer that way if they find her."

"Your mother told me about a little bit about KARP. Listen, she's resting and I have to go feed Hamilton. Can I call you at this number later? There are some things we have to discuss." For one thing, this ridiculous fable about killing a baby before it enters its sixth month, and the small fact that your mother is dead.

"Uh, I might not have this same phone. I'm not sure where I'll be later."

I was getting frustrated by her evasiveness. "Then, how can I reach you? We need to talk about some things."

"Is everything all right? Is Hamilton okay? He's not sick, is he?"

"No, Hamilton isn't sick. In fact, he has an excellent pediatrician taking care of him. Please, let me call you later this evening, or better yet, is there some way we can meet like..." I couldn't follow that thought. Jessica would have to be at a meeting.

"Have Mother call me when she gets up. Leave her a note,

please. I do worry about her. It's an awful lot to expect her to take care of him by herself. And I am glad she was able to talk to you. I truly am grateful." She paused. "Did you say you were 'one of them' before when I asked about taking care of Hamilton?"

"Violet and John are helping as well. John not so much, but he's tolerant. I have to go. I think your son is waking up." And before I could run off at the mouth any more or she could ask further questions, I disconnected and went back to the computer.

The electricity, cable and telephone were automatically paid monthly. The other services were included in the maintenance fees, so those were taken care of. Jessica took out four hundred dollars every fourth of the month, which I guessed was for food and other cash items. One credit card she appeared to pay off each month—online. Only small amounts charged from time to time, mostly gas for her car.

So, we should be all right for a while. It wasn't like we planned to steal from the government. They'd wind up paying for Hamilton anyway, and probably a lot more than the measly fifteen hundred a month that Jessica was getting. We could do it.

Now that I felt some financial relief, I wondered how much to tell Bob. I didn't know if doctors were obligated to report the child as abandoned. If the authorities called, maybe we could say he wasn't abandoned; his mother has given him into our care temporarily while she is job hunting. Or I could present him as my own grandchild. My children were visiting only a couple of weeks ago. That was it! I'd say they went on a cruise and I asked to keep the baby for the duration. Hamilton could be my grandson.

"That's not fair," Violet said a little later when I explained the situation. "I think he ought to be my grandson."

Oh dear, I thought, if Violet's going to start pouting, our little deceptions won't work. "Listen," I tried, "I have dozens of grandchildren's pictures in the guest bedroom. No one could prove whether or not any of them are Hamilton. You don't have any grandchildren, so you'd have to start inventing stories."

"Barclay's old office, you mean," she said. I detected a touch of malice in her voice.

"Yes, Barclay's old office. He wouldn't mind. He loved them as if they were his own."

She sniffed. "If he loved them so much, why did he disappear? Never even a note."

I turned my back on her. "Never even a note," I repeated, my throat closing as I held back tears. I still couldn't get used to the idea that he left that way and having my supposed best friend rubbing it in didn't help matters any. Most days I was all right and could tell myself we'd had many happy years together, but I wanted more. The recent passing of our friend also helped to reopen that wound.

"I'm sorry. But, I do insist on him being my grandchild," Violet persisted. "And all his stuff is at my house right now."

"Fine," I relented, not bothering to hide the anger in my voice. "He's yours. But, only for tonight. By the time he needs another check-up his mother ought to be back."

Chapter Nine

Moira jumped at the sight of the blonde woman in her bathroom mirror—once again forgetting what she'd done to her appearance; the close cropped head of spiky platinum blonde hair and a tan suggested a woman who lived a funky lifestyle. She'd found a job as soon as she arrived three weeks ago, waiting tables at an outdoor café a few blocks up on Collins Avenue. With her short shorts and halter top, she knew she made a pretty astonishing picture—all six feet one inch of her. If only the story she used to get the job could be true, life could be good. But, then, there'd be no baby.

Every day she worried that someone would find her. She worried that her cell phone might be traced. She kept it turned off, only turning it on once a week when she checked up on Hamilton. The past week though all she'd managed was to connect with the answering machine. She hoped that her mother and the other old ladies were taking good care of him.

Her shift ended pretty much with the sun in the late afternoons. She would count her tips, slip on a cotton blouse over her skimpy top and then have supper before walking back to her room at the hotel. The night manager would be coming on duty about then and she'd stop for a brief visit before retiring to her room. If anyone was surprised that the "blonde babe" didn't join the South Beach party brigade every night, no one said anything to her.

She never did speak any more with that woman, Mrs. Reynolds, who was helping her mother with the baby. After the last time she spoke with her, she hadn't had the nerve to make two calls in one day. Just knowing that he was in the retirement park with all those old folks was enough to provide some relief from the terror she'd been feeling ever since Hamid died. She imagined Hamilton being cuddled by dozens of gray-haired senior citizens who adored him. As long as she could lure the terrorists in her direction, evading them as she could, they would never know about the son of Hamid Al Wafiki and her child would be safe.

She played the ditzy blonde for the guests and her customers at the restaurant even though she was sure that at thirty-two she was far too old to be such a dimwit. They had fun teasing her and she earned good tips. The weather continued sunny and warm and she tanned quickly. It all helped with the image.

One Saturday morning she walked in to work at eleven only to find two young girls already working her shift and when she went to the boss, Hugo, a burly fellow with biceps the size of pickle barrels, she was informed that two sixteens beat one thirty-two any day.

"I can go to the labor board about this, you know. Fair employment practices. Age discrimination. Besides, they aren't old enough to serve drinks. You can't get away with this." She could hardly believe herself, complaining to a Czechoslovakian immigrant about fair labor practices when in her other life, she could have bought the hotel and tossed him out on his steroid rattled head.

He grinned at her. "Is a joke. You're working cocktails starting at seven. If you be like the rest of the world and get cell phone, I could save you the walk. And girls are really more than twenty-one years. Now go work on your tan, and I see you later."

He patted her backside when she turned to leave. She considered briefly whirling about and giving him a quick chop that would break his wrist, but chose not to. She'd save that skill for when it was important. As she'd been taught.

With nothing to do all day, she went back to her room and changed into white cotton slacks, a loose fitting orange shirt, donned a straw hat and sunglasses and headed out for a long walk up the beach. She skipped down the stairs, feeling fairly lighthearted considering her situation.

When she reached the landing that led to the lobby she saw two men leaning across the registration desk. Luis, the desk clerk, caught her eye and raised his right eyebrow. She slowed and quietly eased her way down the last three steps, turned toward the back of the hallway and entered the ladies' room where the old-fashioned window could be easily opened. It faced the side street.

Contorting herself like a pretzel, she struggled through it, made sure the curtain fell back into place before pushing the window shut and stumbled around the corner to where her car had been parked all week. Those men could only have an outdated description of her. But she was still a thirty-two year old tall female. She thanked God for Luis.

Pulling the phone from her straw purse, she tapped it against her teeth as she debated calling her mother. A quick check on Hamilton and she would take off again. Dump this cell phone and pick up a pay-as-you-go one at a convenience store. No. She didn't dare make that call. Those men must have traced her through her other calls. She carried it to the dumpster and tossed it. That would take care of that connection. But she still had to get away from the area without being noticed.

Her car! They would most likely know what she drove. Damn. She couldn't take that. She'd had the taillight repaired and now kept the car parked far down the street near a construction site. And her clothes in her room. What about them? She went around the dumpster to the hotel's kitchen door and pulled it open. Nothing much was going on. Breakfast was over and they didn't serve lunch. Dinners were a joke, a pre-packaged buffet that couldn't compete with all the fine dining establishments on South Beach. This hotel was a dinosaur amongst the resurrected art-deco hotels.

She slipped into the dining room and edged her way to the entrance where she could peek around the corner. The two men pushed open the glass double doors. Leaving the building. She waited a moment and then rushed over to Luis, who jumped when she surprised him.

"Senorita! You give me a scare now. What is it you did? They are not so happy mens."

"I didn't do anything, Luis. What did you tell them?"

"Senorita, do not look at me so. I tell them they have a photograph of a beautiful lady. I wish I could meet her, she is so lovely. But, alas, she is not at my hotel at the present time." At this he crossed himself and raised his eyes to the ceiling. "I am not lying when I tell them. I know you go out the bathroom window. You are smart woman."

"Thank you, Luis. Thank you so much. Will you get my bill ready? I have to leave here before they come back."

"No!" He clutched at her wrist as if that would keep her from leaving. "They will not come back. I tell them some good places in Miami and Hialeah where dangerous criminals can hide for many years without discovery. They will not be back to this place, because they have already looked here. You will be safe. You go now. Luis is a good help to you." He smiled, a gap-toothed smile in his young face made him look about twelve years old.

She wanted to pack him up and keep him. Little Ham would adore this boy. She'd consider that later when she was once again in a position to hire people. For the time being, she had a decision to make.

"They were Americans?" She needed to know more about who

was looking for her, KARP, the local cops, the FBI or the CIA. Any one of them would be a good guess at this point.

"Si. Yes. They show identity cards and say names but I am so nervous and my English in reading is not so good. They look official. They say you are Miss Robbins, but I know you are Marie Benedict. But the men, I am thinking most for sure American."

At least not KARP. Hopefully, that bunch had given up on her. She shook her head. Not likely. So much for the good mood she'd been in earlier.

She wouldn't be going for any long walks this afternoon, not with unknown agencies looking for her and still had at least seven hours to kill. She needed to do something to distract herself, to keep from thinking about who was searching for her.

"I'm going next door to buy a book. And, thank you again, Luis." She hoped his idea was right, that they'd already searched this area and gone on to other areas.

Trusting that Luis' lies had sent the two agents back into Miami, she waited a few minutes, until she was sure they'd gone and then slipped out into the shadows of the arcaded sidewalk to walk the few yards to the entrance of the tourist schlock shop.

She picked up two paperback novels and a Kit Kat and then took them with her up to the roof of the hotel, disappointed not to be walking along the beach enjoying the ocean breeze, the water splashing around her ankles, the chatter of vacationers with nothing more on their minds than where they would dine this evening or, in some cases, who they would screw.

She stretched out on a battered old chaise and studied the back covers of the two books; one an Agatha Christie story, the other a romance involving vampires. The selection was pretty grim at the little shop. She opted to start with Agatha.

If only life could be like an Agatha Christie story and she could be the heroine, the sweet innocent caught up in circumstances beyond her control, only to be rescued by a handsome young man who traveled out on the same ship.

A death of... she dropped the book onto her stomach. She didn't even know the name of the man she had shot. He had an accent, that's all she knew. And the fact that he would have killed her had she not gone with him. All those years with her husband, bodyguards always lurking in the background, and she still never fully comprehended the importance, the significance, of being married to a middle-eastern prince.

Hamid always maintained that his was an unimportant title as he had plenty of brothers interested and involved in running his country. Once they were married, he'd given up his work, work he'd said he'd been devoted to, and they spent their time traveling. Hamid loved the casinos. Now, a year after his death, she wondered how innocent all those travels abroad really were. No, too much Agatha Christie.

She would explain to their son that their father had been a good man and would keep her fingers crossed, hoping she wasn't completely wrong. Her mother kept all the DVD's they'd made on their travels and adventures and he'd be able to see his father at his best. Once everything was settled, she would make a home for them, maybe in Colorado or Arizona, and he could go to an ordinary private school and grow up a normal boy.

Thoughts of Hamilton sent her emotions into a deep dive. She wondered if he had smiled yet. Did he giggle or laugh at all? Did he still have the sweetest baby fragrance, just like the flowers, Baby's Breath? She adored him and if staying away from him would keep him alive, then that's what she would do, though her heart felt split in two whenever she thought about him.

Never much good at sitting still in the best of circumstances, she gave up trying to fool herself into relaxing and collected her stuff, slipped her slacks and shirt back on and headed for the stairwell and her room. It was only two o'clock. Five hours before she had to report for work. At least at work she was lost in the anonymity of the crowds. Keeping busy made the time pass. No one knew her or cared who she was, only that she bring their food and drink to them in quick order. There was something comforting in that. She looked forward to the evening.

Chapter Ten

Bob, being a physician first and writer second, was immediately concerned because I had written nothing for the past couple of weeks. I always had at least a little one page fiction, more often a good sized chunk of a longer short story. Despite my pleas of being fine, he insisted on checking my pulse, examining my eyes and peering down my throat while quizzing me on my health until he was satisfied that physically I was all right.

Peg and Minerva fortunately produced enough of their writings to keep us all busy for a couple of hours. Peg, a fairly stout young woman in her mid-thirties, considered herself an expert on vampires and Minerva, a lively woman closer to my own age, was a hopeless romance writer. Not a hopeless romantic, understand, but a hopeless writer.

Bob had a good thing going in a spy thriller and Steven, an older retired engineer, was doing a medical horror story. I had been plodding along with short stories that occasionally sold to small presses.

That Thursday evening moved along at a snail's pace for me as I had no interest in anybody's stories, much less a couple of vampires who wanted to mate and didn't know how and that a couple of thirty-somethings who met on a cruise were mating in the most graphic sense. At least the men's books held my attention for a little while.

I wound up lost in the medical jargon of Steven's story and the spy thriller hit a little close to home when Bob had his hero narrowly escape a bomb exploding under the bed.

Once the others left, I asked Bob to remain behind and then filled him in on Jessica and Ham's story, as far as we knew it. Bob was eager to help but had some reservations, pondering the legality of aiding and abetting the cover up of a death.

"But we're not covering up a death in that sense. We have her death certificate. She was properly examined and declared dead and now she's been cremated and we're keeping her at her house until we find out from her daughter what to do with her."

"And the baby? What's his legal status?" Bob asked.

"Violet is his guardian until Moira returns," I declared in my best Mother Voice, hoping he would accept that as the truth.

"Do you have that in writing?"

"I'll tell Violet to bring the paper with her." I picked up the phone and quickly punched in her number. "Violet, Bob is here. He's willing to take on the care of little Hamilton until his mother returns. He'll need to see the written piece of paper you have that states you are a temporary guardian until Moira Robbins returns. You know, the one that says you have permission to seek medical attention and all that?"

I kept my back to him so he couldn't see my face. I found myself becoming a pretty convincing liar. "Yes, yes. That's the one. The one she signed before she left him with you. When she knew that her mother was too ill to care for him."

Bob poured us a drink from my bar while we waited for Violet to arrive with the paper. "Tell me more about this Moira Robbins. Why did she have to leave her baby with a neighbor?"

"She had to go out of town. I told you." I hoped that Violet understood my message and would show up shortly with the written "proof."

"But, you didn't say why. You said important business."

I took a big slug of my scotch. The golden liquid burned a little as it slithered down my throat. I could trace it all the way to my stomach where it settled in with a warm glow. "It's a matter of life and death."

"Oh, yes. Your terrorist. If you wrote that in a story, I'd yawn." He chuckled, sitting back and crossing his legs, as if to emphasize the point.

"All right. Even though it's true, how about this instead: She left because she killed a man and is running from Interpol." I sat back and waited for a response to that. I didn't know exactly who was chasing her and wanted to steal her baby, but I imagined that was as good a guess as any.

"Okay. You don't want to tell me. Is she hiding from an abusive husband or boyfriend?"

"No. Definitely not hiding from an abusive husband or boyfriend. She had urgent business and had to leave. I hope to speak with her soon." If only the selfish bitch would call and check on her child, I thought. Quite uncharitable of me, I knew, but it escaped me how a mother could leave a baby and not call every five minutes to make sure he was all right. Forget five minutes, it had been more than two weeks.

"Yoo-hoo!" Violet called as she let herself in the front door. "I've got it, Doll." She entered the living room waving a sheet of lined notebook paper. She rushed over to me and pressed it into my hands. "Sorry I took so long, I forgot where I'd put it."

After reviewing the paper that Violet had whipped up and agreeing that it would satisfy the authorities, Bob suggested we call the office in the morning and schedule a physical examination. And to please bring Hamilton's immunization records along so he could make sure he was on track.

We did that a few days later. In preparation for the event, I cleaned out my closet and created a tent of old clothing around the baby carrier in the back seat of my car, making sure there would be plenty of air circulation for Hamilton. He was still at Violet's house, so I pulled into her driveway. Violet came out with her bundle of clothing. It was our little prince wrapped in her old orange bathrobe. Hamilton whimpered.

"You're smothering him," I accused.

"Don't be ridiculous. He wouldn't be able to cry if he was smothering." Violet was cranky and looked haggard.

"I'm guessing he didn't sleep well again last night."

As we worked him into his little nest in the back seat she explained. "When he slept all night for three nights in a row, I thought it was going to be easy. But these past two nights, he's been up most of the night. And then he wants to sleep all day."

"Perhaps today's outing will wear him out. Hop in."

"My hopping days are over," she complained as she eased herself into the passenger seat.

Hamilton's whimper turned to a howl when I started the engine. It hadn't occurred to either one of us that he hadn't been in a car since his mother deposited him with Jessica nearly two months ago.

"Should we stop and get him out of there?" Violet asked.

"Once we get going, he'll realize nothing bad is going to happen." I hoped.

As we drove through the park, residents in their yards, stringing up Christmas lights and creating fake snow around their windows in preparation for the holidays, waved cheerfully. I waved back, hoping Hamilton's cries were sufficiently muffled by the whine of my car engine. By the time we reached the gate, which thankfully raised automatically to let cars exit the park, his cries had settled back to whimpering. Charlie didn't even look up when we passed his hut.

Bob wasn't happy when he learned that Hamilton hadn't had

any shots at all, but did start him on the series required by law. He gave us booklets and pamphlets on modern child rearing as if Violet and I might not know what we were doing.

Friday was uneventful. Saturday afternoon I happened to turn on the *News at Noon*. Not a habit of mine; I was searching for an old movie to watch when the headlines popped out at me. "Police are searching for this woman, Myra Gerstein, as a person of interest in connection with the death of Mohammed Amir Sakir, of Newark, New Jersey. Sakir's body was discovered three weeks ago at a residence in Morningside Mobile Home Park, South Daytona, which had been rented by Ms. Gerstein. If you have seen her please notify..." and they displayed not only the local police numbers but an eight hundred number directly linked to Homeland Security.

And then, to my horror, a New York driver's license photo of the alleged Myra Gerstein, who looked suspiciously like the photos of Moira Robbins that I'd seen in Jessica's house. Not good news.

I'd thought that was all old news, finished and done with. This murder of a New Jersey Arabic man in Volusia County held a lot more significant meaning than I had thought, otherwise why involve Homeland Security?

I realized Violet, John, Judy and I would have to ask others for help. We needed more people to house Hamilton. None of us was getting any younger, and staying up nights with a squalling baby wasn't doing any of us any good.

If we had more people involved, trustworthy and willing people, we could continue to get our necessary sleep and be able to care for him during the days. We'd also have more brains to help consider the ramifications of our actions.

I don't want to give the impression that Ham was a fussy baby. Not at all, but he was still a little guy only beginning to sleep through the night once in a while. Even during the day, all that bending and lifting to change his diapers and feed him, didn't do anyone's back any good.

And then I had an idea that involved Pete, who had been a building contractor in his other life, before he evolved into a senior citizen golf champion. His wife, Alice, was an equally avid golfer. They also kept a boat *Tee'd Off* at the Keegan Bay Marina. Energetic for a couple nearing seventy, I knew they'd be happy to give us a hand. He could make over rooms in our houses for Hamilton.

When I told Violet and John, they agreed, so we called Pete and Alice over to my house that evening to discuss the plans. In the end, it would cost us several thousand dollars, money we could ill afford.

"But to save the child! He's a billionaire. Surely, his mother, once she comes to her senses, will reimburse us." I pleaded with our small group to no avail. It would be too expensive everyone argued.

"Unless…" Violet said.

"Unless?" Alice said.

"Unless we involve more of the community. We could use one house in each court for the project. No one would ever find him," Violet finished.

"Hot stuff!" Alice sat up straight and rubbed her hands together in youthful exuberance. "By God, we can do it, Pete. We got ourselves a project."

"Except for one thing." Pete held up a cautionary finger.

Everyone looked at him.

He removed his baseball cap, scratched his heavily tanned bald head and said, "I got a tournament tomorrow. I won't be able to start until Monday. Think that'll work?"

"No. We don't know how soon those terrorists might come looking for him," I said. "If you read the papers when Jessica's daughter disappeared, you know there was a New Jersey man with a Middle Eastern name found dead in her trailer. He may have been one of them searching for the baby. Now, I suggest we make up a list right now and while you're golfing tomorrow, the rest of us will have to put our heads together to make sure we're including the right people in our plan. Some in here won't approve of our carrying on." I stood to emphasize the next point. "Hamilton is a prince. If word gets out to the wrong people about us hiding him, his life won't be the only one in jeopardy."

"Aren't you being a bit dramatic?" Alice asked.

"I don't think so. Not if you'd heard the news report that I heard this afternoon. Homeland Security is looking for his mother. It's very frightening."

"Well, I don't like to put a damper on your enthusiasm, Doll, but maybe you ought to let them find her and the baby for their own protection," Judy said.

"They'll 'protect' him right back to his own country where he'll be murdered before Christmas. They don't want him to inherit his titles or his wealth. That much I do understand. I think."

"Poor Jessica. If only she'd told us more."

"I don't think she knew more. Moira, scatter-brained fool, was probably 'protecting' her as well." I drummed my fingers on the arm of my chair. "Write the list," I pointed at Pete. "We'll take care of the details."

The others in the room nodded and murmured in agreement.

Pete, looking a bit red-faced, pulled out his carpenter's pencil and started a list of supplies required. "But, I always golf on Sunday. Everyone knows that," he said in a barely audible voice.

Chapter Eleven

Saturday night Moira donned her white shorts and a bright blue, snug fitting t-shirt and running shoes. Carrying her white high-heeled sandals, she stepped out onto the colonnaded walkway in front of her hotel. The old Spanish style arches created dark shadows the entire length of the block. With a little shiver, she crossed the street and headed toward Collins Avenue.

"Moira!" She jumped as a rough hand grabbed her left arm above the elbow.

Reflexively, she dropped her sandals and purse, raised her right arm and whirled to defend herself. Her assailant was taller, stronger and faster. Before she could even register what happened, she was locked in his arms, smelling his aftershave, feeling the heat of his skin.

The man spoke into her ear, but it took a moment for her to recognize the Kushawan language. "Hamid sent me."

"Hamid's dead!" she spat. "Let go of me or I'll scream." She struggled to free herself as a part of her mind wondered why no one bothered to come to her aid. Though it was early, there were a few people out and about.

"Hamburger Boy," he said in English.

Startled by the statement, she stopped struggling. "What did you say?"

"Smile. Smile as if this whole thing is a joke. People are watching from across the street. Hamburger Boy. Remember that phrase?"

Seeing that the only people in sight were senior citizens prowling for an early bird special, she took the opportunity to make him think she'd acquiesced. She looked into his face. Hazel-green eyes in a tanned, cleanly shaved face; high cheekbones, a chiseled nose, and thick dark brown hair, full lips exposing even white teeth as he smiled at her. He seemed almost familiar. She did as he said and smiled, while she simultaneously pulled back and kneed him in his crotch.

He fell to the ground, yowling as he let out a few words in

English and Italian that amused the lookers on.

She scooped up her purse and shoes and then took off across the street, forcing cars to squeal to a stop. Once on the other side, the group of seniors cheered and applauded.

"Hamburger Boy! Hamburger Boy!" a less confident voice squeaked from behind.

She looked back to see the stranger pushing himself up from the pavement. He limped toward her, one hand clutching his groin, the other one outstretched. "Hamburger Boy," he gasped as he reached the curb. His eyes pleaded for understanding.

"Go on, talk to him. He can't hurt you now," an old man called out.

"You showed him," his partner agreed. "He won't hurt you now."

She paused, breathless, feeling fairly safe amongst these people, and waited for him to catch up to her. "Hamburger Boy" had been her private pet name for Hamid and their secret code in the event he was ever kidnapped. It was part of an identification process, forms they'd filled out and provided to the private security firm Hamid employed.

He had assured her the owner and all his employees were carefully screened former government security agents from all over the world. They picked Hamid's name for obvious reasons. Besides the play on his name, he adored American hamburgers cooked in any manner, from the best barbecues to the cheapest fast food; to him a hamburger was American and American equated to Freedom.

"Please, let me speak with you privately," he said, again in the unusual dialect of Kushawa. "Cinderella," he added in a whisper.

Cinderella. That was her code name. She hesitated, wanting to trust him, yet still fearful. Her eyes roamed over the small crowd that had gathered. She and this stranger provided a distraction and entertainment for them.

"Cinderella," she said softly as she held out her arm to help him onto the curb, all the while aware of being observed. "Who are you? Why do you know our code words?" she whispered in English.

"Because I work for Hamid," he responded in kind.

"Bullshit."

He leaned close to her and whispered in her ear, "His security firm, then."

"Try again." Her speech came out throatier than intended. She coughed. He let go of her hand and she stepped back enough to look at him again. "I'd have remembered you if you'd been in our security detail."

He winced as he tried to take a step closer to her. A small scar cut through his hair half an inch above his right ear. He straightened painfully. She had to look up to look him in the eyes.

"Vance Eberhardt, here to serve and protect," he announced.

"You really expect me to believe that? Why here? Why now? Hamid's been dead for nearly a year." She began to walk north on Ocean Avenue.

He limped along beside her, and though she was disconnected from him, so to speak, he kept himself within inches of her so that she could still feel the warmth of his body. His height and his physique, so much like Hamid's, made her want to trust him.

Her feelings about Hamid were confused. She had loved him unequivocally at one time and she missed him, missed his strength, missed how he'd been so gentle and loving at first. At the same time she hated him, angry that he was so careless as to let himself get killed and unable to forget that one explosive moment of violence.

"My contract with the corporation is to protect you for your lifetime. We lost you after Hamid was killed. I argued with my colleagues for letting you remain lost, because if we couldn't find you, then neither could anyone else. Where have you been all this time, if you don't mind telling?"

So, she thought, he doesn't know about little Hamid. How much should she tell this interloper, this so-called protector? And how did he find her now? "After the plane crashed, following the funeral in Kushawa, I began to feel nervous around his family," she lied. "I feared for my life. When I returned to the States I went back to my maiden name and moved around a lot." It was somewhat true. Easier to tell the truth than try to keep up with lies. "Then a man came for me at my house. He was going to kill me, so I ran. And now you've found me. Are you with the two men who were at the hotel earlier today?"

He caught her arm as he stopped. "What two men?"

"Two men in pale gray suits who asked for me at the front desk of the hotel today. Luis sent them to Miami."

He scowled. "Luis is the fellow at reception," he said. "He's a smart kid, but I wouldn't trust that they completely believed him. I didn't."

"What do you mean?"

"I've been keeping an eye on you ever since that traffic stop a few weeks ago in Port Orange, which is probably how they found you, too. I don't know who they are, but they aren't the brightest bulbs or you wouldn't have known about them hunting for you. What else besides gray suits?"

"They looked more European by the cut of their clothing. Western anyway, not Middle Eastern."

"Gray suits. IDIOTS. I'd put my money on them."

"What are you talking about? Why are they idiots?"

"It's an organization, the International Directorate Investigating Official Terrorist Societies. Most likely they're following you, hoping you'll lead them to someone."

Someone, she thought. Someone named Hamilton Robbins. "What makes you think they would be part of that?"

"The gray suits. Were they lightweight tropical wool?"

"Could have been." Moira continued along the sidewalk, angrier now at herself for being found, than frightened of this man. Vance continued to limp painfully beside her.

"They always wear the same thing. And the reflective sunglasses, right?"

"How did you know?"

"When I was a boy my father worked a couple of years in Iran. Their secret police, called SAVAK, always wore black suits, white shirts, black ties and wore the same sunglasses. We thought it was funny, but my father said SAVAK was not an organization to laugh at. The clothing was meant to intimidate. IDIOTS, having a somewhat gentler motive for existence, adopted the soft gray look."

She stopped and whirled on him. He leapt back, hands dropping down, protecting himself.

"Hold it a minute. What do you want with me?" she demanded.

"I told you. My security agency was meant to keep you safe. The contract didn't end with Hamid's death. I'm trying to keep you safe; that's my job. Sorry, if I've been a little late finding you."

She wasn't sure she liked the flippant tone of his voice. "Where are you from? You're not an American."

"Very astute, but wrong. My mother was Italian, father American. They met on the military base in Italy where I was born in nineteen seventy-one."

"You have a trace of an accent," she accused, while noting that that was also Hamid's birth year.

"I work hard to eliminate any traces of accent no matter which language I speak. Would you prefer to converse in French? Arabic? Pick a language and I can most likely speak it. That is, with the exception of a couple of Asian and African dialects."

"I'm not impressed. Lots of people grow up multi-lingual." Only two more blocks to the hotel where she worked. She needed to know more about this man, Vance Eberhardt. Attractive and charming though he might be, he could mean the end of her and her baby. And now, she didn't even have a replacement cell phone. With no idea of who she'd call for help if she did have one, she had to rely on her own instincts to get her through this.

"Very few Americans are like you," he said.

She pondered his comment. "What has any of that to do with me?"

"I know that you're fluent in several languages yourself. If we should have to leave this country and disappear in another I need to know which is the most convenient for you."

She stopped, panic shrouding her mind and body. He planned to take her away from the country, away from Hamilton? He *couldn't* know about Hamilton. "I can't just disappear to another country! I want to live here and keep a low profile."

"You're not making a very good attempt at it. Have you looked in a mirror lately? A six foot Amazon with spiky blonde hair, a St. Moritz tan, who strides along the sidewalks like she owns them. You also killed a man in Daytona Beach. It won't be long before the men from KARP find you."

She gasped; her body stiffened. Her knees went weak before she could stop walking and reach out for support. So he *did* know about Hamilton. "KARP?" she whispered.

"The Royal Princes' organization." He reached out and caught her arm, his brow creased with concern. "You don't look so well."

He eased her back a couple of steps. She turned to see a low wall behind her, stumbled back and gratefully collapsed on to it. He perched next to her, putting his arm around her waist to keep her from falling over backward. She was lightheaded with fear.

"You have to go away and leave me alone. I don't need rescuing. I truly don't." Her heart raced and she wanted to separate herself from this man as quickly as possible. First, she needed to know if he knew about Hamilton. If he didn't, the longer she could keep it that way, the better. She couldn't think how to ask him.

"How long do you think it'll be before others find you? After learning that you were in Florida, we then tracked you through your cell phone. "

"I got rid of it. By Monday it'll be out to sea or wherever they take the trash in Miami."

"By Monday you could be on the same garbage scow or on your way back to the Persian Gulf. Where did you throw it?"

"The dumpster behind the hotel. Luis told them he never saw

me. I thought that if they'd already been there, then it would be the safest place to stay. Why should they come back?"

"Where are you headed now?" he asked.

"To work. I'm a cocktail waitress."

"A cocktail waitress?

"It's honest work and I earn good tips. At least enough to take care of myself for the time being."

"You're a wealthy woman; this doesn't make sense. What do you know about waitressing?"

"I wasn't always wealthy. I had to work from the time I was in high school. There's a certain security living and working amongst anonymous people."

"But what about your money? I'm still receiving payment from your corporation, why aren't you using your own to protect yourself?"

"You said it right from the start. Hamid was killed. He didn't just happen to die in a plane accident. It was his own plane; it had been serviced that morning, and so far the NTSB has found no reason for it to have crashed. It seemed safer to get away from my former life as quickly as possible until I could learn who killed him and why."

"And what have you learned?" he argued.

"Only what you know. KARP. The royal princes never liked the idea that Hamid married an outsider, and I'm afraid they had him killed so we'd never have any children." She couldn't tell him that she'd spent the better part of the last year hiding out in a convent, waiting to have her baby.

"But you two had already been married nearly ten years and showed no signs of becoming parents." Vance puzzled over her statement and she worried that she'd given it away.

She nodded. "True."

He scratched his head. "I'm not completely sure what's going on here, but I know people who can help you access your funds."

"No! It's not as simple as it seems. I have to consider my family. My mother." She couldn't go on, not without betraying her secret. "Look, I have to get to work. You want to talk later, you can wait."

"You want to work tonight, go ahead. I'll walk you home when you're finished."

"That's around two o'clock. You can't hang around without ordering." She didn't know what to think. Her mind raced as fast as her heart. Maybe he was all right. He did know the code names. She led him through the hotel lobby to the patio out back where musicians warmed up for the evening. It would be a loud, raucous night. Her first

Saturday as a South Beach waitress. She hoped she could survive amongst all these kids. The other members of the staff, all five of them in their twenties, paid more attention to Vance than they did to her.

She felt like their mother, prepared to warn them about talking to strangers, but remembered that she herself had only met him barely half an hour ago.

She picked up her miniscule apron, tied it around her waist and waited to wait. Work.

Chapter Twelve

I was exhausted; we'd been meeting at my house and it was already one o'clock on Sunday morning, and the group, though as exhausted as I, was eager to get to work. John and Violet had taken turns to stay at the house with Hamilton, who slept through, oblivious to the international activities his existence stirred up, Canadians and Americans joining to protect him.

"We'll start work on Monday morning. Tomorrow, you each have your assignment," I said as everyone rose and stretched.

"Are you sure you want me to talk to Michael Garrett? You realize he's a retired Marine and likely to want to take over," Judy said.

"If he was a good Marine, he'll work well with the group. Plus, he may have some further ideas on the logistics of our plan," John said.

I opened the door for them. "I have no doubt he was a good Marine. Look how he maintains his property. He's precise and regular in everything he does. Military precision. He'll be an asset. And good for Hamilton."

They left and within moments Violet appeared at my door. "I'll help you clear up. I'm afraid this is going to be too much for you, Doll. When's the last time you managed such a large project?" She began collecting empty glasses and taking them to the kitchen.

"We have you and John, Judy, Pete, Alice to start with. And by tomorrow night we'll have added Michael, Justine, Larry, Al, Hannah and Beatrice. I'm hoping that Pete and Michael will draw in more of the men, the younger ones. I'm sure old Howard would be delighted to be a part of it all, but ninety-one is a bit old to ask him to take on such responsibilities."

We loaded the dishwasher and wiped the surfaces so the ants wouldn't figure out we had a little party and try to create one of their own.

~ * ~

It seemed like half an hour later when someone knocked at my door, but when I looked at my bedside clock, it was already eight thirty.

With a newfound energy, I tossed back the covers, slid my slippers on, grabbed my robe and headed to the door.

Alice stood there with a large box that looked suspiciously filled with donuts. "Breakfast," she announced with a chipmunk grin. "I thought we ought to start off on the right track. Pete will be along in a minute with the big coffee pot and get that going. It would be easier if we could do this at the clubhouse…"

"Keep talking," I interrupted her. "I need to run to the lady's." I disappeared into my master bathroom while she continued chattering in the kitchen.

"What happened to Pete's golf game?" I shouted over the noise of my handwashing.

"He decided to forego it. But just for today, he said. I think he's having too much fun with this project. He already talked to Michael and he'll be here. He has some drafting paper that he'll donate to the cause."

"Drafting paper?" I wondered aloud as I opened the cupboards to search for enough mugs and cups for an unknown number of people.

"It would be a lot easier to meet at the clubhouse. We already have everything we need over there. The cups, sugar and creamer. All that stuff." Alice opened the donut boxes and set them on the dining room table.

"You know why we can't."

"Yeah. I know you all think Carol would throw us out of the park, but she couldn't really, could she?"

"Maybe not, but she could call the authorities about Hamilton and he'd be taken away from us. We promised to look after him and keep him safe until his mother comes back."

"What if she doesn't?"

I looked at Alice. She was a skinny little thing and I could probably pick her up and toss her out the door. "Don't even think that." I'd worried about that enough for myself ever since Jessica died and I wasn't in a mood to be reminded of that possibility.

Violet soon arrived followed by the rest of the group, including the new invitees. Michael marched through the door precisely on time at nine thirty, dressed neatly in creased tan shorts and starched sport shirt.

Justine, unlike the rest of us Florida transplants, showed up in a pale yellow linen suit and heels. Not a hair out of place, shoes and purse matching. She placed a delicate tissue lined box of petite fours in the center of the dining table, right next to the box of donuts, making the donut box look like a rhinoceros next to a fragile butterfly.

"I'm going to church as soon as we're through here. We're going to need all the help we can get considering the undertaking." She placed herself daintily at the dining room table.

Maybe it had been a mistake to include her ladyship. I somehow couldn't see her changing a poopy diaper. Or even saying such words.

Once everyone settled I tapped on my water glass to gain their attention. Before I could open my mouth, Michael stepped away from the bookcase where he'd been posing in his best John Wayne stance. "Listen up!" His voice boomed. "Doll has a plan, but before she begins I want every one of you to take an oath of allegiance to the cause."

This created an uproar of mixed comments. I heard, "Asshole, who does he think he is?" "I can be trusted without taking oaths." "Great idea. Create a secret society in the park." "We'll need a password."

"Hold it!" Michael's voice boomed again. "Anyone who refuses to agree to the rules and take the oath will be asked to leave. No offense, but there are important things at stake here and before we divulge the entire story and the complete plan, we need to know where your loyalties lie. It's that simple."

I smiled across the room at him. So different from my Barclay. I admired Michael, but no way in hell would I ever been able to live with someone like that. "Thank you." I carried on, "This won't be in writing. We want no paper trails. The schedules will be word of mouth and please don't, whatever you do, use your computers to communicate. They can break into them easily. Now, Michael will give the oath. Is there anyone who objects? There being no objection, Michael, if you please."

"Everyone stand and raise your right hand." To my surprise, they all did as ordered. I followed suit.

"Repeat after me. I, state your name, do solemnly swear to do my duty to preserve and protect the child known as Hamilton Robbins, also known as Hamid Al Wafiki."

They swore, some of them exchanging surprised glances at the foreign sounding name.

Michael continued, "Should any person, including those in authority, ask any questions regarding the child, I swear to notify one of our leaders immediately in order to prevent his discovery in this community. Moreover, should I be found guilty of divulging any of our secrets, I recognize that I will be shunned for the rest of my life or as long as I live here. I will work in collusion with my fellow members no matter how long it takes, to care for the child until he can be recovered by his mother at which time I will willingly relinquish any and all claims to him. This I swear before my fellow members and before God."

Everyone waited for more, but Michael dropped his own right hand and the rest sank back onto their chairs.

It was my turn to lay out the plan and a work schedule. I asked for a computer expert, someone who might be able to do a little entrepreneurial hacking for us and Scott Simon's name came up. He is one of the younger residents in the park, newly moved in a few weeks ago.

"Good man, Scott," Michael declared. "Former Navy, but that's all right. Still a good man. He'll be trustworthy. I'll see him after the meeting and have him contact you as soon as possible."

"Now, what about Charlie? Isn't he going to notice that Jessica isn't coming and going?" Violet asked.

Charlie is our guard at the gatehouse. He reads a lot. There are two lanes to get in to the park, one for visitors and one for residents. Residents have a thing in their cars that automatically raises the gate. Visitors have to stop for Charlie to raise it manually. I doubt he ever looks up when a resident car comes or goes and I said so. "We should, however, move her car every couple of days and make sure it doesn't get dusty."

"On my list," Michael said as he tapped the side of his head. "Consider it taken care of."

"John said to tell everyone that he'll do whatever it takes. He's prepared to work night and day, if necessary, to get this show on the road." She blushed. "Those were his words, not mine."

"May I speak?" Justine raised her hand like a schoolgirl.

I nodded in her direction.

"Why is Michael in charge? We didn't have an election, did we? I thought this was all your idea, Doll. You ought to be in charge." She looked defiantly around the room before sitting down.

I cleared my throat. "This isn't a formal organization, Justine. We have only one goal and that's…"

"If you don't have a leader, you have anarchy," she interrupted.

"She's right, Doll," Pete offered. "We should make it official. Give ourselves a name and have officers."

Oh, Lord, I thought. Here we go. "All right. As I began this thing, I'll be the president pro-tem until we have an election. And as we've already agreed not to put anything in writing, who has the best memory to be secretary and keep track of the 'minutes' of our meetings?"

"I can do that," Judy said as she brushed donut dust from her face.

"I'll second that," Justine said.

"Good work. Robert's Rules," Michael added.

We then voted on a treasurer, sergeant at arms, a president and a vice-president.

"Now, what shall we call ourselves?" I asked as the new officially elected president.

"It can't have Hamilton's name in the title," Alice said.

When we all looked at her, she added. "In case we get caught and questioned about our meetings. Someone in the park is bound to notice that we meet at each other's houses. Think what would happen if Wilma Van Hess caught us. She's like a ferret."

"That's being kind," Pete said.

"Okay. You call him Ham for short. How about The Ham and Egg Club?" Hannah suggested.

"Then we could only meet for breakfast," Beatrice giggled.

"What about Duplicate Bridge Builders?" Pete put in. "We're building duplicate rooms and a way to connect all of them so we can move the baby quickly from house to house."

Groans from the group.

"Wouldn't it be cool if we had someone from World War II who was familiar with underground operations in Europe?" I said.

"We do!" Justine piped up.

Everyone looked at her.

"Old Howard. He worked in France with the Resistance!"

The same Old Howard I'd considered and rejected from my list of group members; I hadn't known of his activities in World War II.

There were cries of "No!" "Not really!" "You're making that up."

"I know he's quiet, but he still plays cards on Mondays and Wednesdays. He never talks about his experiences because he was captured and doesn't like to remember, but one day I walked him home from the clubhouse. He's such an old sweetheart. He invited me in for tea saying in the old days he would have said, 'rendezvous,' but as I was such a young girl, and I blushed, he thought tea would be nicer."

"And then?" I asked.

"Well, we chatted for quite a while and he told me all about his experiences in Paris during the war. That's all. We can include him. And if you like, I shall speak with him. In the mornings he still enjoys a strong cup of coffee and in the evening he will want a crepe with butter and brandy." She folded her hands on her lap when she was finished speaking.

I shrugged. "I think we have our expert and I think we have a name," I added as a thought popped into my head. "The Blenders. It sounds like a social club, but the meaning is clear."

"You want to explain that one?" Hannah asked.

"Remember Hamilton Beach appliances? I used to own a blender made by them. So 'blender' can be our secret password and the name of our group."

"Hold it a minute," Michael stood up. "The name for the group is a good idea, but it can't be used as a password. A password should be totally unrelated to the exercise."

"For example?" Beatrice said.

"I know. A bee in her bonnet!" Alice offered.

"That's stupid," her husband, Pete, said. "What's that got to do with anything?"

Michael held a hand up to stop them. "She's got it exactly right. It has nothing to do with the baby or our secret building project. If one of you needs to speak about the project and an outsider is present, you make sure to use that phrase. The other person will know to see you privately later."

"I don't get it," Beatrice frowned.

I jumped into the conversation. "Supposing you find a great bargain on diapers and need to deliver them to whoever has custody of Hamilton? If you see me on the street walking with Carol, for example, you would say, 'Have you talked to Judy lately? She has a bee in her bonnet about something.' Then I would call you or go to your house after I'd finished talking with Carol. It's simple."

"Why wouldn't I just bring the diapers to your house and ask you who has the baby this week?"

"What if my writing group were here? What would they think of you bringing me a bag of diapers?"

"They'd think you were incontinent," Violet said with a laugh.

I shot her a look that cut that laugh short. "We are the Keegan Bay Blenders. The password is 'bee in her bonnet.' We'll meet again tomorrow night."

Once everyone left except Violet and the house was again reasonably tidy, I asked to visit our little ward, just to reassure myself that this whole idea wasn't a hallucination.

We crossed to her house and John let us in. We tiptoed into her back bedroom where I could see Hamilton's tiny form by the light from the hallway.

How precious a sleeping baby can be. Oblivious to the world

and the turmoil that surrounds his little life.

I wiped a tear from my eye as I left Violet's house, knowing that somehow, some way, we would keep him safe, no matter what the future might bring.

Chapter Thirteen

True to his word, Vance remained at a table as far removed from the center of the action as possible. Much further and he would have been in the ocean. He occasionally used a cell phone and often disappeared only to magically reappear a little while later. Moira never saw him leave or re-enter the patio. There was something terribly familiar about him, but she feared that her mind could be playing tricks on her. Hamid had been gone for nearly a year.

As the night wore on Moira had to drop any thoughts of Vance. Groping hands, suggestive leers, and outright crude invitations peppered her evening. By midnight she was ready to throw in the towel.

From time to time she delivered a cranberry juice with ice and a twist of lemon to Vance, who smirked at her efforts. She would let him know just what she thought of him once she was off work, except she wasn't sure what she did think. He had the security code that she and Hamid agreed they would never share with anyone but the agency he'd hired to protect them; he even reminded her somehow of Hamid.

Not just his stature or his personality—there was nothing professorial about Vance—but she couldn't quite put her finger on it. Maybe she was too eager to feel safe again. To let someone else take over the worrying.

By two o'clock in the morning, exhausted, she wanted nothing more than to crawl into her bed. She had made good tips, but her feet, her back, her arms, her everything, ached. As she turned south on the sidewalk to head back to her hotel, Vance cautiously took her elbow and switched her direction.

"I'm just taking you to my car. You have a new room."

"Oh, please. I need my stuff…"

"All taken care of."

Bright neon lights kept the district festive even at this late hour. She stopped and pulled a chair out from a sidewalk table. "I need to rest. Be like a good reporter and give me the who, what, how, when, where and most especially the why."

Vance looked at his watch, tapped on it, and then joined her at the table. He waved off a weary waiter when he stepped out of the nearby hotel. "Won't be here more'n a minute, son."

Moira closed her eyes. "I'm waiting."

"I have help, that's who. They took care of moving your things to a new location. That's what. It was simple. Your hotel doesn't have the best of security. Luis, your faithful watchdog, was off duty. The night manager didn't give a hoot who came and took your stuff as long as the room was paid for and he received a generous tip. That's the how. We did it while you worked. That's the when. You know the where, well, except for where we're going. We're headed for my car which is parked a hundred miles north of here—at least it seems like a hundred miles. You'd think the powers-that-be around in this city would organize better public transportation to keep the cars away. And why? Because you're my job. That's why."

"I'm not paying you."

"You don't have to. I'm being more than adequately compensated. And I have the bonus of being in your company."

She glanced over at him to see if he was joking. He smiled at her. She giggled and then caught herself.

"You know if you didn't have that butch haircut, you'd be downright pretty." He took her arm, helped her up and led her across the street. "But, it gives me an idea. We can deal with that on Monday. Maybe tomorrow."

"Listen!" She yanked her arm away from him. "I never agreed to let you run my life! I have enough money to take care of myself. There are some things you don't know and I'll be damned if I want you interfering anymore. So, tell me where my things are so I can collect them and then try to find another room."

"Hold it. If you have money, why are you working at that place?"

"That's how I get my money. I need to work. Okay? We went through this earlier." Eyes burning, she rushed ahead of him. She couldn't weaken and cry now.

"All right, you need to work. I had the idea that you had plenty of money stashed in Swiss accounts or in Lichtenstein, one of those places."

"We did; still do, I suppose. At the moment, I'm trying to stay out of sight so I'm not even accessing my own personal accounts. Look, I worked my way through college so it's not exactly foreign to me to take care of myself." She paused. "It's just that I kind of got out of the habit over the past ten years."

Vance nodded as if he understood. "The car's up on Twelfth Street. Places are shutting down. It'll be quiet soon."

Being off the streets once the lights went out would be a good idea. She hadn't considered that when she accepted the promotion to working nights. How lucky that Vance showed up when he did. Or was it luck? He arrived the same day as the other two men at the front desk. Good cop; bad cop?

But, if he wanted to kidnap her or kill her, he could have done so already and been long gone. He didn't seem to know about Hamilton, either, but that could also be a ruse, a ploy to gain her confidence. Right now she needed to soak in a hot tub and get some sleep.

Between the drinks she slopped all over herself during the evening and the cigarette smoke out on that patio, she smelled like a nightclub. And felt like a nightclub that had been run over by a truck.

"Right here. Well, left actually," Vance said from behind. She turned into the public parking lot not knowing what to look for. "The Beemer in the back. Keep going."

He guided her through the lot and once settled into the car, comfortable and weary, she yawned. "All right, before you start your engines, just where are we going?"

"You remember when you filled out that paperwork? Cinderella and Hamburger Boy?"

"Of course."

"Then you'll remember that if we need to remove you from a dangerous situation, you agree to cooperate in your evacuation."

"I don't perceive the same dangers as you do, obviously."

"I told you, IDIOTS and KARP. If one can find you, so can the other. And anyone else looking to do harm to the," he hesitated briefly before finishing, "the widow of the heir."

"Fine," she said, too exhausted to argue. "Just take me wherever. I'm tired."

"Your slave, madam."

Twenty minutes later he pulled into a driveway with enormous wrought iron gates that slid apart to let the car through. It rolled to a stop under a softly lit portico surrounded by tropical foliage. Spanish style wooden doors marked the entrance to the house or hotel, she didn't particularly care which. She stepped out on to the red tiles and waited for him to open the door for her.

She felt like she'd been transported to another country once they entered the foyer. With no concierge or reception area, she realized it was a private residence. It was elegant and Spanish, with a curved staircase to the right, more red tiles on the floor, muted gold stucco walls with alcoves containing brightly colored ceramic pots filled with more tropical plants.

A parrot stood on a wooden t-bar on the left near an open door that led into a large, also softly lit room filled with overstuffed leather furniture, dark wood tables and more greenery and colorful planters. Large paintings decorated the walls and she wanted to step into the room and pretend it was home; home with no troubles.

"Upstairs."

"What?"

"I had your things put upstairs in the master bedroom. You'll be comfortable there. And safe."

"Shut up and let an old man sleep."

Moira stared at the parrot. "Did he really say that?"

"Hello, Hidalgo. And good night."

"Sleep well, children," the parrot responded. It shifted its weight, ruffled its feathers and settled back into its sleeping position, eyes closed, shoulders hunched.

"And you?" she asked, already starting up the stairs.

"I had a cot put into the adjoining nursery."

Her heart stopped. *Nursery? So, he did know! He planned to bring Hamilton here! Could it be that he was already upstairs sleeping soundly?* She didn't know whether to laugh with relief that her baby would be safe or cry that her secret was no longer secure. "Nursery," she said dully.

"That's what they call it, though as far as I know there's never been a baby in it. The owners were divorced before their marriage certificate dried and the ones before that were retired billionaires. If it makes you happier we can call it a dressing room."

"How do you know all about this place? Was it your friends who couldn't face the commitment of a long term relationship?"

"Actually it was me. This is your room for as long as you need it," he said as the reached the top of the stairs. He pointed to a door on the left. "The guards sleep in the two rooms across the hall. There's another guest room at the end of the hall. You share a balcony with it, but don't get any ideas about leaving; we lock all the doors every night. This door between our rooms has no lock. You'll have to trust me." He held up both hands like a magician proving he had no cards up his sleeves.

"Trust is not a word I can relate to these days. But, thank you."

The room was large. The heavy Spanish oak headboard of a

king-sized bed with lavish brocade spread stood against one wall. The bed appeared small in the beautifully tiled room.

Her overnight bag rested in the center of the bed. Next to it was a large plastic bag with the rest of her clothes she'd bought since settling in to the hotel. Plush red draperies stood open to a balcony with a wrought iron railing. Two paintings on the wall to the left looked like excellent Picasso copies, their brilliant colors standing out against the muted tones of the walls.

She could be happy in a room like this, if only she could have Hamilton with her.

"Good night."

Vance gave a half wave. "I'll go downstairs and double check that everything is secure. Fernando and Vern will take turns keeping watch."

"Vern and Fernando?" She refrained from laughing. "Vern and Fern. Who are they?"

"Security. I wouldn't suggest laughing when you meet either one of them. They take their work seriously. The nursery has a door leading into the hallway. I'll use that one when I'm done with my rounds. So." He shifted from foot to foot like a shy schoolboy. "Well. Good night."

She smiled as he left the room. If only she'd met him... but she couldn't think that way now. As soon as she heard him heading down she raced over to the connecting door, hoping and yet not hoping. But, just as Vance had said, there was nothing more than an adult sized cot made up for him and a bureau with men's personal items on it. She turned back into her room and scanned it for a telephone.

Disappointed at not finding one, she vowed to call her mother first thing in the morning. She knew Hamilton was safe in that senior citizen park, but still, she'd feel better if she could hear her mother's voice.

"Nice house," she said as she opened the bathroom door.

Once again startled by the leggy blonde who faced her in the full length mirror, she quickly turned away and headed for the sink to remove her contact lenses, then the excessive eye make-up she applied daily in an attempt to alter her appearance.

Though her 'butchy' blonde hair should have been enough, she knew anyone really searching for her would recognize her within moments of seeing her. Besides the height, slim build and eye color, she had a long scar on her right upper arm, the result of a skiing accident five years ago in Switzerland.

Though the surgeons did a fine job of saving her arm, which

had been broken during a tumble down the steep slope, even the talents of the finest specialists couldn't make the scar completely disappear. Being out in the sun every day didn't help either as her skin turned a lovely golden tone, the scar appeared whiter and whiter.

No, she would not disappear easily into a crowd. She brushed her teeth and slipped on an oversized T-shirt, and then slid between the softest sheets she'd encountered since leaving her own homes.

Her mind wanted to worry about Hamilton and her alleged rescuer, Vance, but before anxiety could take over, she fell asleep.

~ * ~

For the next three days she remained a prisoner in the compound. Vance explained that his duty was to keep her safe and out of sight until he could figure out their next step. In her fear for the safety of her baby, she complied. Whatever Vance had in mind, he still didn't act as if he knew about Hamilton. He spent his days prowling the grounds, taking turns with Vern and Fernando, the other two guards. She had met them on her first morning there when Vern brought her breakfast in bed.

Vern turned out to be a five foot four power-house of a woman. Well-muscled, short dark hair, sparkling icy blue eyes and a New York accent and attitude to make the strongest man quake. When Vern spoke, Moira listened.

Later that morning when she ventured out of her room, Moira found Fernando drinking coffee by the swimming pool while he watched Vance do his laps. Anyone observing the group would think they were a bunch of lollygagging vacationers instead of international mercenaries.

Fernando jumped to his feet when she stepped out onto the patio. "Good morning, miss. Can I get anything for you?"

"Do you think I could swim?" She needed to expend pent up energy.

"Of course. It is not necessary for you to remain in your room all day. You are not a prisoner here."

Though Fernando was as huge as Vern was small, he moved with the lightness and grace of a cat. He headed into the kitchen. "You go swim, then you eat."

When she returned to the pool, Vance still worked on his laps. She stepped to the deep end of the Olympic sized pool and dove in. The cool water flowed over her skin, refreshing rather than chilling and she came up ready to do her own laps.

Vance headed toward her and turned to keep pace as she made her way across the pool. They swam companionably until she figured she'd done a mile. Breathless, she pulled herself out of the water while Vance flipped himself up onto the edge of the pool, reminding her of a seal at the zoo. She half expected him to begin a flapping applause for a fish someone might toss.

"You keep in shape," she commented. Vern tossed her a towel. Fernando was nowhere in sight. As soon as she said it, she realized she'd been staring at Vance's rock solid body with pleasure. Her face burned.

"I try," he laughed. "You're in pretty good shape yourself."

His gaze roved over her body, and she was glad she'd chosen a one-piece suit so he wouldn't see the slight but obvious scarring left from her pregnancy. The longer Hamilton remained a secret, the longer he would be safe.

She needed Vance to trust her so that when she was ready, his guard would be down and she could leave this place. First, she needed to find a way to get a cell phone. With the three Musketeers watching at all times, that was going to be tricky. At this point she didn't know if she was really being protected or she was a prisoner.

Chapter Fourteen

Nearly another entire week had passed and we still hadn't heard from Moira Robbins. Thanksgiving had come and gone and she had no idea that her mother had died. Christmas was only a few weeks away. She had no way of knowing that Hamilton was safe. The selfish brat was probably already at one of her homes overseas, happy to be free of her obligations. Once she murdered that man in her seedy little trailer...

But, no. I couldn't go on thinking so negatively about Ham's mother. He would grow up sensing my hostility. I told myself to trust that she'd got caught up in something beyond her control and was unable to call. I forced myself to even say it aloud two or three times a day. One of those times when I was with the baby.

"Your mommy loves you so much and as soon as she can, she'll come get you."

I only hoped I wouldn't be saying that as we sent him off to college.

Old Howard arrived at our next meeting in his bright blue golf cart and was duly served his brandy, following which he was eager to participate in our clandestine activities.

Michael Garrett took control as the chairman in charge of logistics, and explained how, in the event of an emergency Hamilton was to be transported from house to house, before taking the last most desperate step in the event we ran out of houses. The last house in our underground railroad was at 28 Keegan Bay Marina Way, adjacent to the gates to the marina.

If the danger persisted, then Hamilton would be placed aboard Pete's boat. Michael informed us that he would keep the next step secret from all but a few chosen people for security purposes.

"It is essential that I be kept in the loop at all times. Pete and I'll prepare the boat with all the essentials for the subject's care for not less than three days nor more than ninety, by which time he should have reached his final destination."

"We can't work on Thursdays," Pete added.

"Why not?" Hannah asked.

"Lawn service."

"What's the lawn service got to do with our work?"

"Them boys are all over the place, in the back yards, first with their edgers, then with the mowers and blowers. They could get wind of what we're up to."

While we had our own three employees, it was true that an outside lawn service came in on Thursdays for mowing and vacuuming of the lawns and streets in Keegan Bay. The attention to detail is what kept the park in such first-rate condition.

"They can't even speak English," I said.

Old Howard cleared his throat and everyone turned to him. "Pete is right. Observe, if you will, when you see them next, that these young men who scurry about like hyperactive robots are mostly Latino. If I were from the Middle East and spying on this community in search of Miss Robbins or her child, I would certainly find it easy to mingle with that lot."

"You'd last long enough to open your mouth. They mostly speak only Spanish," Michael said.

"You have a point," Old Howard conceded, but then added, "However, I go along with Pete and suggest that we not work on Thursdays. We don't need one of those fellows catching you passing lumber in through a back window and reporting to Carol."

I listened in awe. This thing was becoming larger than I had ever dreamed.

Pete took over explaining how much lumber and nails and such we would require for each room. Considering that there were fourteen streets in Keegan Bay, and Michael wanted to have a room on every street, we'd need quite a bit.

Judy sat upright on a dining room chair with her hands folded in her lap, looking for all the world like an attentive schoolgirl. But as Pete finished itemizing his list of supplies required along with his estimate of the cost of each item, she came up with a total.

Personally, I found it hard to believe and went immediately to my computer and recalculated the numbers. She'd been exactly right. We'd made a good choice when we appointed her secretary and treasurer. How she could do that without writing anything down, was beyond me. She should have been working for the CIA, or the Canadian equivalent. Come to think of it, that's exactly what she did before retiring twelve years ago.

Justine offered to provide her version of food and drink to the working crews. "Every day I'll prepare a fresh salad for the workers, fruit for dessert and refreshing vitamin enriched flavored water."

I could tell by the looks on the men's faces that they weren't particularly thrilled with that, but we didn't want to discourage anyone or make them unhappy at this point. Disgruntled people can cause problems.

I looked around the room and saw Alice grinning. She waggled her fingers as if giving a secret code. It took a moment, but I caught on. She was letting me know that when Justine's "lunch" was finished, she would bring along real food, hearty roast beef heroes, donuts, beer and soda.

Our plans moved along pretty smoothly considering everything had to be done in secrecy. That meant all our debris from the building projects had to be removed under cover of darkness.

Instead of putting the scraps in our own dumpsters, the men hauled them over to a neighboring community and used those dumpsters. We knew it wasn't right, but on the whole, what is a life worth? We would pay the fine, should we be discovered. Pete used his golf bag to bring materials into the park when he had work during the day. Screws, nails and other small hardware fit nicely in our cloth grocery bags.

Each member had already recruited at least one person from every court so that in the event of having to transfer Hamilton quickly, we wouldn't have to travel far at one time. There would be a total of twenty "safe" rooms for him.

Nine of the streets were exceptionally long so we decided to have two safe havens on each of them. At least five of the houses had small walled gardens in the back, put in during a lax period when a previous manager preferred Jack Daniels to Keegan Bay and so neglected to uphold all the rules. Another small group, six, had enclosed their carports and made garages out of them.

We had use of three of those homes, which was a blessing, as that's where we hid our building materials. As construction on each secret room was completed, the decorating teams consisting of Larry and Al, Hannah, Beatrice and me with the help of Michael and Pete, who did the heavy labor, took over and painted the walls, carpeted the floors and placed decals so that all the rooms appeared exactly alike. Our thought was that Hamilton would be less traumatized if we had to move him often.

During the building process I couldn't help but wonder what Carol, our park manager and her good friend, Maggie, thought of all the sudden activity in the park. Golf carts and scooters scurried up and down the streets. Neighbors saluted one another, frequently beginning their conversations with, "So and So has a bee in her bonnet."

When The Blenders gathered, if Hamilton was awake, we would place him on a blanket on the floor and let him become familiar with all of us. What a lot of grandparents he would grow up with, though I confess it seemed more of us were far more intrigued by the challenge of hiding him from the authorities and whatever dark faction of society were searching for him.

On Thursday morning Violet and I were working on a quilt for Hamilton when she gasped. I looked at her and saw that she was staring out the window. I didn't have to ask to know that there was trouble outside.

I turned and saw it immediately. Wilma, that venomous, pinch faced piece of work, stood in Jessica's driveway talking to two men dressed in gray suits. Both wore reflective sunglasses. This was not a good omen. Moving as one, we quickly stowed the quilt, scraps and sewing supplies in the drawer beneath the sofa. Hamilton was spending a few days with Larry and Al, where his room was habitable, if not completed.

"She's pointing out this house," Violet said needlessly; I could see that for myself. I could also see the supercilious, smug smirk on Wilma's face as the men left her and headed in our direction.

My mind whirled and quickly settled on a plan. "You go into the back bedroom and turn on the intercom so you can hear me. Make sure you don't put it on the two-way channel. If it sounds like I'm in trouble, then you can sneak out the back door and get one of the men, Pete or Michael, to create a diversion. Or something," I added lamely, the idea fizzling out as the two men came up my walk.

With my heart in my throat, I waited for their knock before going to the door.

"Yes?" I tried to look surprised to see them on my step.

"Doris Reynolds?" The one on the left said as he held out a business card. "I'm from The International Directorate Investigating Terrorist Societies."

I took it. "Sam Smith, Investigator, IDIOTS," I read it aloud, and then handed it back to him. "Mr. Smith? Then, you must be Jones," I said turning to the other one while trying unsuccessfully to suppress a smile.

He removed his sunglasses and stared at me in surprise. "How did you know? Have our men already been around?"

"Just a lucky guess. What can I do for you, gentlemen?

"May we come in? We have a matter of utmost delicacy to

discuss and it would be better if we weren't observed."

"You've already spoken with Wilma; the entire community will know about you within ten minutes, but do come in. Can I offer you some iced tea or coffee?"

"No, ma'am." Smith sat on one end of the sofa while Jones prowled around the living room like a cat inspecting its new surroundings. "We're trying to locate Jessica Robbins. Your friend suggested you might know where she is?"

"Why do you need to locate Jessica?" I asked, trying my best to look like a stern mother protecting her child.

Jones spoke from directly behind me. "This isn't a joke, Mrs. Reynolds. We need to find Mrs. Al Wafiki before the terrorists do."

"Oh, my. I thought you were looking for Jessica. Who is Mrs. Al—"

"Al Wafiki. Her daughter."

"What an unusual name. What do you want with her?"

"Don't think you can toy with us, Mrs. Reynolds. We know there is someone else in this house with you. Would Mrs. Robbins happen to be slightly plump with thin white hair? Thick eyeglasses?" Jones moved like a dancer as he whirled in front of me and squatted gracefully at my knees. He lowered his eyeglasses and smiled, an evil, thin lipped smile, a Wilma smile.

I felt my lips curl in a smile of relief. They had no idea what Jessica looked like. "How did you know?"

"We've been watching the neighborhood for a while now. One of our skills is to be able to observe without being observed," Smith said.

"Very clever," I said.

"Jessica!" I called as I pushed myself out of my chair and headed down the hall. "She's been helping me with my laundry all morning. Such a dear."

I stuck my head into the room. Violet cowered in the corner, eyes huge, lips trembling. "Don't make me do it, Doll. I'll mess everything up."

"Remember Anastasia? How you played the Dowager Empress?"

She removed her glasses and looked at me through watery eyes remembering her days of glory on stage. "I was good, wasn't I?" The transformation was amazing; she tossed aside the glasses, brushed me out of the way and strode into the hallway. I followed her.

Jones put an end to that. "We'd like to speak with Mrs. Robbins alone, if you don't mind."

Violet perched regally on the edge of my best Victorian lady's chair and waved a royal hand in the air. "Go along, dear. I'll just have a little chat with the gentlemen. Perhaps later you can make some tea."

I bowed out and returned to the bedroom and put my ear close to the intercom, heart pounding as I waited to hear how Violet would respond to their questions. She was in her actress mode and anything could happen.

"Such a good friend to me—quite like a real sister. I don't know what I would do without Doll."

One of the men cleared his throat. "Well, it's clear that you're good friends."

"Very good friends, indeed."

"I can see that." He apparently didn't know how to start his questioning. I was tempted to run out and prompt him, but Violet opened the process.

"What is on your mind, young man? You realize I am a very old lady; I haven't got time to sit here all day waiting for you to dream up questions. If you have something to ask, ask it."

"We wonder if you know where your daughter, Moira, is?"

"I know my daughter's name and what difference does it make to you whether or not I know where my daughter is? Suffice it to say, we stay in touch. Now, if you'll excuse me, I must help my friend. We do that, you know."

"Do what?" That sounded like the first one, Jones.

"Help one another. That's what friends do. Give me your cards. I shall make Moira aware of your interest in her. Idiots, indeed." Her voice faded and I realized she was coming down the hall, moving away from the intercom. "You may let yourselves out. I'm sure Doll won't mind."

She burst through the bedroom door and flung herself into my arms.

"You were quoting from an Agatha Christie murder mystery!" I accused as I hugged her.

"I think it was *Appointment With Death*."

"Oh, my." Suddenly, I didn't feel like laughing so much anymore.

Chapter Fifteen

Sunday morning Moira sat with the others out by the pool. They had finished the breakfast Vern had prepared and Fernando served and now they were reading the newspapers, taking turns sharing the various sections. There had been no further news about the dead man in Daytona Beach, neither on the television, nor in the papers.

She assumed the event was considered a burglary gone bad. That didn't mean whoever had sent him to find her and or her baby wasn't still searching. As long as these three people continued to watch her, she felt fairly safe. The problem she had was not knowing what they had in mind for her.

Vance hadn't been forthcoming yet about why he "helped" her to get away from the two men at the hotel. He spent his days locked in a room he called his office. Fern and Vern took turns patrolling the grounds and periodically joining them for meals, as they were this morning, which left her to converse with Hidalgo. They were short conversations as his vocabulary, though extensive for a parrot, was pretty limited.

"Good morning, pretty lady," whenever she came down the stairs, no matter the time of day.

"Good night, pretty lady," when she went up the stairs.

"Sleep well, you two," if she and Vance happened to go up the stairs together.

"My name is Hidalgo," she repeated to him day after day.

"Hardy har har har and yo-ho-ho," he responded.

There were a few other phrases and occasionally he would surprise her with a cognizant response to a real question. One morning she asked, "What does Vance do all day?"

"Vance monitors computers," he answered.

~ * ~

Moira threw her section of paper onto the table. "I've had it with being stuck in this house. I need to get out. I've admired every flower and plant in the place, I've learned the names of at least eighteen birds, sidestepped two snakes, and counted the tiles in my bedroom four times, coming up with a different number every time. I've spent so much time with Hidalgo, he thinks I'm another parrot."

Vance peered at her over the top of the financial pages, blinked once, and then put the paper up again.

She leaned across the table and yanked the paper, tearing it in half. "Talk to me, dammit!"

"Be nice, and I will," he said pleasantly.

"I don't feel like being nice. I appreciate that you helped me lose those two men at my hotel, but I can't stand this inertia. Why are we just sitting around like this? Why aren't we doing something? Going someplace?"

"You're shouting."

Vern pushed her chair back, stood and stretched. "My turn," she said to Fernando. "Later," she said to Vance with a small wave.

She shifted her shoulder holster into a more comfortable position, checked her watch and headed toward the opposite side of the pool and faded into the foliage. She would patrol the outer boundary of the compound for the next two hours.

Moira watched the spot where Vern had disappeared while she tried to compose herself. She needed to convince Vance the importance of her connecting with her mother without giving away her secret. "Vance, please tell me what's going on. I need a cell phone so I can let my mother know that I'm alive and well. She's probably out of her mind with worry by now. Do you want to be responsible if she has a heart attack?"

Though she truly was concerned for her mother, she needed to know that Hamilton was still with her and safe and well. If she could only call.

Vance looked at her, studying her for a moment before speaking. "All right. Let's go over to South Beach where we can pick up a cell phone and you can make one call. After that, it goes into the ocean. Is that a deal?"

This time when she reached across the table she grabbed his hands and squeezed them. "Thank you. Thank you!"

Her heart skipped with joy as they crossed the causeway. It wouldn't be long before she could actually call her mother and assure herself that Hamilton was thriving.

As they drove, Vance explained that the IDIOTS were most likely checking other places for her by now, not having found her anywhere in South Beach, so that was the safest place for them to go.

"That's what I tried to tell you when you first found me," she shouted over the noise of the traffic.

"It was too soon then."

He stopped the car, dropped her off at a convenience store on Fifth Street while he drove on around the block, promising to be back within five minutes.

Her chance to escape. But, first she had to buy a cell phone so she ran into the shop and shifted from foot to foot as she watched the secondhand sweep around the large industrial clock on the wall five times while the clerk dawdled. The instant she paid for the phone she rushed out into the brilliant sunshine ready to run. The problem was, where to?

She had seventy-five dollars and change left from her tips after buying the phone. Her escape bag with her secret stash of money was still in the closet in the bedroom at the house. Now, she had to figure out what to do next. The first thing would be to get off the street before he returned.

She looked up and down the crowded street. Plenty of cars going in both directions but she didn't see his BMW. She started walking eastward, toward the beach when she felt a tap on her shoulder.

"Don't you want a ride?" Vance smiled at her.

Her shoulders dropped. "I was just pretending I'm my own person and can come and go as I please."

"Your highness isn't her own person, Moira. You're safer with me. Trust me."

"You keep saying that," she scowled as she climbed into the car. "I have a phone. May I at least speak with my mother in privacy?"

"We'll have Vern set it up for you."

"I can do that myself!" she replied, indignant that he seemed to think her a fool.

"And what address will you use when they ask? What ZIP code? What name?" He wheeled the car in a U-turn and they were now heading west again, back toward the causeway and the compound.

She hadn't thought of that. Somehow she figured the phone would be completely anonymous. She tried to read the directions, but the motion of the car made it impossible to make out the fine print. She tossed it back into its plastic bag and resigned herself to waiting another hour before finding out about her baby.

"Are we just going to spend the rest of my life living in that compound?" she asked for the umpteenth time.

"Rest assured that everyone has your welfare at heart. I'm happy enough to have you as a houseguest. Fernando and Vern are happy to have something to do besides play housemaid and butler, so relax and enjoy yourself."

Enjoy herself! How much she wanted to explain to him about Hamilton. She took a deep breath, fought back the ever-threatening tears and tried to enjoy the ride. A blimp was preparing to land up ahead. That proved a temporary distraction until they got home. God! Now she was thinking of his house as her home!

As soon as the car stopped she leapt out and headed for the house in search of Vern. Within minutes that felt like hours, she had the phone operational and retreated to sit on the diving board to call her mother. She punched in the numbers and waited. And waited. The answering machine was the same generic male voice that told her to please leave a message.

She disconnected and redialed. Again the generic answering machine. Unsure if she remembered her mother's number correctly, she looked around to make sure the others weren't watching her and then called information. The number was right. Where would her mother go with Hamilton?

She went into the house and reported to Vance about the answering machine, but without expressing any alarm. "She must have gone to church. I forget that people still do that." Trying to make light of the situation. She knew damn well that her mother wouldn't risk taking Hamilton out to church. "I'll try again in an hour or so."

"You'll try again in fifteen minutes and if you don't reach her then, you'll get rid of the phone and we'll get another one in a couple of days," he ordered as he chopped greens for a lunch salad.

She sat on the tall stool at the kitchen counter and rested her arms on the cool ceramic tiled surface. "Do you really think they can trace a brief call to an answering machine?"

"It could be a set up. They don't let her answer the first couple of times you call, then when you call again, they're ready and waiting, so they let her answer."

Her eyes grew large. "You think they might have my mother?" As soon as the words were out she had to bite her lips to keep from telling him about Hamilton.

"I don't know that they do, but it's a possibility we have to consider. Now, do you want these little grape tomatoes in your salad?" He held up the tiny red vegetables for her inspection.

"I'll try the phone again." She stormed out and punched the redial button. Same thing. What the hell were the names of her mother's neighbors? Most of them were Canadians and probably weren't even there yet. Some old ladies lived year round across the courtyard. Doll and Violet. She remembered Doll with a last name that begins with R. She could telephone the main office and ask. She was punching in the number for information when Vern emerged from the bushes.

"Who are you calling?" she asked.

"My mother."

"You know you're mother's number; why are you calling information?"

Moira looked at her in astonishment. "You are observant, aren't you?" Before Vern could force the issue, she tossed the phone into the pool. "I guess that's why Vance keeps you."

Her phone had barely hit the water when she heard Vance's voice from the kitchen, "Moira! Get in here. Now!"

The urgency of his voice sent her rushing inside. Vern rushed beside her through the patio doors, her weapon at the ready. Fernando dashed in from the front of the house, gun drawn. He kept sweeping the room with his eyes as his gun moved back and forth.

"Lunch is ready," Vance said. "Put the artillery away. You'd think you never had a call for food before."

"That's not funny, boss," Fernando grumbled.

"It's not," Vern agreed as she reholstered her weapon. "You ever hear about the boy who cried wolf?"

"Point taken. Sit down. Who wants milk and who wants a soft drink?"

Moira pulled out the stool she'd been sitting on earlier. "I want to speak with my mother. If I can't reach her by Wednesday, do you think we can send someone to at least check on her?"

"That's fair enough. You're probably right, though. She's gone to church. We'll get another phone this evening. Maybe we can even go in to Miami for dinner," Vance said. "Get you some different hair color. A wig or something until your hair grows out."

"If I change my hair back to dark brown, or if it grows out, I'll look like myself again. What's the point?"

"All right, stay blonde, but you really need that mop styled. Butter?" he asked as he handed her a hot roll from the oven.

"My sister is a hairdresser," Fernando said.

"Your sister lives in Guatemala," Vern replied. "We can hardly pop over there for a do."

"If I can't reach my mother, I don't care what my hair looks like, I'm going to find a way to go see her—"

Vern said, "That's a four hour drive."

"I have an idea, but it'll have to wait until—" Vance began.

Moira cut him off "—until Wednesday, at the latest. That's when I go on strike. " She buttered a roll. "I need to know that my mother is all right."

"I have an idea. Let's finish lunch and get some more sun. You've been tanning beautifully. Makes a nice change in your appearance. Once you're dark enough, maybe you can go back to black hair and look like a Latina."

Moira looked at her reflection in the toaster at the end of the counter. "I was rather pale when this all began. You may be right, but this scar shows up more viciously now."

"I have an idea about that, too. I hope you get in touch with your mother by Wednesday so we don't have to go out."

Chapter Sixteen

There had been fourteen calls on Jessica's answering machine since this whole thing began. The only message was from a carpet cleaning company. I hoped the other calls were from Moira and for some reason she couldn't talk.

In the beginning, when I pressed the call back button, I got a message that the number was unavailable, but more recently the message was that the number was out of service. In spite of the evidence, I refused to accept that Moira was a killer who had abandoned her child.

After erasing the messages, I dusted around Jessica's house so it looked lived in and then remembered it was Wednesday and the trash men would be around shortly. I had to gather some trash to put out so they wouldn't become suspicious.

Before I could find anything, I saw Old Howard coming around the corner leaning heavily on his walker. He wore the fur-trimmed overcoat that he normally took with him when he went North.

I watched as he approached the house, wondering if he'd forgotten that Jessica didn't live here anymore. He sidled up to the driveway and into the carport where he glanced around before opening his coat and dropping an empty milk carton into the trash can. After replacing the lid, he stood a little straighter as he left the driveway.

I added a plastic bag full of cleaning rags to the garbage before heading home.

As I walked back to my house, I saw Michael emerge from Violet's. He carried an enormous purple duffel bag on his back.

"Morning, Doll." He saluted briskly, though I could tell from the perspiration dripping down his face and the way he was limping, that the bag was probably more than he should have been carrying.

"Michael."

"Any news from Moira?" he gasped as he settled the bag next to his Jeep.

"No." I was about to explain about the hang-ups on Jessica's phone when I thought I saw movement behind the hibiscus bushes at the side of Violet's house. That would be the space between her place and mine. "Hush a minute, Michael. I think someone's watching us."

"Well, I'll just take these old clothes down to the Thrift Shop for old Vi," he shouted at me and then whispered, "Who is it? Where is he?"

The bushes stopped moving, but in the mid-morning brightness, dark shadows remained. "Right behind you. They know we've seen them. They're being still at the moment."

"Open the vehicle door for me and place yourself behind the Jeep," Michael said.

I did, feeling a bit silly.

"I don't see anyone," he said.

"They were there!" I replied as I stepped out from behind the Jeep. Just then Wilma and Carol appeared from the far side of the empty house. I jumped back, sure that guilt was written all over my face.

"Morning, ladies," Michael said with a small salute.

Carol approached us while Wilma remained on the sidewalk. She was sure she'd caught us at some nefarious activity. Actually, she had, but I'd never tell and I knew Michael wouldn't either.

"I've been wanting to talk to you, Doll," Carol began. "Do you have time now or would you prefer to come down to the office later?"

That was a surprise. "Talk? About what?" I looked at Michael as if he'd have the answer.

"About your position as Block Captain for Sunset Court."

"What about it?" Behind her Wilma stood with folded arms, watching. I knew she was wishing she could hear what was being said.

"Wilma tells me that you didn't report a death. The passing of Mrs. Robbins. I'm on my way there now to find out what's going on."

"Jessica's dead?" I gasped.

"Jessica?" Michael echoed. He stopped, apparently at a loss for words. One thing a good Marine probably didn't know how to do was lie.

I had to think of something fast. "What makes her think Jessica's dead?"

"She read it in an obituary."

"No," I said in a shocked voice as I sidled closer to Carol so that there'd be no way for Wilma to eavesdrop. "She must have misread it. Robbins is a fairly common name. Did you see it yourself? You know Wilma's reputation, of course."

Carol frowned in thought. "I've tried calling her several times and received no answer; then I tried her emergency number, her daughter in Switzerland, but that number's been disconnected. No one has notified me and the boys haven't reported any unusual activity at her house." She paused and then added, "Or lack thereof."

"Last I heard she was going to visit the daughter. For a month."

"Or two," Michael added.

"Or two."

"So, you've seen her?"

"We had a meeting at my house the other night and she was the center of attention."

Carol looked across the way at Jessica's. "Who drove her to the airport?" Her tone and the raised eyebrows suggested she probably didn't believe us.

"Me. I did." I said, before Michael could make the same claim at the same time.

"Good. You should have told me in the first place. I wish you people would tell me when you're going away. It would make my life so much easier. Wilma has at least one false report a week about a resident. Last week, she told me Flora on Dawn Court had terminal cancer and there I went with a huge bouquet of flowers and she told me her birthday was three months ago and what was I doing bringing her flowers anyway. I didn't know how to ask her about the cancer story."

I let her ramble on, unable to follow the story but totally relieved that Wilma had developed an unreliable reputation with her.

"So, then she told me she had just been diagnosed with fibrocystic disease and had to stop drinking so much coffee."

"Fibro...?"

"Benign lumps in the breast. Usually happens in younger women. Wilma didn't get past the name of the disease and jumped to conclusions. Have Jessica give me a call when she returns. By the way, Michael, what have you got in that bag? It looks like it weighs a ton!"

Michael wiped his brow with a handkerchief. "Bunch of clothes for the Thrift Shop that Violet asked me to take out for her."

Carol studied the house then looked back at Michael. "Is John not well?"

"John?"

"He's fine, why?" I interjected.

"Just wondered why he didn't take the things himself."

Pete wandered out of Violet's Florida room just then, tool belt on, hammer in hand. "Hey, Michael, before you go..." He stopped when he saw Carol.

By now, Wilma had drifted within hearing range.

"What a busy neighborhood," Carol said. "Good morning, Pete. Doing some work for the folks, are you?"

"Closets. Never enough closet space," Pete said.

"That's why she has to get rid of all these clothes," Michael added.

"I have to start lunch." I said as I turned toward my own house, hoping that would break up the conversation.

It did. Carol admonished Wilma as they walked away.

Wilma's whiny voice carried back to me. "…in the obituaries. Not the paid ones, the public announcements. I threw it away before I realized it was our Jessica Robbins. I don't remember which day."

~ * ~

When they were gone and I was inside behind my closed door, I collapsed onto a chair. Michael wasn't far behind. He tapped and entered before I could respond.

"Have you ladies been doing what we agreed on in Jessica's house?"

"Oh, it still looks quite lived in. I make sure of that. I even erased all the messages on her machine to make it look like she checks them. If anyone were to walk in there right now, they'd think she was still living there."

Michael pulled himself to attention. "What do you mean you erased her messages? She had messages?"

He can be quite intimidating when he gets into his former master sergeant mode. I cringed a little when I answered. "She only had one, really. The rest were hang-ups."

"Did you check to see who called?"

"I told you, they were hang-ups. The only real message was a cleaning outfit."

"But, what about the caller ID's of all those hang-ups? Surely you checked those," he said, folding his arms and taking a wide legged stance. I could easily imagine his recruits trembling in their boots. He wasn't very big, but he was fierce. Barclay hadn't liked him much.

"Do you think I'm stupid? She doesn't have caller ID on her phone." I considered flipping him the bird, but turned my back on him instead.

"That was a close call," he said, changing the subject. "We have to alert everyone tonight that Jessica's away for a couple of months. A good idea you came up with, telling Carol that. Took care of the nosy one, too."

"Thank you, Michael. I'll see you this evening."

I chuckled to myself as I watched him climb into his Jeep

wondering what my sons would say if they knew their mother was the president of The Blenders, a secret club whose sole purpose was to hide the heir-apparent to a Middle Eastern throne.

Personally, I felt pretty damned good about it. The boys had made their own lives over twenty years ago and since then I'd spent most of my time catering to Barclay and writing travel articles and fiction.

That last, I liked, making up characters and giving them adventures that I would never have. Sadly, no one else wanted to read my stories, but now, here I was, living an adventure of my own; one that I didn't have to make up.

I had thrown together a pasta salad for the evening's gathering, knowing that Violet would bring her marvelous tossed green salad, Justine her expensive petite-fours and Alice a serious pot roast or beef stew. Judy was unpredictable. She might bring along a bottle of apple juice or she might suddenly decide to create a massive pan of homemade lasagna; we never knew.

Hannah and Beatrice were good for making the coffee and tea while the boys, Al and Larry, generally brought a pitcher or two of mixed cocktails; tonight they brought Hamid.

We made ourselves comfortable in the living room, and I opened the meeting with a short prayer that Hamilton would continue to thrive and be safe under our charge. The little prince gurgled and cooed on his blanket, appearing content to be surrounded by a group of admiring adults. Judy recited the minutes of our last meeting and as we had no specific budget, she also recited the amounts being spent on our various projects.

Justine raised her hand to ask, "If Jessica is meant to be away for a couple of months, shouldn't we do something about her house?"

"Such as?" Michael asked.

"Well, if Carol does go in, Jessica's luggage will be there. The fresh foods and milk will be in the fridge."

"She's not allowed to enter our homes," Hannah protested.

"She can if she thinks we're in trouble. Remember poor Carrie? No one saw her for nearly a week and finally Carol went in. She had a boyfriend in there with her that she didn't want anyone knowing about."

This apparently happened before I moved into the park. "Why do you say 'poor' Carrie?"

Nearly everyone in the room laughed.

Justine began the explanation. "Carrie was in her eighties and having what she called one giant last fling. She'd hired a young man and, according to him, paid him well to… you know."

I could guess.

"She was a sweet old gal. Deaf, but never missed a Bingo night except for that one week. She always heard the numbers but could never hear a word you said right up close to her," Pete said. "Anyway, poor old thing had a heart attack a couple of days after the boy left. Then Carol really had to enter her house. Carrie had no relatives so we went in to clean it out."

"That's the 'poor Carrie' part. All her sex toys were still strewn about the house. Not just in her bedroom where you'd expect to find them," Beatrice said, and then realizing what she'd said, blushed.

Al dove for the floor and covered Hamid's ears. "Please. Not in front of the child!"

Hamid, startled by the sudden attack, began to cry, so Al picked him up and cradled him in his arms. The baby quieted instantly.

"Sounds to me like she died happy," I said. "Anyway, Justine's right. We've been maintaining the illusion of someone living in the house. Now we have to make it look like she hasn't been there."

Alice and Violet volunteered to help me take care of that after the meeting.

Bob Stewart, our Dr. Bob, raised his hand to add, "Once this is all over and word gets out about the little prince being hidden in your homes in secret rooms, they'll come clamoring to the park to try to buy one of your houses. You'll be famous all over the world."

"I wouldn't count on that," Michael said. "When we made the second bedrooms smaller…"

"Not by much."

"But they are smaller so that the baby's rooms in all the homes extend out into the sheds. Cleverly done, if I do say so myself, but they do make for an unusual configuration of rooms in those homes."

"The rooms are adorable. Little six by eight cells with tiny cribs. Blue clouds on the walls and plush blue carpeting." Al sighed with delight at his own decorating talent.

"We can call them offices. Or even guest rooms," Pete said.

Larry said, "I think the addition of the skylight in the utility sheds was a brilliant touch. Carol thinks we've all gone out of our minds, but just that little bit of natural light makes such a difference for our boy."

"Our boy," Al sighed. "You all have no idea how happy you made us when you included us in your plan. Our boy. Something I never thought Larry and I would ever be able to say."

Michael cleared his throat. "Now, what about the guardhouse?

Did someone say they thought the guard is becoming suspicious?"

Justine raised her hand. "I did. I worry about him. He's terribly loyal to Carol. You think he's reading all day, but I'm not so sure. I think we need to find another couple in the park who has grandchildren legitimately visiting and have them include Hamilton in their excursions so that the guard will come to view him as one of theirs."

There were cries of "stupid," "silly idea," "what's the point?" and other negative comments until I stopped them. "Wait! Think about it and you'll see that perhaps it's a good idea. Who has young grandchildren that visit on a regular basis?"

They discussed it for a few minutes. "Maggie Brown! She has three grown daughters living in the area and they're constantly coming over and dropping off their children for her to babysit."

"But, Maggie is a good friend of Carol's. She'd tell her in a heartbeat," Violet said.

"It's true. They are friendly," Judy added.

"I think Maggie is just polite to everyone," Alice threw in. "I've never heard her gossip about anyone or tell tales out of school."

"When you think about it, she's right," Justine said. "I move that we include Maggie Brown in The Blenders so that Hamilton will have playmates and she can provide a safe exit in the event of an emergency."

"I second," John said.

"Before we vote, is there any discussion?"

Michael stood. "We have our contingency plan in the event of an emergency. We don't need anyone else nosing in on our business."

"She'd be helpful for bringing him to my office," Bob suggested.

"You always see him when you're here. He doesn't need to go to your office." Even with all this activity going on, I had managed to make time every morning to write for a couple of hours and we continued our weekly writing group meetings.

Four more people raised their hands. The biggest problem with including Maggie was the concern that we were becoming too large and unwieldy for much control. The plus side of having her was that if we needed to get Hamilton out in a hurry, we could pop him into her car amongst her other grandchildren and no one would ever notice.

"Except," Michael interjected again, "most emergencies occur at night and she rarely has them stay overnight."

Almost to a person they slumped like a bunch of disappointed school children until Justine stood. "But, she's perfect! She's like a female Michael. Forgive me, Michael, I didn't mean that as an insult.

Did you ever see her disorganized or flustered? I bet if we take her into our confidence, we'd have a really strong ally."

Eventually, we voted to include Maggie in our circle and the meeting ended. Our new schedule was updated based on the status of the construction of bedrooms for Hamilton in individual homes. Everyone left happy.

Violet, Alice and I went on to Jessica's after the meeting. Alice thought we'd made Jessica's bedroom too neat, so we left a couple of pairs of stockings on the bed as if they'd been forgotten when she packed.

Satisfied that we'd made a good job of it, we each took a filled suitcase and left. Violet and Alice stepped out ahead of me and waited for me to lock the door. As I dropped the keys into my handbag, the telephone began ringing inside the house.

"It might be Moira!" I said, trying to untangle the keys that had become mixed up with my own house and car keys. "Damn!"

"Take your time," Alice cautioned. "It's still ringing."

I got the keys out, unlocked and opened the door just in time to hear the machine announcement and the click of someone at the other end disconnecting.

"It might have been Moira," I said, feeling hopelessly saddened by that thought.

"She should leave a message!" Violet said.

"She should, but she didn't. Maybe we should sit here for a while in case she calls again."

"We don't know it was her," Alice said gently. "We can't spend our days and nights worrying about what Moira is up to. We can only hope that she's all right and will come back for Hamilton when she can."

Chapter Seventeen

Moira slammed around the house after drowning yet another cell phone. Vance refused to listen to her demands to be taken to her mother's home immediately. He reminded her that her mother was well over twenty-one and could come and go as she pleased without sitting around waiting for her daughter to call.

"But, she never goes out at night and when she does, she's home by nine thirty at the latest."

"She never went to a movie that lasted a little later than that?"

He had a point, but she refused to budge, because she knew her mother would never leave Hamilton alone or with strangers. She wished she could trust him enough to tell him about her boy.

After so many days with Vance, she found she liked him and under other circumstances would probably have been attracted to him, but her body had barely recovered from having a baby and she'd yet to even fully process the grief of losing her husband.

Eventually she gave up sulking and went up to her room. She glared at the closed door between their sleeping quarters and hoped he would have a lousy night. Dressed in an oversized Dolphin's T-shirt, she slid between the sheets and turned out her light.

Her mind raced with pictures of her mother and her child caught in a car wreck, of KARP torturing her mother to learn where she, Moira, was hiding. Her poor mother had no idea and they would eventually kill her. Her baby screamed for his mother. She tossed and turned. And woke up several hours later in a cold sweat.

She brushed her forehead. It was soaking wet. She could barely catch her breath. The room was still pitch dark with the exception of the glow from the clock beside her bed. Three fourteen. She watched the numbers roll until they reached three forty seven. Giving up on sleep, she threw back the sheet and padded to the bathroom.

The quiet house soothed her. Looking out from the balcony, she watched as clouds reflected in the pool drifted across the moon. She heard rustling in the jungle-like foliage that bordered the property.

During a brief period of light she caught the movement of either Fern or Vern patrolling the grounds. With a sigh she returned to the bedroom but was unwilling to return to the bed and her nightmare thoughts.

Instead, she headed downstairs. She'd gained Vance's trust enough that he left her room unlocked. The cold tiles felt good on her bare feet. Ever since she'd been in the house she'd behaved like a proper guest, never snooping around, only using the rooms she'd been shown such as the bedroom, bathrooms, cabana, kitchen and dining areas. There was a lot more to the house than those few rooms. Curious, she headed around the curved staircase to the far side of the house where there were several closed doors.

A light leaked out from under the one on the left. She approached it silently and pressed her ear to the door, hearing only a soft whirring like the fan of a computer. But it would have to be either an awfully large computer or maybe several for her to be able to hear the noise through a solid wood door.

The door opened and she fell into the room, the light temporarily blinding her.

"Why didn't you knock?" Vance said.

Hidalgo laughed.

Vance's bare, hairy legs filled her vision now. Foolishly, she found herself wanting to rub her hands over them. Then she looked upward to see him grinning. She began to push herself upright. "I told you I was going stir crazy. I need to find out about my mother and I need something to do!"

He pursed his lips and scowled for a moment before coming to a decision. Rather than push her out, he turned her toward the desk and gave her a gentle shove in its direction.

Scraps of paper and colorful sticky notes, like a rainbow gone crazy, covered the entire desk as well as the surrounding cabinets. In the midst of all this a laptop screen showed a word processing program open, but no words. To her left, another desk, much neater, contained another computer, this one a colorful Mac that appeared to be running a black and white film, until she watched it for a minute and realized it was monitoring security cameras inside and outside the house. She turned her gaze to Vance.

He smiled again. "I caught you sneaking up on me."

"That's not fair."

"It wouldn't be fair if I'd not had it on and someone else snuck up on me. That wouldn't be fair because then I might be gone and then you'd be gone and who knows what might have happened to Fernando and Vern."

"They'd have killed whoever it was by then," she said confidently.

"You put a great deal of faith in those two."

"They seem trustworthy; you trust them." She wanted to say more, but standing so close to him had become distracting. First she wanted to touch his legs, now her entire body wanted to move closer to his. She resisted the impulse by twirling the chair around and dropping down on to it.

"Unlike me?" He pulled up a stool and perched on the edge of it. "You don't trust me and that won't help if we find ourselves in a crisis because then I won't be able to trust you."

"You're here to protect me from a certain element of society that deplores rich widows of wealthy sheiks. But, you can't know the entire story."

"Do you want to go out on the patio to talk?" He moved to the door, assuming she'd follow.

She did. The bright lights bothered her eyes, and she didn't like him being able to scrutinize her so clearly. On their way past the kitchen he stopped and picked up a bottle of wine, a corkscrew and two glasses, stepping aside to let her open the screened door.

"Pinot Grigio. Nice. I can't remember the last time I had a glass of wine." She took a seat in a chair instead of lying on a chaise.

He raised one eyebrow.

"On my own, trying to elude whoever was following me, I needed to keep my head clear."

"Then you do trust me," he laughed.

"At least for a glass of wine." And, she thought, maybe a chance to go back to sleep without the nightmares.

Once settled, he said, "Now would be a good time for you to tell me what happened to you after Hamid was killed. After the funeral you returned to your New York apartment for about two weeks and then we completely lost track of you. It's as if you dropped off the face of the earth."

She sipped some wine while she debated about how much to tell him. "There was no body to bury. His family held a traditional memorial service for him at their palace. I didn't want to go, but I flew over with my mother. They all shunned me, permitting me to attend as a mere courtesy. They were barely civil. The oldest brother, Manoush, insisted on everyone following protocol. They all blamed me for his death, saying that if I hadn't lured him away from the family business, he never would have died. They conveniently forgot that he was already a professor of archeology when I met him. Mom and I left as soon as the memorial service was over."

"But if he was already a professor when you met him, how could they blame you?"

"I think his father, in particular, believed he would eventually return to the fold, but when he married me, an infidel, they effectively banished him. They couldn't cut off his personal funds, but they were able to make life difficult for him." She twisted the glass on the table as she spoke, surprised to find it already empty.

Vance refilled both their glasses.

"I know his plane was sabotaged. He was too careful a pilot to let any faulty wiring get past him. And he completely trusted his mechanic. Who, by the way, disappeared the same day. That wasn't in the news."

Vance nodded.

Vern slipped from the shadows and crossed to them, stopping at Vance's shoulder and whispering in his ear. She then retreated as quickly and quietly as she'd arrived.

"What was that?" Moira asked.

"Bathroom break."

Sipping at her wine, she studied him. He was lying. She leaned across the table. "Tell me who you're really working for. You don't expect me to believe you are loyal to Hamid's memory? You could have taken the money and run once he was dead. Who would have known?"

"I would," he said with a scowl on his face. "Listen to me, you remember those men who found you at your hotel, the day I found you?"

She nodded. "IDIOTS."

The bottle poised for a brief second above his glass before he continued pouring. "It might not be such a bad idea if we let them find you."

She slammed her glass on to the table, wine spilling over. "What did you say?" she asked, hardly able to mask her terror.

"You heard me. I told you about them the day I found you." He mopped up the wine with a napkin while he continued. "If we let them find you, it could bring KARP out into the open. With any luck, the IDIOTS could wipe them out, leaving you free to run your own life."

"Let the IDIOTS find me," she repeated, in shock at what he was suggesting. If she agreed to that, then there would be no way to keep them from finding out about Hamilton. "I don't think I can agree to that. There has to be a way to reason with KARP."

He set his still filled glass down and leaned across the table.

"We're talking about a lunatic fringe of not-so-bright fanatics who are being well paid to do their job."

She cleared her throat, glad that the table separated them. She was supposed to be frightened of something he just said. Whatever was going on with her, her body was certainly out of control. Her baby would be five months old the end of the month. This entire year, ever since Hamid's death, she never thought about becoming a sexual being again.

Vance was a good-looking man, but he had yet to indicate any interest in her other than as a protectee. Maybe that was what she found sexy. Instead of talking any more, she held out her glass.

"We seem to have spilled quite a bit," she said as he emptied the bottle.

"There's a lot more inside."

"Later." Grasping for control, she tried to stand, wobbled a bit, and flopped back onto the chair. "Tell me more about KARP. All I know is that they wanted to kill my husband. And probably did," she added sadly, thinking that they must have thought by eliminating him they'd be eliminating any chance of more royal princes.

"We don't know that, yet. They're trying to keep their group small, under twenty. Had you produced an heir, the numbers would grow again. There is only so much oil to go around," he added sarcastically.

"The oil," she repeated, not following. "Hamid told me they weren't interested in financial gain."

"The economy of the world. Do you think anything happens without the royal princes' approval?"

"You sound like one of those conspiracy freaks. Just let me go back and get my... mother safely away. Then you can tell me all about the oil goblins." If anyone had asked her to explain, she probably couldn't, but she was disappointed in Vance. Disappointed in his ridiculous theory and annoyed that she was suckered into his world. Well, at least he had kept her safe for a while. First thing in the morning, she would have to find a way out of this place.

He ignored her remark and continued. "Did your husband ever explain why he didn't want anything to do with his family?"

"He thought they were far too ostentatious and grand while there was so much suffering in the world." She knew she sounded like a student reciting a lesson. "He studied anthropology and archeology in an effort to understand the past. He wanted the world to be a better place. A place where the haves and have-nots weren't so far apart. And before you go on about him being some sort of left wing liberal, let me tell you, he wasn't! I need another glass of wine!"

She paused, her anger building as she waited for him to return. He came back with two more bottles, one in a bucket of ice, a box of crackers, cheese, and a fat candle on a tray. He lit the candle before opening the fresh bottle of wine.

"You were saying?" He saluted her with his glass.

"Zimbabwe." She had a thought about it before he left to get the wine.

"What about Zimbabwe?"

"You know how prosperous it used to be?"

"I do. The breadbasket of Africa."

"Then the farms were nationalized and given away to the friends of the people in power who knew nothing about farming. Poor people killed the remaining small farmers and took over their places, still not knowing how to farm. Not knowing how to make the land produce. Now they have inflation so bizarre and out of control it could be a joke if it weren't so tragic. And people dying. Either from starvation, cholera, AIDS, or by being murdered. And it isn't the only country in Africa where chaos reigns. Nobody cares."

"Can we get you back in focus here? You were talking about Hamid's beliefs, something to do with have's and have not's."

"Yes. Well, you see, even the States aren't immune. Poor, uneducated people want what the educated, wealthy people have. First they need an education, but don't want to take the time. They want handouts and the government wants to give them handouts because that's how they'll get votes. And what happens next? The rich people get to pay for it all, not like the rich farmers in Zimbabwe." She knew she was slurring her words but didn't seem to be able to stop talking.

"You ought to run for political office."

"Hamid's family run a lovely country. It's all clean and well cared for but not by its citizens. No. They import people from the poor countries around them and have them work. The workers have no rights, but they are happy to have money to send home to their families, who are not allowed to emigrate. The citizens have money and go to school to the finest universities. The women become doctors, lawyers, or just wealthy women who decorate their husbands' lives. They are all seemingly happy." She hiccupped. "Seemingly" came out as "sheemly."

"And your point is?"

Her mind was a bit fuzzy now. She did have a point when she started. "They have oil. They have control. But, what are they going to do when the world runs out of food?"

"Lots of poor, starving people in the world. At the moment, my only concern is to keep you safe until we get rid of the threat hanging over you. This week, we'll worry about getting KARP out of your life. Next week, you can worry about the rest of the world."

Moira moved to a chaise to get more comfortable. "No. I can't worry about the resht of the world. I have to worry about Ham..." Oops. She lowered her head and tried to put Vance's face back in focus. She'd had entirely too much to drink.

"Ham, what?" Vance said.

"Ham? Did I say Ham?" She carefully set her glass on the low table next to her and tried to think. "Hamlet! Did you know New York has hamlets? Where I grew up, Paris, is a hamlet in a village that's in a town—township."

There, that ought to put him off the track. Though at the moment she couldn't quite recall what the track was. She laid her head back and shut her eyes. And then opened them as a wave of nausea overwhelmed her.

"We'll talk more in the morning. Come on, let me help you to bed."

She held out her hand and let him pull her up from the low seat and then fell into his arms. "Did I tell you that I'm frightened and lonely?"

"You didn't have to." He shifted her weight and assisted her up the stairs to her room where he dumped her unceremoniously onto her bed. She felt the comforter fall lightly over her before she passed out.

In her dreams she raced across a river in a human skull, fleeing from a bunch of Catholic nuns. Before she could reach the opposite shore where the uniformed students at West Point would protect her, the current changed, and she drifted, rudderless, down the river toward New York City, but when she arrived, she was in the middle of the Everglades and crocodiles, not alligators, surrounded her with open jaws. Behind them rows upon rows of hollow-eyed starving children stared blankly at her.

She awoke with a start, rolled over and had to stop herself from falling out of bed in her haste to escape the nightmare.

Sunlight filtered into the room through a space between the drawn curtains. Her head ached; her mouth felt fuzzy.

What had she done last night? Same T-shirt, same underwear still on. But, she remembered the touch of his body next to hers. "Oh, boy." A quick trip to the bathroom and then she showered and dressed for the day. She hadn't been able to reach her mother and her plan to go to Daytona today was nebulous, but first she had to get downstairs find some aspirin and quench her thirst.

"Pack your things," Vance greeted her.

"Don't shout. Why?" she groped in the cupboard for a glass, noticing that any evidence of last night's rendezvous had been cleaned away.

"We're going to find your mother. I told you I have an idea. By the way, do you remember any of our conversation from last night?"

She dropped a tea bag into the mug and reached for the teakettle. "I know I probably owe you an apology."

"You owe a lot more than that," he grumbled. "We leave in twenty minutes. Be ready. I have some gear for you in the foyer."

Chapter Eighteen

The palm trees sparkled with Christmas lights and the baby Jesus lay in his manger by the swimming pool.

Michael and I stopped Maggie Brown outside the clubhouse one afternoon to invite her to join The Blenders.

Maggie is a New Englander, bred from sturdy stock, solid as Vermont granite, yet I knew she had a heart softer than warm Jell-O. She spent three days a week reading to first graders at the local elementary school and loved every single one of them.

"Are you people crazy? Turn it over to a children's service and be done with it." Apparently, Maggie Brown was not impressed with us.

"It's nearly Christmas, Maggie," I said. "Do you want to be the one to turn a baby out three days before Christmas?"

Michael cleared his throat. Was he choked up because of what I said or was he trying to silence me? I couldn't tell. I was too busy wondering how I so seriously misjudged a person.

Maggie folded her arms and scowled, a sign I recognized from past experience with her that she was weakening. "How are you keeping it a secret from the office?"

"*Its* name is Hamilton," Michael interjected. "Apparently we've been successful at keeping him a secret from the office so far. If you don't know what's going on, then for sure nobody else does."

She raised her head and looked down her nose at us as if debating whether or not she'd just been insulted. Her eyes went from one to the other of us. Her pinched lips reminded me of my kindergarten teacher, Mrs. Benedict, who liked to twist ears if children spoke out of turn. I began to dread our plan to include her and I could have kicked Michael for being so rude; she might go straight to Carol.

"A baby. Hamilton?" She made it a statement, as if she'd pondered it carefully and come to the conclusion all on her own that we had a baby named Hamilton.

I nodded.

Michael took her by the arm and led her to the side of the street. "Jessica Robbins's grandson."

I gasped, knowing exactly what Maggie would say next.

"Why isn't Jessica taking care of it—him?"

Michael knew he'd stepped in it then. But, too late. He had to explain the rest of the story to her. And so we placed her between us and as we escorted her home, took turns explaining how we came to be hiding a baby in the park.

About three quarters of the way to her house—she lived at the other end of the park—I saw Larry and Al coming toward us from Keegan Bay Lane where they shared a house. Between them they carried a large laundry basket. They have their own washer and dryer so I doubted they were going to the community laundry.

When they saw Maggie with us, they stopped in their tracks, looking unsure of which way to turn.

"Good evening, Larry. Al," I said.

Michael nodded curtly in their direction. An old Marine, he was still having trouble with their relationship.

"Good evening, ladies. Michael," Larry said taking an awkward step forward, Al in tow, the basket between them.

Then I heard a whimper. Hamilton. In the basket. The look of alarm on the boys' faces might have been funny if it hadn't been from fear.

Maggie started to speak, but before she could get a word out, Larry began to sing. "We are poor little lambs who have lost our way, baa-baa-baa." Al joined in and they continued walking away safely masking the sound of Hamilton's gurgling. They were up to "Gentlemen shepherds off on a spree, Doomed from here to eternity…" when Maggie recovered from her astonishment.

"Ham in a basket, like 'pig in a blanket'?" she managed to say as she tried to suppress a smile.

"They're going to Philadelphia for Christmas," I said. "Justine will have the baby until after the New Year and then it's either Hannah or Bea. Judy keeps the schedule in her head. If you let us fix your house…"

"I don't like babies. I raised my own and for reasons known only to them, my daughters seem to think that I owe them. I don't know what I did wrong, but they are perpetually bringing their children to me. They're whiny little monsters. So, if you thought I'd want to take care of another baby, you'd better think again." Maggie stood firmly in the middle of the street, once again using her Mrs. Benedict expression.

"But, we thought you'd love to include him in your outings

with your grandchildren!"

"You thought wrong. When you see me driving out with those babies, then I'm probably taking them to a sitter, whom I pay so I don't have them messing up my house."

"Oh, dear," was all I could manage. Maybe the reading to school children story was nothing more than a rumor.

In the distance I heard Al and Larry. "Lord have mercy on such as we-e-e, baa-baa-baa."

"Thank you for your time, Maggie," Michael said. "I trust this conversation will be kept confidential." He held out his hand and they shook on it.

We left Maggie at her doorstep and started back. I was enjoying Michael's company. "You think you know a person," I began.

Michael chuckled, something I hadn't yet heard him do. "Like my first wife, Julie. Thought I knew her, too."

"Maggie Brown is like your first wife?" That was a surprise; I hadn't heard that he'd ever been married much less to a stern woman such as Maggie.

"No. Silly woman was a ditz. Before you ask, I met Julie right after boot camp. She was working at a bar near the base. I was twenty. Julie was gorgeous. When she got pregnant, my father threatened to kill me if I didn't marry her."

"I didn't know you had children."

"Don't. Three months after the wedding when there weren't any obvious changes in her, um, anatomy, I confronted her. She never was pregnant in the first place. Two weeks after that I went to Viet Nam and never saw her again. That's all I meant; I thought I knew her."

A grounds keeper wearing a bandana across the bottom half of his face headed toward us. Grabbing Michael's sleeve I pulled him to one side. "They only wear those when they're mowing."

"He's carrying clippers. Maybe he's allergic to the hedges," Michael said.

The man came closer and I stepped back into the middle of the street. "*Feliz Navidad*," I said to him as he passed.

"*Si*, een the morning. *Mañana.*" he replied and continued walking.

Now it was my turn to fold my arms and look grim. "That's a first. Imagine that, a groundskeeper allergic to the hedges. Also, a Hispanic without a clue what *Feliz Navidad* means."

"I don't like it, either."

We hurried to my house to call a special meeting of The

Blenders.

I didn't bother to call Justine as she would have our little ward. Larry and Al would be in the midst of packing for an early morning flight so we decided not to notify them. But still, within the hour we managed to bring together quite a few members.

Being so close to Christmas, many of them had brought along cookies, eggnog and other treats. Several of them had already imbibed seriously. Old Howard kept tilting sideways onto Hannah's shoulder. She pushed him upright with one hand while feeding herself cookies with the other.

I called the meeting to order and explained my fear that the terrorists had infiltrated the park in the form of the latest part time gardener. I noticed that Michael didn't correct me, nor did he accuse me of being paranoid.

Hannah, ignoring the gardener, stood and announced that she heard that Wilma was calling everyone in the park to remind them about the Christmas Eve party at the clubhouse. "I think she's looking for information. Nobody put her in charge of making the reminder calls. She thinks she knows something."

Old Howard's head landed on the seat of Hannah's chair just as she sat. With a screech she was up again in a flash and Old Howard rolled onto the floor where he snored throughout the rest of the meeting.

I then explained that Maggie would not be joining our club.

The telephone rang. I looked at the caller ID. "Keegan Bay."

"It's the office," I said with a trembling voice as I hit the talk button followed by the speaker so everyone could listen.

After the standard greetings, Carol got to the point. "I'm beginning the annual inspection early this year. December 26th to be specific."

"The day after Christmas?" I shouted into the phone. Everyone in the room went silent.

"I'm calling all the court captains so you can inform the rest of your neighbors. You are the Keegan Bay Central Court captain, aren't you?" she asked with hostility in her tone.

"Yes! Oh, indeed I am. Are you starting early for any special reason?"

"Stay calm," Violet mouthed at me.

"Last year, my first year here, it took me far longer than I anticipated, so I'm starting early," she responded curtly.

"I see." I didn't. Violet shrugged. She didn't understand the reason for the call either. All the others exchanged glances. No one had any idea why she might begin her inspections so soon.

"There seems to have been a great deal of home improvement going on in the park these past few months. I know I won't find debris from all that work lying about in the back yards, nor will I discover evidence of any illegal additions to any houses. I'm sure of that."

She was warning us! Why would she warn us if she didn't know anything? I looked at everyone in the room, hoping for any hint of what to say. No one had anything to offer. "I can't imagine what you might find in any other court, but we're fine here. Half the snowbirds still haven't arrived." Thank heaven for that!

"All right, then. I just thought you'd like to know. And by the way, Maggie Brown and I are about to go out for dinner. She's such a nice lady. Don't you work together in one of the homeowner groups?"

"Maggie Brown?" I choked out. Eight pairs of eyes widened in shock. Old Howard snorted from his position on the floor.

"Yes, you know the nice lady on Keegan Bay Marina Way. Number sixteen. Lots of grandchildren always visiting."

"Oh, yes. That Maggie Brown." I said with a forced laugh. There were a couple of wan smiles in the room. "No, we're not on any committees together. I hardly ever see her. How is she?" I shrugged toward my audience, all of whom were looking increasingly alarmed.

"Very busy with her family, I gather. Well, I won't keep you. Please let your neighbors know that I'll be coming through on the twenty-sixth to inspect."

"I will," I said.

After disconnecting, I stared at the roomful of people. "Now what?"

Everyone began to voice an opinion and amongst the din of babbling voices, I didn't hear the telephone. The blinking light caught my attention. The caller ID showed Justine's number. With a raised arm I silenced the room and picked up the phone.

"There's a bee in a bonnet. My package hasn't arrived," she said.

Chapter Nineteen

I covered Old Howard with a blanket and the rest of us split into teams. Hannah and Bea would take the northeast quadrant, Violet and John the southeast, Pete and Alice, southwest and Michael and I northwest. Scott, our computer expert, promised to remain by the phone and to keep an eye on Howard. Armed with flashlights and cell phones, we set out in the dark to find Al, Larry and Hamilton.

"They were fine when we last saw them," I repeated as Michael led the way, retracing the same path we'd taken from the clubhouse to my place earlier.

His cell phone beeped. "MC," he murmured into it. "Roger that." He flipped it shut and stopped short in the center of the street.

"What?"

"That was Scott. Two gray suits have been spotted."

"Oh, no! They think Violet is Jessica! If they see her, we're going to have a lot of explaining to do."

"Start your explanation with me," he said in a low voice as he pulled me into the shadows of the foliage in the center island that ran the length of the park.

"A while back two men in light gray suits showed up on my doorstep looking for Jessica." I continued whispering my story about their visit, rushing so that we could carry on searching for Hamilton. I promised Jessica to keep him safe and now, all of a sudden, practically right before my eyes, he'd disappeared. With my abbreviated recitation of events complete, I took the lead and headed toward the clubhouse where we'd last seen Larry and Al. I was having a hard time breathing as we rushed along the darkened streets.

It was nearing ten o'clock and soon the Christmas lights would be turned off and the gates around the pool locked. The life-sized Nativity had been presented to the community by a grateful relative of an elderly resident. While the life-sized crèche was generous, the figures were far too life-like to suit me. Every time I walked past them, I could swear they moved and breathed.

A breeze came up sending leaves skittering across our path. The colorful robe on one of the wise men flapped gently. Another movement caught my eye. Michael must have seen it at the same time. He froze beside me.

"Walk calmly. Hold my hand. We're just out for an evening stroll. Enemy at two o'clock," he said, nodding his head away from the wise men.

"Stop for a moment, will you? I have to catch my breath." As we stood on the verge of the grass, I scanned the landscape before us. I have to admit I'm old enough to have seen all those old war movies so I knew he meant the gray suits were slightly to the right in front of us. I spotted them. Only their backsides were visible as they were bent over, searching in the bushes for something.

We continued walking toward them, pretending not to notice. Our soft soled shoes made no noise as we approached them.

"I'm telling you I heard a baby cry," one of them said.

"I didn't hear anything."

"Those two fools with the laundry were making so much noise, it's a wonder I heard anything at all."

"You think they're—you know—gay?"

"Why?"

"Well, it's late at night. They're out walking around together. Kind of makes you wonder."

"Idiot."

"Watch it."

"You and I are out late together."

"I meant to watch it, there's an animal in here. It's staring at me."

By now, Michael and I had stopped walking and stood less than two yards from them listening to this bizarre conversation. I hoped they'd run into an angry raccoon rather than a timid armadillo. Either one was a possibility.

The bushes rustled violently as the two men backed out. The one on the left stumbled and landed at our feet.

"Good evening," I said.

Michael stooped to help him up. His partner brushed leaves from his suit.

"Are you still searching for Jessica Robbins? I can assure you, you won't find her in the bushes."

"We called Mrs. Robbins repeatedly today and received no answer, so we came to look for her ourselves to find out if she's heard from her daughter." Tweedle Dee and Tweedle Dum stood before us.

"She's gone for the holidays," I assured them. "To Switzerland to visit," I hesitated briefly. "Family. Relatives."

"Well, then. Thank you for your time. Can I ask you a question?" Jones, I believe his name was, asked.

"Sure," Michael answered for both of us.

"Is there an animal that lives in Florida that might sound like a baby?"

Michael and I exchanged glances. I smiled. "Sometimes at night, when an owl catches a rabbit or a squirrel too stupid to stay in their nest, you can hear them cry out. The sound could be construed as a crying baby."

"Peacocks sound like babies," Michael offered, "but I don't think any live around here."

"So, what were you looking for in the bushes?" I challenged them, feeling brave with Michael at my side.

"Jones heard a baby cry, and I saw movement in the bushes."

"So you jumped to the conclusion that a baby had crawled in there?" I scratched my head. "Amazing what babies can get up to these days. What would a baby be doing in the bushes so late at night?"

"We were worried. It might have been a child in distress. An infant in need of help."

I laughed and hoped I didn't sound as artificial as I felt. "What would a baby be doing in a retirement park?"

"That concerned us. Which is why we searched." Jones stood awkwardly for a moment then turned and walked away.

Smith tugged his jacket into place and then quickly joined his colleague to walk in lock step down the street toward the entrance to the park. I assumed they'd left a car in the guest lot.

Once they were out of hearing range, Michael and I skirted around the clubhouse searching for any evidence of Larry, Al and Hamilton. For the first time I was truly frightened for Hamilton.

As we came around on the far side of the swimming pool, I noticed that the door to the pump house stood open.

"Should we call for back up?" I whispered to Michael.

"I'll do some reconnaissance first."

The lights in the nearby palm trees went black. This was no longer a fun adventure; I was not only worried about Hamilton, I was scared for myself. I stuck close to Michael as we moved down the four steps to the entrance to the pump house. The machines purred.

He entered first and shone his flashlight around the small cluttered space. "Oh my," he said, sounding in awe.

I peered over his shoulder and said the same thing. Two men

stared, glassy eyed, back at us.

"Does José put them away every night?"

"I never checked. This is only the second year we've had them. Do you think he locks them up?" My voice trembled.

"But, they were still outside a few minutes ago. I haven't seen José locking up."

"The lights went off."

Michael turned and pushed me gently back out into the stairwell. "He does that from inside the clubhouse. Why would he put only two of the figures away?"

"Because he didn't!" Without waiting for him, I charged painfully up the steps and shoved open the pool gate. "So much for locking up at night." The entire Nativity scene stood in the shadows before us.

"They probably haven't made the rounds, yet," Michael gasped behind me.

The Nativity appeared just as we'd seen it ten minutes ago. Three wise men standing outside a stable. Mary and Joseph knelt beside a cradle that contained a sleeping baby. A cow and a donkey lay nearby inside the scene. I tiptoed over and peered down into the manger.

Hamilton opened his eyes and grinned at me. Then he cooed. "Ga. Gee. Ga," he said as he raised his little arms.

"Don't say anything," the wise man closest to the stable said under his breath. "There are two men prowling the grounds. Dressed in gray suits like you described."

"But, what are you doing here?" Michael could hardly contain his laughter.

I had to cover my mouth.

"Are they gone?" Larry asked.

"They headed down toward the entrance. I think it's safe to say they've left the park. Do you want to explain this?" I was still trying to puzzle out where the robes they wore came from.

"We'll wait a few minutes. Oh, my God, here comes José to lock up the pool." Al shifted his weight, ready to run.

"Stay put. I'll take care of this." Michael went off to have a word with José while I moved into the shadows of the crèche.

"Where'd you get the robes? And why didn't you just hide down in the pool house? Do you know what a fright I had seeing those statues in there?"

"If José had locked the pool before we could get away, we'd also be locked down there all night. It seemed safer to be here."

"Safer than what? What did Smith and Jones do to suggest they were suspicious of you?"

Only their eyes moved as they contemplated an answer.

"They asked us if we knew Mrs. Robbins and I said we didn't," Al said, looking like a rabbit on the first day of hunting season.

Larry took a shuddering breath. "Just as I was saying that we did know her and were on our way to her house to deliver her laundry."

I closed my eyes and drew my own shuddering breath. "And I just told them she'd gone to Switzerland. And Violet is wandering around the park unaware that they're here. They think that she's Jessica Robbins."

"Oh, dear," Larry said. "Can we get out of here? We have a flight to catch first thing in the morning.

I pulled out my cell phone and called Justine first, to let her know that the baby was fine. Then I called Scott so he could alert the troops to return to base. I was getting good at this espionage stuff.

Next, we had to extricate the boys and the baby from their predicament without José realizing what was going on. We waited for Michael to return. He'd gone off, seeming to have a plan.

"Where's the baby Jesus?" I asked.

"Behind the cow."

I peeked into the depths of the crèche and sure enough, there he was in the laundry basket.

"And the robes?"

"Don't you recognize them?"

"Why would I recognize them?"

"They're Arlene Esteban's slip covers. She left them on the clothesline."

Five minutes later Michael returned, a wise man tucked under each arm. "Let's get out of here before José comes back. I sent him to the front gate to make sure those two suits hadn't broken it when they entered earlier. I gave him a song and dance about them being vacuum cleaner salesmen."

The boys quickly replaced the slipcovers on the clotheslines next to the clubhouse laundry room. We then moved as a well-oiled unit to Justine's house to drop off the baby, who'd gone back to sleep.

"Just for the record, Al," Michael said as we headed down the driveway, "How long did you two plan to stand out there?"

"Until someone came to rescue us, I suppose."

"And what if we didn't find you until morning?"

"That never would have happened. Look, you found us in less than two hours. And that was quite fun posing as a wise man. At least three couples passed us, to say nothing of the gray suits, and never noticed."

"I vote we all reconvene at my house and have a drink," I said. The thought of the masked gardener still bothered me. We needed to resolve that.

Chapter Twenty

Moira gaped at the leather jacket, chaps, boots and helmet lying on the bench in the foyer. "That smacks of motorcycle!"

"So long, it's been good to know you," Hidalgo sang from his perch.

"Put them on and let's go," Vance said.

She looked at him, astonished at his angry tone. "Do I have time to get my things?"

"I told you; you have twenty minutes. If you can be quicker, do it!" he barked.

Vance was already dressed in leathers, bouncing on the balls of his feet, like a fighter waiting for the bell to ring.

She passed Vern on the stairs. The woman, also dressed in motorcycle leathers, kept her eyes downcast as she went by.

"Oh, we're going for a ride; going riding near and far," the parrot crooned.

Moira slammed into her room and quickly jammed whatever she could fit into her backpack. The rest didn't matter. She could always buy new clothes as long as she had her cash and ID. Puzzled by Vance's anger, she tried to remember the night before but all she could recall was a stupid conversation about the state of the world; a condition neither one of them could resolve. And something else niggled at the back of her mind.

Vance held out the leather jacket. "Get this on quickly. We've got to leave."

"I don't know how to ride a motorcycle! I've never even been on one." She backed into the living room away from the attire as if it might bite her.

"You don't have to drive the thing, just ride pillion."

"Bitch seat," Vern laughed from a doorway to the left.

Vern had a pack slung over her shoulder. So, they were all vacating the house. "Where are we going?"

"Our destination is Daytona, but we have a couple of stops to make first," Vance grumbled.

Her heart lifted. Night and day, she thought. Ten minutes ago she was ready to kill herself with frustration and boredom and now, within hours, she could be holding her son. "Definitely Daytona?" she said, unable to hide a grin, ignoring the warning signals in her head.

"Definitely Daytona. Fernando will close up the house and catch up to us in a couple of hours," Vance answered. "He has some cleaning to do before the housekeeper arrives."

Confused by the sudden change in character, she quietly followed Vance out into the courtyard where three large black motorcycles stood.

Exhausted from their late night conversation, excessive drinking and the bad dreams, she clung to Vance, unable to find any pleasure in riding on a motorcycle in the heavy Miami traffic, especially when he got onto the expressways. Much to her horror, before she could relax enough to take a deep breath sitting on the back of the bike, her arms around Vance, he pulled up to a tattoo shop in Hialeah. Desperately hoping that they'd stopped for coffee, she searched the row of shops in the strip mall for a café, but she only saw two pawn shops, a motorcycle supply store, a bar and the tattoo parlor. All the signs were in Spanish.

"Why are we at a tattoo parlor?" she asked suspiciously as she scanned her surroundings looking for an escape.

"We need to get rid of your scar. Come on." He reached out to help her off the bike. "You can remove the helmet now."

"I don't want to. I'm not getting any tattoos. Not on your life." She crossed her arms and remained firmly in place.

"You will get a tattoo and it *is* on my life. My job is to keep you safe. Now, get off the damned bike."

"People are watching," she said, wondering how he could risk a confrontation in public.

"We're in a territory where women do what their men demand. You're the one who screwed up when you killed Mohammad Sakir."

She didn't budge. "Who the hell is—" She stopped, remembering the dead man in her trailer. That he had a name never occurred to her. He was a killer out to get her. And she got him first.

Before she could react, Vance was behind her. He used his booted foot to dislodge her right leg so that he could drag her from the seat, and then, before she could react, his arms surrounded and hugged her close to him. He hiked her up off the ground and carried her into the tattoo parlor while Vern held the door open, carefully keeping a straight face.

Vance threw her into a chair that reminded her of an old dentist's chair and then unsnapped her helmet and waited for her to remove it.

"Not until you tell me what's going on here!" She clamped her hands over her head and glared at him. He had the nerve to stand over her grinning.

While their eyes locked in stubbornness, a burly man in a worn 'wife-beater' shirt entered the small cluttered room from behind a curtain. Every visible part of his body except for his face was covered in tattoos. Soaked in perspiration, she looked around for escape but was faced with Vance, Vern and the new occupant of the room.

Surrounding them were walls covered with designs—crosses, hexes, Stars of David, devils, pitchforks, angels, wings, banners, flowers, rock stars, movies, stars, and objects she didn't recognize. They couldn't do this to her.

"Take your jacket off and show Alistair your scar," Vance ordered.

"Alistair? Not for real." She looked up into the face of Alistair. He wasn't grinning. She choked back the laugh that had been about to follow her comment, sat up and removed her helmet and jacket, handing them to Vern without comment.

Alistair took her arm and probed it with surprisingly gentle fingers. "I got something that'll work here. Want a few more just for authenticity? Maybe something on the neck and a unicorn on the butt?"

He wasn't talking to her, so she kept her mouth shut and waited for Vance's response.

"Just where they can be seen when she's in regular clothes. How about one on the ankle, too?"

Her heart sank. Why didn't Vern speak up, after all she was a woman? Moira looked at the short woman with the huge biceps and reconsidered seeking help in that direction.

Alistair left the small room but he whistled while he worked in the back of the shop. Anxiety, something close to what Moira thought may be an actual panic attack, made her eyes burn with perspiration, her heart race and her fingers twitch. No one seemed to notice.

The art displays closed in on her. It felt like an hour had passed when Alistair called from behind the curtain. "All is ready. Come on in."

Vance and Vern each took an arm and led her through to the back where an open door led off a short hallway. They pushed her through where Alistair waited garbed in a clean white lab jacket, looking like a doctor from the Hell's Angels. He held a shiny stainless steel object in his right hand. He indicated a seat, similar to one in a hairdresser's salon. She balked and Vance gave her a little shove in the back.

"Go on," Vance said from behind her. "He doesn't bite."

She gaped at the array of miniature stainless steel bowls resting on an immaculate counter. Tubes of color were lined up in a rack along the back of the counter, just below a plate glass mirror. She felt sick to her stomach. Easing herself into the chair, she closed her eyes, wondering how she could have been so trusting of Vance these past few weeks.

"Don't close your eyes, yet. You still have to pick out your artwork."

"I can't." Her scalp crawled with the thought.

"Hey, kiddo, it isn't like it'll last a lifetime. Six weeks at the most, provided you don't take too many showers and stay out of chlorine treated pools."

An icy cold sponge wiped down her arm over the scar.

"Six weeks!" She popped her head up and stared at Vance in the mirror. He was leaning against the door jamb. "You knew all along you planned a temporary tattoo. Why didn't you tell me?"

"Wanted to see your reaction, that's all. Now, let the man do his job. How about a skull and roses? He does intricate artwork, prize winning stuff."

Skulls. No skulls, she thought as she remembered her dream. She scanned the book Alistair had placed before her and settled on a picture of an upright dragon with a castle in the background. "Can you do that one on my arm?"

"Sure. It'll take a while, but your wish, kiddo, is my command." He set to work dispensing colors into the bowls, following a formula from the book. Moira prayed he knew what he was doing. He pulled out stencils from little drawers in a nearby cabinet and laid them out on the counter, and then plugged in the gadget he'd been holding.

"You'll have to stay still while I do this."

"I realize that." She was annoyed and angry at Vance, still wondering what had ticked him off.

Alistair reminded her of a chemist as he rummaged through the tubes of color, arranging and rearranging things until she was lost trying to figure out what he was doing. Eventually he placed one of the stencils on her arm and she felt a cold burst of sprayed paint. He pulled the paper away, apparently satisfied with the first stroke of color. She watched for a few minutes until her eyelids grew heavy.

She rested in the chair with her eyes closed. Her head

continued to ache. While Alistair did his artwork she tried to remember all that they talked about last night and why Vance should still be angry this morning. She was sure nothing had happened between them. She'd drunk too much wine, but that shouldn't account for his hostility.

Her mind wandered. Soon it would be Christmas. Could she buy a present for Hamilton? How would she explain him to Vance? *Could* she explain him to Vance? A baby is a baby. What's there to explain? But if Vance and his employees learned about him, then surely others would.

She dozed, half asleep, half hearing the background music. All of sudden it came to her. Last night.

Last night when Vern whispered to Vance as they sipped their wine. She recognized now that Vance sipped; she chugged. Vern had been explaining something that caused her concern. Moira tried to focus on the conversation but fatigue won and the next thing she knew a solid lump of something cold and damp landed on her stomach. Her eyes flew open. Vance sat beside her in another chair, opening a sandwich for himself.

"Vern bought you lunch," Vance explained. He popped open a diet cola for her.

Moira yawned; her eyes felt gritty. "What happened to Alistair?"

"He's taking a break. Take a look."

Still half groggy she tried to view the tattoo by looking down at her arm. What she saw looked like an outline of a grungy green animal with plant life surrounding it. She rubbed her eyes and turned so she could see the artwork in the mirror. It was definitely a grungy green animal, not the dragon she'd requested.

"What's going on here?" She scowled at Vance who looked too amused to suit her. At this point she preferred him angry.

"I decided you needed something more biker-like. Ladies have cute dragons; biker babes have gargoyles and ominous images."

"Ominous images?" She picked up the wrapped sandwich and threw it on the counter. "What the hell do you mean by ominous images?"

Vance moved to the other side of her chair and examined her arm more closely. "He's actually going to be kind of cute."

She couldn't figure what was going on. Earlier he'd been angry with her for some unknown reason, now he was teasing her as if they were friends.

"Eat your lunch. When he's finished with your arm, he's going to put barbed wire on your ankle. You prefer right or left?" Vance sipped his soda.

Unsure whether to laugh or cry, she tore open the wrapper and picked up her sandwich. "Bastard," she grumbled.

"Look, maybe I ought to explain," Vance began.

"Explain what?"

"Last night."

Her heart lurched. "What about last night?" Had more happened than she realized?

She caught movement behind her. Vern straightened in her chair, a look of alarm on her face. What was going on?

"We had company, that's what happened. We thought about not telling you, but since we've been sitting here, I've been thinking it over. It's time we let you in on the entire story."

She looked from face to face and realized something more serious than her idea of a flirtation was going on. The piece of sandwich stuck in her throat and she took a swallow of soda to wash it down. "I've been hoping…" she began lamely but couldn't finish.

She didn't want to know the truth. All the years during her marriage Hamid had sheltered her and later, at the convent, the sisters took care of her. She foolishly thought when she left Hamilton with her mother that she could disappear again. Luring any harmful elements away from her son, that's all she had in mind.

"Last night while you and I were lounging comfortably poolside, Fern and Vern apprehended two men planting explosives around the perimeter of my property."

"Apprehended?"

"Yes, ma'am," Vern stood. After exchanging glances with Vance, she stepped over and leaned against the counter, arms folded as she continued the story. "I'd just gone out to relieve Fernando, when he signaled a warning to me. We outflanked them and took them down with little fuss."

"I certainly never heard anything," Moira said.

"You weren't supposed to. If you had, it would've meant we weren't doing our jobs right. Cuffed, hogtied and gagged, we stashed them in the garage until this morning. Fernando drew the short straw. He's depositing them with the authorities."

"He should catch up to us along the way. We'll take it slow until then. We don't want to meet any more surprises," Vance added.

Moira felt her eyes widen in terror. "You said we were going to Daytona. To see my mother."

"We are. We're going to get her out of there before KARP figures out that you might be heading that way."

"Why would they think that?"

"I'll back up," Vance said. "We've known your location since you reappeared at your apartment in New York City. I have to confess, we did lose you for several months before that. Since shortly after your husband died. As long as you were safe, we felt it better to maintain our watch, keep you out of harm's way. Until you showed up on the radar after getting a parking ticket in Daytona and that same night you murdered someone in your trailer. Some digs, by the way. Couldn't you find anyplace worse to live in?"

"I was trying to stay out of sight!"

"No need to shout," Vern cautioned. "Alistair doesn't need to know our business.

More quietly she continued, "I didn't want anyone to know I was living near my—" She took a furtive glance around for Alistair or another pair of snoopy ears and whispered "—near anyone I care about."

"I sent Fern and Vern to check up on you, but you had already left town. Luckily for us, we picked you up on your cell phone about the same time everyone else did."

"Everyone else?"

"The IDIOTS and KARP. That's when I decided it was time to get you into protective custody."

"Is that what you call it?"

"I've told you. My job is to do just that. The company didn't die with your husband."

Moira drew a deep breath, trying to absorb the information. "You were watching me the whole time I was working in South Beach?"

"And at the café in Port Orange. The whole time. But, you seemed to be safe. Then the afternoon you were stopped, the police officer did a computer search on you. We keep an eye on those and my people notified me that you'd been exposed. If we learned your whereabouts that way, so could anyone else seriously interested in finding you. That night KARP paid you a visit. If Sakir had lived—if you could have just wounded him—we could have questioned him to learn the whereabouts of his cell, his colleagues. Also, what the news never informed the public was that your trailer was wired with enough explosives to take out the entire trailer park. In any case, you left for Miami before I could have anyone step in. Once again you appeared to be safe for a little while. Until the IDIOTS found you."

"Hamburger Boy and Cinderella," she murmured, feeling a sudden rush of tears. "I never dreamed we'd have to use those words."

"Look, I'm not happy about those two people showing up last night. If you hadn't killed that guy at your trailer…"

"I would have been dead and you wouldn't have a job," she finished for him. He might be angry at her for killing the intruder, but in the end, he did work for her. And, she realized, it was about time she began treating him as an employee. Before she could say anything she heard the bells over the front door jingle.

"All right, time to get back to work!" Alistair's gruff but cheerful voice boomed from the entrance.

By three in the afternoon Alistair finished. The barbed wire anklet wasn't as offensive as she thought it might be. She reserved judgment on the gargoyle surrounded by anonymous ogres, swirling vines and flowers. She never would have dreamed of putting a picture down the side of her arm, but it did cover the scar. She had to acknowledge that it had been a good idea. No one would be seeking a tattooed princess.

She donned the biker's gear, mounted the bike behind Vance and they took off. More comfortable, Moira took time to look around. Unlike riding in a car, she was surprised at the odors and sounds all around. Already gaudy bodegas decorated for Christmas looked like overdressed hookers.

The sidewalks were mobbed with people doing last minute Christmas shopping. The sounds of salsa and traditional music blaring from shops, the fragrance of Cuban coffee and frying foods assaulted her senses. The streetlamps all bore Christmas decorations.

She longed to be with little Hamilton, to share his first Christmas with him. And then at midnight they'd be free. On December 26th, Hamilton Robbins would no longer be prey for KARP.

Now that she understood their relationship more clearly, she had to figure out what she really wanted Vance to do as her employee. So far, it appeared that he had kept her as safe as anyone might have done. The thoughts churned as they rode west. West?

"Why are we headed west?" she shouted into his ear as they sped along the street.

"The road less traveled," Vance answered. "It's a little rougher, but it'll get us there just the same. I gave Fern this route. Relax."

"That's not an easy thing to do back here."

"You'll get used to it."

"I hope not." Once they reached the open road where cars became few and far between, she did begin to enjoy the sparse scenery, sugar cane fields, old houses, an occasional sign leading to a Native Village. "Visit a genuine village; see craftsmen and women at work."

They traveled Route 27 and by the time they reached Lake Okeechobee, the second largest freshwater lake in the United States, or so the signs said, it was dark. All she saw of it in the sporadic light from passing vehicles was the grassy slope that rose above her like a dam holding it back. As time passed she found herself relaxing, even resting her head against Vance's back for a while.

Fernando caught up with them shortly after they crossed into Hendry County. When they reached Clewiston, Vance slowed to the speed limit and they kept their eyes out for a place to eat. A pass through the town only showed them a couple of chain fast food places and two food shacks where no one wanted to stop.

The Clewiston Inn on the main highway looked a bit fancy for them, considering their clothes, but in the end, they decided they were hungry enough to incur the wrath of the hotel dining room staff, parked next to a shiny Lexus and paraded into the hotel lobby.

In spite of the elegant lobby displaying elaborate Victorian Christmas decorations, the hostess, dressed in black shirt and slacks, welcomed them graciously into the dining room. She led them to a linen covered table and seated them, offered a full range of drinks and then left them to look over the menus.

"What a great place," Moira said.

"It's eight thirty already. I say we stop here for the night," Fernando suggested.

"I don't know," Vance began before Vern added her two cents.

"I go with Fernando. We're at least another hundred or more miles from Orlando and I for one, don't like the idea of riding tired."

Moira said, "I agree with them. We shouldn't drive tired. And remember, I'm in charge from here on out. I'll respect your opinions, but I make all the final decisions."

"What's your problem? You're not doing the driving." Vance scowled at his menu. She thought after his explanation earlier, that he was over his annoyance.

She turned to Vern. "We could all use a good night's sleep. It's been a stressful day for all of us."

"To say nothing of last night," Vance muttered. "I'm getting the fried chicken. Excuse me while I help myself to salad. With your permission." He hesitated a moment. "Boss."

Moira watched him push away then looked to Fern and Vern for support. They both avoided looking directly at her.

"Maybe he's concerned about having to be too far away from you in a separate room. When we check in, I'll see if there's a suite available, if not, you and I become bunkmates. You're still our number one priority, you know," Vern said. She left the table.

Moira watched as Vern headed to the salad bar and then turned to Fern. "What took you so long to catch up to us?"

"I thought Vance told you, I had some cleanup to do."

"He said you and Vern caught two men outside the compound. Where did you take them?"

"There are some things you're better off not knowing," Fern said as he, too, went to the salad bar.

Now she began to feel angry. "He said you took them to the authorities. Which 'authorities' was that?"

Fern fidgeted with his water glass, then got up. "I must eat. You should get something for yourself."

Feeling more like an intruder into their private club than their boss and the focus of their attention, Moira glanced at the menu. She wondered what they would think when they found out that her son was probably more important to KARP than she was. That is, if KARP knew about Hamilton. So far, it seemed like people were looking for her alone.

Still angry, she stormed over to the buffet, avoiding the others and scooped food onto a dinner plate. She ate without being particularly aware of what she was eating. More annoying than ever, Vance assured her the food was excellent. He had a beer with his dinner and stretched his legs out to relax while he waited for her to finish.

After dinner, Vern registered them and then they walked into the bar on the opposite side of the historic building. Moira wasn't so angry that she couldn't appreciate the extraordinary 360-degree mural featuring the flora and fauna of the Everglades.

She picked up a brochure from the bar to learn the history of the mural. Painted in the 40's it had been valued at well over a million dollars and was carefully preserved during the renovations. She read some of the information aloud, but as no one was in a particularly chatty mood, they each had a quick nightcap, Drambuie for her, hot chocolate for Vern and ginger ale for Fern.

Vance's fingers drummed on the bar top while they drank. He was clearly not in a mood to socialize tonight.

Her room proved to be luxurious with soft sheets and a mint green goose down comforter. The only annoyance was the guards' insistence that their adjacent room doors be kept unlocked. As she prepared for bed she thought about the change in their roles for this mission. Her goal was to get to her baby and find a safe haven for him. Vance and his team still thought they were only rescuing her and her mother before heading to a foreign country where Vance considered they'd be safe.

"I'm the boss," she said to herself in the mirror, staring at a biker babe, not the head of a billion dollar corporation.

Was she? Did Hamid really leave her in charge? She'd never been in charge of anything in her life. First she was her parents' child, then a college student. Though she'd been away from home, it wasn't all that far and she went home weekends.

Funny, she thought, Colgate is in Hamilton. Then while working in Kushawa, she met and married Hamid. He decided when and where they'd go on their trips; he decided he didn't want children, though for the sake of his family, they had to keep up the pretense that they were always trying to produce an heir. He decided, he decided.

She wet her hair and brushed it flat against her head. Now she looked like a dominatrix. Not good. She fluffed it out again, but it stood up in spikes.

Biker babe beat dominatrix any day. She left it alone to grow, still mulling over the concept of being in charge. Vance took to calling her "Boss." She wasn't sure if he mocked her or was showing respect. Maybe he really was deferring to her now that he let her know she was actually his employer. Hamid had taken care of security arrangements along with everything else in their life. Had he told Vance what to do? Or did he leave it up to Vance's judgment to know what was right?

~ * ~

In the morning, they were once again greeted by incredibly cheerful and hospitable staff. Moira's head still ached. Fern and Vern were already in the dining room feasting on huge portions of eggs, sausages, bacon, potatoes and pancakes. They were her employees, friends to each other, but they would never be her comrades or companions. She approached their table.

Through a mouthful of food Fern spoke to Vern, "Did you know the lake has an average depth of only nine feet? Today it's at 14.3. They post the levels every day. I also learned a new word,"

"I'll bite. What's the new word?" Vern asked.

"It's actually two words. Tertiary quintipoint. How's that?"

"Once again, I'll bite. What's it mean?"

"Five counties meet in the center of the lake," he responded like a little kid who did well on his homework.

Moira cleared her throat. Fern and Vern both stood as she took a seat at their table.

"Morning," Vern said. "Can I get you some breakfast? This food is outstanding! I think I like it even better than dinner."

Moira wondered if Vern had been thinking over the changing situation as well. She hadn't offered to get her dinner for her last night. "I'm going to have coffee and juice. Thanks just the same, Vern," Moira said as the waitress came to pour. "Have you seen Vance this morning?"

"He's outside taking a walk. He's been ready to leave since daybreak."

She headed out in the bright morning sunshine.

Chapter Twenty-One

I awoke, unsure what time Michael and I had parted company last night. Crawling out of the dim interior of my darkened bedroom, I groped my way to the kitchen in search of a glass of water. Anything to quench my parched throat. Far too much alcohol last night.

As I yanked open the refrigerator door, a loud snort came from the living room. My first thought was of old Howard passed out on the chairs, but John and Violet had escorted him home after the meeting, after we'd found the boys with Hamilton.

Stepping lightly, headache forgotten, I peeked around the corner into the living room. Michael lay stretched out on my sofa, his legs draped over the arm, his head lolling to one side.

I whipped back into the kitchen and checked the level in the Scotch bottle. Oh dear. We'd consumed a vast quantity, but the time had passed so quickly.

I recalled talking about so many things other than sickness, spouses, children and grandchildren, the usual topics in the park. He surprised me by saying he also liked to write and had published several "how to" survival manuals and was working on a techno-thriller a la Clancy. He was amused to learn that my mother's maiden name was Clancy. Everything amused us last night.

The phone rang. The phone was always ringing these days. I grabbed it before it could do more damage to my head.

"I had dinner with Carol last night," Maggie began without a greeting. "She's wise to something going on in the park. I never let on. Just in case it leaks from another source, I want you to know I never said a word."

"Good," I groaned. And in three days Carol would be seriously snooping around all the houses. "Thanks for warning me. I'll let the others know."

"I can do that much. I won't take care of any kids, but I can certainly sympathize with your situation. I'll be your inside man with the office, how's that?"

Maggie was also obviously enjoying life again, even though she was only on the periphery of our plot. It occurred to me that everyone in our group was enjoying life again. None of us were talking about spouses, late or otherwise, or grandchildren. We didn't even talk about our medical problems. We each had a role to play and we relied on each other.

I smiled in spite of my throbbing head and poured a glass of tomato juice and then added a little Worcestershire sauce.

Another snort followed by a groan emanated from the living room. "What the f…" Michael stopped when he saw me smiling at him from the doorway. "Sorry. Did I really sleep here all night?"

"Not all night," I said. "Only since around two or three o'clock. Coffee? It can be ready in a few minutes."

He rubbed his hands over his face and head. "Coffee'd be great. Mind if I use your bathroom?"

"Go ahead. I'll get the coffee started. Want an egg or something?" Why did I say that? Damned if I wanted to cook for anyone else again. I liked my independence. I ate when I wanted to, slept when I chose, and watched movies in the middle of the night if I felt like it. Come to think of it, I could do all that when Barclay was still around.

"Don't bother." Michael groaned. "I'll grab something later. Just coffee with a little cream and sugar. I gotta go home and shower and then we have to make some plans."

Plans? I wondered what we talked about last night that required plans.

My lack of response or the dense expression on my face brought Michael into the kitchen. "The inspections. We've got to make sure all the houses are secure so Carol can't tell what we've done. The secret doors, any disturbance in the lawns around the new construction. There are so many telltale signs of our activity that could be seen if anyone looks too closely."

"Oh lord," I said handing him a cup. "Maggie called. Carol will definitely be looking closely, very closely. She said Carol is suspicious of the activity in the park and the diminished numbers at cards and bingo. She's wondering what everyone is doing on those nights. And Pete's not golfing anymore. He used to always go into her office to brag about his scores because she likes to golf as well, but apparently isn't very good."

"Maggie? Didn't she and Carol go out for supper last night?"

"Maggie kept your agreement. In fact, she's planning on spying for us. That's why she called, to let us know Carol is suspicious."

"We've got to ask everyone to watch her movement in the park. If she gets anywhere close to Justine's house, Justine's got to be warned to keep Hamilton quiet." Michael frowned. "We've also got to learn more about that masked groundskeeper we saw last night."

I'd forgotten about him.

We both headed for the front door at the same time. I reached out to undo the locks but before I could unlock it, I heard the toot of the little horn on Carol's golf cart, the cart she used to move about the park. She rolled into my carport. "Uh-oh."

"Where can I hide?" Panic stricken, Michael backed away from the door. It tickled me to see a tough ex-Marine frightened of being caught in a woman's house, both over half a century beyond the age of consent.

"Why should you hide?" I whispered. "We're adults."

"Then why are you whispering?"

He had a point. "Get in my bedroom," I said. "I'll find out what she wants."

I waited until he was out of sight, and then opened the door for her. There would be nothing for her to see at my house today. Ham was with Justine. "Hello, Carol! You're out and about early today. Is this a social call?"

"In a way, it is. Do you have time for me to come in for a few minutes? There's something I need to talk to you about." In her hands was a clipboard similar to the ones she used when inspecting.

"I'm getting ready to make Christmas cookies, but I can spare a little time." I lied with a smile, remembering Barclay's mantra, "Let the others get the ulcers." I hadn't done anything wrong, unless you called saving a baby's life wrong.

I showed her to a seat in the most uncomfortable chair in the living room, a Shaker straight-backed hardwood. I took a seat in my overstuffed old recliner. As I lowered myself I spied Michael's shoes on the floor near the end of the sofa. If she didn't turn around, she wouldn't see them.

We sat, and I waited. I kept myself from looking at the shoes, but they were prominent in my peripheral vision. It was like telling someone not to think about something.

I wasn't about to offer her a drink or a coffee. She might mistake that as an invitation to stay.

"This is difficult for me because I know you're friends with her," she began in a hesitant manner, unusual for her.

"With whom?" I asked.

"Didn't I say?" The poor girl was truly nervous.

"No. You only said you had something you need to talk about."

"It's Justine Chambers. I know you're friends with her and I wouldn't be talking to you if I weren't genuinely concerned with what's been going on."

I thought of the expression one of my grandsons had used. *Busted!* I waited, palms sweating.

"You do know that she's been having a difficult time financially lately?" she said.

"No, I didn't know. We tend to keep things like that to ourselves. Is there a problem? Something you want me to help her with?" Maybe this wasn't going to be as bad as I thought.

"I'm not sure, that's why I wanted to ask you about it. You see, you're not supposed to run a business from your home here in Keegan Bay. You know that, don't you?"

"She's running a business?" I couldn't imagine what business Justine could be running. Maybe selling her petit-fours?

"Childcare."

"No." Uh-oh. Hamilton was at Justine's.

"I think so. At first I thought she was babysitting a grandchild, but when I looked up her application to live here, she doesn't mention any close relatives. For an emergency number she lists a sister in Iowa. Do you know anything about this?"

I didn't. "No, I didn't know she had a sister. Maybe she's just helping a young friend?" I offered.

"I asked her outright when she was in the office last week. I said very specifically, 'Justine, are you babysitting?' She denied ever having a baby in her house. I didn't say anything else. I wanted to wait until I had an opportunity to ask some of her friends. I worried that she might be in some financial trouble so turned to childcare for additional income."

I shrugged helplessly. "I suppose she could have done that, but what made you think she had a child there overnight in the first place?"

"Did I say she kept a baby overnight?"

I cringed inwardly and tried to cover the gaff. "I-I was thinking of something else entirely." The shoes mocked me from the edge of the sofa.

"You'll keep this between us?"

I nodded, curious. Carol was not the type of person to share confidences with the park residents. She had to know I wouldn't keep a management secret. And I was sure the others would need to know whatever Carol was about to tell me.

She leaned forward. "Wilma told me she heard a baby crying

late one night two weeks ago when she was out walking."

"Maybe Justine had her television too loud. She is hard of hearing." If there were a hearing competition in the park, Justine would win. She could hear a misplaced footstool three houses away.

"Wilma claims she walked up on her lawn and peeked in the living room window. She saw Justine rocking a baby."

"You know how trustworthy Wilma is. And what business does she have looking in people's windows?" My mind tried to backtrack and recall any suspicious movements outdoors while we had our clandestine meetings. How would I know if Wilma had been outside my windows?

"That's why I want to verify her story and why I didn't go straight to Justine. I wouldn't want to evict her without just cause."

"Evict her?" I pressed my hands on the arms of the chair and pushed myself to a standing position, joints snapping, knees aching. My version of jumping up. "Carol! You wouldn't evict a woman on the mere suspicion of keeping a child overnight."

With a sad tilt of her head she replied, "I have to follow the rules of the owners. I'm only the manager. If she is harboring a child, an unregistered child no less, for more than two weeks, she will have to either get rid of the child or move. That's the way it works. You all know that. It's in the prospectus you receive when you buy your houses. You own the house; we own the land."

I nodded. "She enjoys her evening television programs too much to be disrupted by kids. You have nothing to worry about there."

"You're sure? Wilma seemed very confident."

"Is there something more you're not telling me, Carol? Because if Wilma saw a baby there one night, that hardly comes close to the two weeks limit."

"She did report another incident prior to that, but she wasn't sure so I told her not to be making false accusations. I told her to come to me only if she had proof. That's why she went and looked in the window the second time. I know she's not everyone's favorite person, but rules are rules. If I let one of you get away with something, then everyone would feel entitled to break the rules."

Oh dear, if Carol only knew how true that was.

I mentally promised myself to strangle Wilma next time I saw her. Maybe Michael would help. As an ex-Marine he would know ways to kill people silently and permanently. Meanwhile, we had to get Carol off the scent.

"If it will help, I'll have a word with Justine and I promise to report back to you immediately." As I spoke I walked to the front door, rude maybe, but I wanted to get her out of the house.

She stood. The shoes were right behind her. "It's not urgent, but when you do, I'd like to know. I need to be clear about whether or not she's keeping any children beyond the allotted times permitted or if she's being paid to babysit. I'll be off three days for Christmas, but I'll be at my house if you learn anything you want to tell me. We can talk again on Monday when I start my inspections. Will that give you time?" She spoke as if she just given her employee an assignment.

"Sure," I responded, knowing I sounded weak willed, like a wimp giving in at the first sign of danger. My mind raced, willing her out of my sight so I could get busy on the phones.

As soon as she left, I called Michael out. I pointed to his shoes before I told him about Carol's visit. "We have to go see Justine immediately and make sure there isn't any evidence of Hamilton around her house."

"Except for his secret bedroom," Michael added as he donned his shoes with a sheepish grin.

"Do you think Carol would really evict her?"

"Damned Nazi! I'll kick her snooping-ass butt from here to the lighthouse and then dump her body onto the rocks! The vultures can dine on her entrails, and the crabs can munch on the rest of her." He stood and stomped his feet as if testing to make sure he had the right shoes on.

That was a side of Michael I hadn't seen before. Perhaps, being an ex-Marine had a downside to it. I tried to hide my dismay and my nausea at the thought of anything munching on anyone's body.

I called Justine, still with the picture of vultures munching on Carol in my head, and told her about Carol's suspicions and that Michael and I had to see her. She was quick to remind me that we weren't supposed to discuss anything over the phone.

"All I said is that Carol is becoming suspicious. I didn't say about what!" I hated when others were right.

"I think," Michael began as soon as we arrived at her house, "we need to pull you out of the mix. We can't have you investigated at this point. We've done all right so far and Hamilton is flourishing. We've got to maintain the status quo until his mother gives us some signal of her intent." In his distracted state of mind, he'd picked up a sponge and began wiping off Justine's already immaculate counter tops.

Hamilton sat in his highchair poking Cheerios around on the tray. I picked him up and sat him on my knees. He grinned at me, drool dripping down onto his shirtfront.

"His mother has dropped off the face of the earth," I reminded Michael. I quite liked the way he stood practically at attention, rinsing and wiping his way around the small room. Barclay rarely entered the kitchen.

"With good reason, you must remember."

I sighed. "I suppose. But if Wilma is going to be snooping around and reporting every little thing to Carol, Ham is definitely going to be discovered sooner rather than later. We have to do something about her." Before he could respond, I added, "And while your earlier suggestion was colorful and creative, I think something a little less dramatic will have to suffice."

"Suffice, humph." He accepted a cup of coffee from Justine, who so far, had barely said a word. I shook my head when she offered me a cup.

As she passed him the milk in a delicate china pitcher she said, "I suggest that we include Carol in our program. She's a mother herself and would understand our concerns. That way, we wouldn't have to fear discovery."

That was a shocker for me. Carol, the park manager, the woman who worked for the corporation that owned our land as a member of The Blenders? I couldn't imagine it.

"I don't think so. Carol does have the power to remove her from the park and until we hear from Jessica's daughter, management mustn't know about Jessica's death or the baby being with us. Though she's a mother, Carol is still responsible to the corporation."

Justine took her seat at the kitchen table across from me, a scowl creasing her eerily wrinkle free forehead. Not an attractive woman at the best of times, she was frightening when she was unhappy. None of us wanted to confront an angry Justine. I worried how Wilma would fare at their next encounter. If Justine was upset enough she might inadvertently spill the beans.

"Michael, you have any other suggestions on the topic of Wilma and Carol?"

"Justine, we're going to have to remove Ham from your place for a while. At least until Wilma settles down. But, that won't stop us from using your house as part of our underground railroad should the occasion arise," he answered

Justine's back was up now. "Ham loves my little Jeremy and Skipper. It isn't fair that he can't play with them." Jeremy and Skipper are her cats.

"Babies his age don't play. They eat, sleep, and grow," I reminded her. "He'll be fine without playmates for a while. It's not like a puppy that has to be socialized in the first three months."

"When did we say Jessica would be back from her trip?" Michael asked.

As I jiggled Hamilton on my knee, the baby threw up on her spotless floor. Before I could move, Michael grabbed a paper towel to clean it up.

"After the new year," I answered. "Justine, please get the shopping cart. We really have to move him. We'll take him to Bea's for a few days."

"It's his lunchtime," she said, tears making her eyes glisten. "May I at least give him his lunch first?"

I looked to Michael. He nodded.

When they were finished, we bundled Ham into a four-wheeled net shopping cart and piled fake presents around him, perfect camouflage this time of year. I wondered as we walked down the street what kind of person he'd grow up to be. He seemed to like being stashed in unusual places. His cooing and gurgling attested to that.

"Hard to believe anyone is looking for him, isn't it?" Michael said as if reading my thoughts.

"I wish Jessica was still alive so she could tell me again about Moira's marriage to a rich potentate slash professor who loved skiing at St. Moritz. Too unbelievable and yet, we have the baby as evidence."

"And the gray suits and an unknown groundskeeper," he reminded me.

Chapter Twenty-Two

Moira's mind raced as fast as the motorcycle. Within hours they would be at Keegan Bay Park and she would have to get rid of Vance and his employees. If she could have them buy her a car, a good car, first, she could get her mother and Hamilton out by morning and head west toward Montana or Wyoming. Surely, there was a place no one would bother to look for her.

When they reached Orlando and turned east she was glad she couldn't see the speedometer as they rushed across the I-4 corridor toward Daytona. Her teeth rattled as Vance kept up with traffic.

They reached Daytona Beach shortly after four o'clock. Vance led the group over to the beach and stopped at a waterside bar and grill. She dismounted awkwardly, unused to sitting in that position for hours. Her legs felt rubbery as she limped across the parking lot toward the restaurant. The glass entrance doors reflected a bunch of grizzly, worn out bikers. If it hadn't been for desperately wanting to see her son, now that they were so close, Moira might have enjoyed playing the role of a hard bitten biker babe.

"Why'd you bring us here?" she asked as the four of them were led out onto the deck overlooking the ocean.

"To reconnoiter. We need a plan before we approach your mother. And there are some things you ought to know." He pulled out a chair for her.

She plunked herself onto it, antsy and anxious to be on the move. "Tell me. A root beer," she said as a ponytailed waitress approached.

The others ordered drinks and food. Exasperated, but still needing their help, she went ahead and asked for some curly fries and a shrimp salad, reluctantly admitting that she needed to eat something before the "long night" Vance had in mind for them.

She leaned on the table and drank root beer from the bottle, fighting the urge to sit up straight and demand a chilled glass.

"While we're waiting for our food, you ask to use the phone to make a local call, and try your mother's house again. I hate to say it, but I'm beginning to agree with you; something's up." Vance hesitated then added, "You're absolutely convinced she wouldn't have gone on a cruise or taken…"

She thought of Hamilton and nearly leapt across the table to throttle Vance. "I told you! She never goes anyplace!" When she realized what she'd done, standing there poised as if to strike, she straightened and forced herself to look composed, trying to look casual as she removed her leather jacket and hung it on the back of her chair.

"I've had a man in the park ever since you arrived there in September. His name is David Abramowitz, a good man who can pass in several ethnic groups. He hasn't reported anything unusual."

Moira's whole body tingled with excitement. Someone had been watching her mother all this time? Relief, joy and a strong desire to kick Vance in his privates again for keeping this information from her surged through her all at once. "He's seen my mother?" Even as the words tumbled out, she thought, *then if he's any good, he must have seen Hamilton.*

"He said there was nothing unusual going on. He did see two men from IDIOTS a couple of weeks ago. They never even went into her house. He overheard them talking about meeting with her at a neighbor's place. I can't imagine what she told them, but they left."

"But how does she look? Is she well?" She desperately wanted to ask him about the baby, but still had some reservations about explaining Hamilton to him.

"He didn't actually see her, but he later heard the IDIOTS thanking the manager for pointing out her friend's house. It seems they had a good interview. From the lack of activity on the part of the IDIOTS in the interim, I surmise that your mother didn't divulge any useful information."

"She doesn't *have* any useful information. I haven't spoken to her in weeks and even when I did, I never told her where I was staying."

"They managed to find you in South Beach."

"Actually, they didn't, if you recall. I evaded them and then you 'rescued' me."

"True enough." He pointed at Moira, "Now, go inside and use the phone."

"You're ordering me about? I thought we four were going to reconnoiter, discuss a plan!" She was still having a hard time trying to figure out how to behave toward them. She'd been comfortable enough with servants, but Vance and his crew didn't really quite fit into that category.

"We'll discuss it when you get back. First, we need to know that she is at home and will be there when we arrive. Tell her around eight-thirty. Now, go."

She shoved her plastic deck chair back so hard that the weight of the jacket made it topple over. She didn't care. Let one of them pick it up. As she strode angrily between tables back to the interior of the building she was aware of the looks she received from men at the tables. With the spiky hair, her black jeans, form fitting T-shirt, biker boots and now a tattoo decorating her arm, she must make an astonishing appearance.

Fighting the urge to stick her tongue out at them or mash their faces with her boots, she found a waitress who pointed her in the direction of a pay phone next to the restrooms.

Frustrated, she had to head back to get coins from Vance before trying to make the call. Still to no avail. She tried the number three times before giving up.

Their food arrived just as she returned to the table. Vance pulled out a pen and began drawing on a napkin. "Based on what my operative tells me, this is what we're facing when we arrive. A security gate with a guard. Your mother's place just about dead center in the development."

"Park. They call it a park," Moira grumbled. "Keegan Bay on the south side."

"A small strip mall on the north," Vance added. "Give me any and all details that you can recall about her house. David was never able to get inside. At the moment, word is that she's taken a trip to Switzerland to visit you, but we know that isn't true."

Alarm bells. Moira's head shot up. "What do you mean, 'word is'? Are you saying she's not even in the park?"

"I'm not saying that at all, but David hasn't actually laid eyes on her for a long time, even though her house is lived in and she has occasional parties and meetings there. I'm just trying to cover all bases."

"Who said she took a trip to Switzerland?"

"I don't have the names in my head. We can ask David when we see him later."

"He's at the park now? In Keegan Bay Park? What's he doing there?"

Vern spoke up. "He's pretending to be a Mexican gardener. I said we should send Fernando, but Vance thought we needed him in Miami."

When Vance scowled at Vern, she smiled and shrugged, picked up her empty lemonade glass and signaled the waitress. That was the first time Moira had seen Vern actually interact with Vance. Although she'd behaved like a tough soldier since they'd met, it was nice to know she had a thought of her own now and then.

"The choices were," Vance said, "Fernando who looks too much like a heavyweight prizefighter to be a yard boy but speaks Spanish or David, an Israeli who can pass for an Arab or even a Latino, but doesn't speak Spanish. David is physically like a chameleon; he fits into any surroundings."

Moira held her head in her hands as her food was placed before her. "What a mess. And Hamid hired you to protect our family?"

"You're still alive, aren't you?"

She stared at him.

"Oh." He cleared his throat. "Hamid's death was an accident."

"Unproven." Moira picked up a fork and murdered a slice of cucumber.

Fern and Vern focused on their food.

After a few minutes Moira said, "All right, let's talk about my mother's house. First, doesn't anyone have a decent piece of paper?"

Once she had outlined the layout of the interior of the house and noted the two live oaks between Jessica's house and the neighbor on one side and three palms in the front yard, she made her first decision as their employer. "First we buy ourselves an SUV, either a new one or a recent model. And we do that before we go into the park, is that clear?"

Vance gave a half-hearted salute. "Already in the works, Boss. David has one waiting for us behind the diner next door to the park."

"It needs to be prepared with a…"

"A baby seat, infant carrier," Vance finished.

The pencil dropped from her fingers as she looked around at the three of them now facing her. "You know? You knew all along?"

"How could we not know? You returned to your New York apartment with it. What we don't know is its sex and how you managed to elude us during the entire pregnancy," Vance said. The other two nodded.

They all looked at her expectantly, waiting for her story. Her eyes traveled from one to the other, trying to ferret out which of them could be a true ally. She felt betrayed and alone, seduced into trusting them.

Looking down at her nearly empty dinner plate, she felt the food roil in her stomach. An anger she never experienced before erupted. She grabbed the edge of the round table as she stood and flung it upward so that all the food, drinks, and condiments slid and splattered over them. The three of them were left stunned, covered in the remains of their meals.

"*Its* name is Hamid Al Wafiki. He's my son! You knew. You knew, and you didn't tell me!" She turned and ran down the outside steps of the deck onto the beach.

She didn't pay any attention to where she was going, she just ran. She wanted her baby. She wanted him to be safe, and these fools her husband hired had left him behind while they were 'protecting' her. Tears blinded her as she stumbled along on the hard sand.

It didn't take long for Vance to catch her. He grabbed her and pulled her to the ground with him.

"Let go of me!" she shouted at him as she scrambled to get away. "You knew... you knew all along..."

He caught hold of her ankle. "You caught me by surprise once before and again today. Stay still and let me explain," he gasped, breathless from the chase.

"Why?" she cried as she pulled herself to a sitting position. "Why didn't you let on that you knew about him? What else have you been keeping from me?"

"Why didn't you tell us?" he asked in response.

"Why should I? I thought if you didn't know, then surely KARP and the IDIOTS, no one knew. He's been in danger all this time because of you!" She dropped her head onto her knees and cried. "I left him in a senior citizen park on purpose because no one would expect to find him there. You knew. *You knew!*"

"He's been in no danger. I've had David watching the house. Her friends and neighbors bring food into your mother on a regular basis. They even take out her trash for her so no one can tell there's a baby in there."

"David? The gardener who can't speak Spanish?" She wiped her eyes with the backs of her hands.

"That's the one. We thought, in spite of the importance of mother-child ties, that it would be better to leave the two of you in separate locations. When you went to that dreary trailer park, I had to admire your spunk. We checked out Arly Hitchens, your neighbor. He's a former Marine and a member of the NRA with two well-trained German Shepherds. We figured if any prowlers came around there, you'd be safe."

He paused for a moment. "Stinks about Sakir. If he hadn't been so determined to move up the ranks of KARP he might still be alive today. His orders were to keep an eye on you, not to bring you in."

Moira remained huddled on the sand with her knees drawn up to her chin, her arms wrapped around them. "How do you know all that?"

"Part of my job is to know what's going on in any area that might affect you. And your son."

"Except you didn't know he was a son until a few minutes ago."

"All right, I'll give you that. Now all we have to do is get to the car, collect your mother and the little Al Wafiki…"

"His name is Hamilton Robbins so people won't know who he is."

"Hamilton. Because it starts the same as Hamid or after Hamilton, New York, where you went to school?"

She turned her head so that her left cheek rested on her knee. "You know about Colgate and how Hamid and I met?"

"He told me the whole story."

"I miss him." Tears dripped onto her hands.

"He loved you."

She stared out at the ocean in the twilight. "Maybe."

Vance stood and held out a hand to her. "Come on, boss. We have to pick up a car and a family. Vern and Fern ought to be cleaned up by now. I'm glad nobody ordered chili or soup."

She let him help her up and the two of them started back down the beach. They used the public walkway to get back to the bikes. Fern and Vern waited there for them.

"We took care of everything, boss," Fernando said.

Moira turned to see to which boss he spoke. He was talking to her. She nodded her thanks as she mounted the bike behind Vance. They headed across the Dunlawton Bridge, back to the mainland. Sand from her tumble on the beach chafed at her skin inside the jeans, but she wasn't about to ask for anyone to wait so she could change.

When they stopped for a red light she looked over at a crowd of people waiting in long lines to get inside Aunt Catfish's restaurant. Men, women, old and young, with dozens of children of varying ages milled about. Ordinary people with ordinary lives that were unique to themselves. She envied them. No matter how she played it in the future, there was no way she wouldn't be a billionairess with a son who was heir to a throne. He was her baby boy, and within the hour she would be holding him in her arms again.

Chapter Twenty-Three

Hamilton had been successfully secreted at Bea's house. Though Justine was put out, we assured her that tonight we'd speak with Carol and try to feel her out about Hamilton.

I reminded her that we had to continue to be vigilant and cautious because we still didn't know where his mother was. Justine insisted on being present when we spoke with Carol. Michael disagreed. I agreed with her. We left it that we'd talk with Carol after dinner, but didn't make it clear whether or not we'd include her.

Michael and I had just finished an early supper when there was a knock at the door. I automatically rose to answer it, but Michael held out a warning hand.

He peeked through the blinds before announcing, "Old Howard. I'll deal with him."

Barclay would never come out of his den unless I shouted "Food!" or "Fire!" This was novel for me, having a man take charge and I wasn't too sure I liked it.

Old Howard stepped in after checking behind to make sure he wasn't being followed. He leaned against the door, out of breath, eyes glistening. "Enemy in the compound," he managed to rasp.

Michael led him to a chair while I pulled out the brandy. I could tell by the look on Michael's face that he didn't approve, but I opened the bottle anyway and poured an ounce or so into a crystal glass for Howard.

"What enemy?" I asked as I handed him the drink.

I was thinking of the phony gardener and the gray suits we'd seen last night. As far as I could tell he wasn't providing any new information except that they were back. Hamilton was safely ensconced at Bea's with Pete, Alice and Scott remaining at her house until Bob Stewart worked out a living arrangement for him outside the park. Only Bob and I knew about this plan. I hadn't even confided in Michael.

The others thought this would be the status quo until we got rid of the invaders, though how they could believe that was beyond me.

It took Howard several seconds and some of his brandy before he could speak. "I was heading for Jessica's with my nightly trash contribution…"

"What?" Michael and I spoke together.

"I give her one milk carton every other day. On the other day I put in a paper plate. That's all I use since Peggy passed."

"Howard, we all agreed that Jessica's taken a trip to visit her daughter in Switzerland. You were right here when we discussed it."

He looked from one to the other of us, completely baffled. "I was? That's a good plan. Did I suggest it?"

I patted him on the shoulder. "You could have." More likely he was passed out after too much brandy.

"What about enemy present?" Michael barked, unsympathetic to the old man's dilemma. I remembered his outburst about Wilma.

"I'll have to get the trash back without anyone noticing. I was a bit disappointed to note that the rest of you weren't contributing your fair share." He shook his head, lips pinched, as he appeared to consider his trash retrieval scheme.

"The enemy, Howard!"

"Ah. I spotted two of your gray suited gentlemen on Keegan Bay Midway and two more on Keegan Bay Lighthouse Court. They seem to be multiplying. And there's more." He held up his empty glass.

I rolled my eyes but refilled it anyway. "Keep talking." That was half prayer and half order. We didn't need him passing out if he had more to tell.

"I saw Carol arguing with three groundskeepers. All new men. I don't think she was winning. I hid behind the shuffleboard sheds until things quieted down and when I came out, she and the three of them were headed toward her office. I would almost swear that they had her in custody. For Carol, she was very quiet."

"What are you talking about? How did it look like she was in custody?"

"Well, one of them had his hand over her mouth while he carried the upper part of her body, and the other two had her legs. I would say they were carrying her off. Not a good sign."

"When did this happen? Where did they take her?"

"Just after dark, it was."

"Michael, call nine-one-one," I cried in alarm, my first thoughts going to Hamilton and hoping they weren't after him.

"We have to take care of this ourselves," he said, a hero waiting to relive his past.

"Nine-one-one," I repeated as I reached for the phone in a state of near panic.

He slapped my hand aside. "No!" he bellowed.

I knocked his arm away. "Watch it, buster. I managed to lose Barclay in the Galapagos. You want to be next?"

Startled, he took a step away from me. "You can't alert the police until we know what's going on. We only have the rambling of a drunken old man."

My hand turned red where he'd struck it and I was preparing to slug him when Howard's voice croaked.

He made a serious effort to stand, but failed. "A little brandy in the evening hardly justifies that insult, sir. I went straight to Justine's to make sure Hamilton was safe and what did I learn? That you two removed him this afternoon without consulting the membership. What if I were to tell them about that?"

"You're right, Howard," I said, my anger at Michael temporarily forgotten. "What did Justine tell you we gave as a reason for moving him?"

"Some nonsense about Carol being suspicious of her having a baby."

"Did she tell you where we placed him?"

"I don't think so. Certainly not back with the boys. They're heading North in the morning. I think."

Old Howard was listing to the side. We could safely leave him alone for a while in order to find out what was going on in the park. Four gray suits and three unknown groundskeepers who had captured or kidnapped Carol? And there was still the question of the masked gardener from last night who had disappeared. This required immediate checking.

Michael threw an afghan over Old Howard while I put on my walking shoes, fingers trembling with excitement and fear as I tried to tie the laces. I noted Michael's gentleness to the old man even as my hand continued to sting from the slap.

Chapter Twenty-Four

Moira and Vance pulled up behind the diner next door to Keegan Bay Park. A dark colored SUV waited for them next to the dumpster. Under the security lights, the van could have been black, blue or even dark green. As she dismounted, a seedy looking young man dressed in soiled blue jeans and a dirty tee shirt stepped out of the shadows of the building and headed toward them.

"Hey, Vance," the man said.

"David. What's the news?"

"Are you sure you're ready for this?"

"How bad?"

"At least four IDIOTS and three KARP."

"Great. What have we got?"

"I've called Granger and Milkweed. They're in Ohio, but everyone else is in Kushawa or Europe."

"ETA?"

David scratched his stubbled chin. "They should be landing in Daytona by nine p.m."

"Two hours. Have them come straight here. We'll wait for them."

"Already ordered."

Moira listened impatiently to this exchange. "We're not waiting another two hours."

"You people get out of there. Go to the Salvation Army. They'll feed you," a man shouted from the other side of the wall separating them from the retirement community.

Moira looked up at the top of the six foot stucco wall, from where the voice came. "Must be the dumpster. He thinks we're homeless people searching for supper."

"Thanks for the advice, mister," Vance called back to the man.

"Where are the keys for the car?" Moira asked, her voice raised.

"I said we'll wait for Milkweed and Granger. They're two of

my top operatives."

"What were they doing in Ohio if I'm your only client?" she demanded, her voice growing louder by the minute.

Vance looked to Fern and Vern as if they might explain but they remained silent. David folded his arms and waited with a smirk on his face.

"Well?" she shouted.

"I called them in from Europe two days ago. Told them to book their tickets to Daytona. They—um—made a mistake and wound up in Dayton, Ohio late last night."

"According to Granger," David said, "Milkweed drove around the city for hours looking for the racetrack where they run the five hundred until a kid at a gas station caught on to their mistake. I authorized them to rent a plane. They're flying themselves in tonight."

"That does it." Moira removed her jacket and tossed it on the SUV. Before anyone else could react she took a run at the wall, grabbed the top and began to pull herself over.

"I'm calling the cops right now!" the voice shrieked from the other side. "Get out of here!"

Vance caught the waistband of her jeans just before she would have made it over and dragged her back to the ground. "What do you think you're doing?"

"I'm going to get my baby and my mother out of there. And then I'm going to fire you and your band of incompetents!"

"Really? This is now the third time you've surprised me, Mrs. Al Wafiki."

"What were the other two?" She shoved him away and checked her elbow where she'd scraped it on the rough wall.

"The first was when you killed the guy in your house and the second when you kneed me in the *cojones*."

"You deserved both. Now, I'm sick of all these delays. I'm going into that park!"

Vance's eyes narrowed as he studied her for a moment. "If you're that intent on going in now, then let's go before that old coot does bring in the police."

She eyed him suspiciously. "You really mean it?"

"You people leaving or not?" The old coot shouted.

"Did you call the police?"

"I got the phone in my hand. You're all crazy."

"We're going," Vance shouted as he pulled Moira toward the car. "Let's do it, Cinderella."

She laughed out loud with relief. They were going in.

"Hamburger Boy and Cinderella—where are the keys?"

"I've got them," David said as he pulled them from his pocket and tossed them in her direction. Vance caught them in mid-air and tossed them right back to David.

They piled into the SUV with David taking the wheel. Vance opened the rear door for Moira. She slid in behind the driver. Vance climbed into the front passenger seat. She noted that there was already an infant seat in place in the back. Fern and Vern mounted their Harley's, but didn't start their engines.

"They'll follow in ten minutes, unless I call them. No point in alarming the residents if there's no problem," Vance explained.

David started the engine and they rolled out from behind the diner onto U. S. One, about fifty yards to get to the entrance to the park. She couldn't stop herself from smiling now that Hamilton was so near.

Chapter Twenty-Five

"Doll, you get Violet and round up the others," Michael spoke in a stage whisper as we stepped out into the night. "I'll scout around the office and Carol's house to see what I can learn."

"You can't go alone!" I whispered back. "Let me get Violet and John and then we can all go together." I was becoming distinctly annoyed at his bullying manner. "And you'd better alert Bea and the others to be on their guard."

"I'll stop at her house on my way to Carol's. You three come along when you're ready. Got your cell phone handy?"

My cell phone—something I'm always forgetting. "I'll be right back." I dashed into the house and then stopped short. When had I last used it? My eyes moved up and left as I mentally retraced my steps and tried to picture myself with the phone in my hand. Frustrated at this senior moment, I remembered my daughter-in-law's technique and used the house phone as a locater, quickly punching in the number and then following the sound of Beethoven's Fifth to the master bathroom counter—one of the few places it worked—where, I now remembered, I'd used it to call Bob two days ago. When I opened it to stop the ring tone I saw there was a message waiting for me. The number and name were unfamiliar and I wondered if I ought to take the time to return the call. It could be important considering all that had been going on in the park. I walked back to the front of the house and looked out the front window. Michael had already gone. I stepped outside and pressed Redial.

"Marilyn Anderson," a southern woman's voice drawled.

"Doris Reynolds returning your call." I hoped it wasn't a marketing ploy.

"Doris? Not Doll?" she said.

"My friends call me Doll. What do you want?" I responded in annoyance, anxious to leave and find out what was going on. I peeked into the living room where Howard continued to sleep soundly.

"That's what Bob said. He said you need a home for a baby for an undetermined length of time?"

That's was fast work on Bob's part. Thank goodness our baby could be safe sooner than I had thought possible. As much fun as the people in the park were having protecting Hamilton, Bob had convinced me he'd be better off in a stable environment until his mother returned. "Oh good. Oh, thank you. Praise the Lord," I said, something I don't do often enough.

"There's a situation going on here at the moment. Hamilton is currently at—" I knew he was at Bea's house but I couldn't for the life of me remember her street address. Besides, I still didn't understand or trust cell phones. Anyone could be listening, for all I knew. "Instead of wasting any time, just come to Keegan Bay Park and meet me outside the manager's office. It's the first building you come to in the center island. How far away are you?"

"Christmas Eve, no one on the roads. About twenty minutes, I'd guess."

"Christmas Eve," I repeated. "We planned a party for him tomorrow."

"Do you want to wait until Monday?"

I had moved out onto my front lawn by then. Torn with indecision, I tried to figure how much danger Hamilton might really be in. Biting my lower lip, I looked at Violet's house and the Christmas lights twinkling in her shrubs, as if staring at her house would bring her out to help. All I thought was that I hadn't put any decorations up in my house. I stopped doing that the year Barclay disappeared. *The baby. Think about the baby.*

I took a deep breath. "Come over now," rushed from my mouth before I could change my mind. "Call Bob and have him come with you," I added.

"He's right here; do you want to speak with him?"

"Right there? No. Bring him with you. We can always call the police if we need to," I blurted, my mind racing in a jumble, mouth moving before I could sort things out.

"Why would we need the police?" I could almost hear the wheels spinning in her brain during a brief silence. "Then what Bob said was true. There really are terrorists after the baby?" She didn't have to add, *you're not just a delusional old woman*, though I was pretty sure I heard the subtext in her tone.

"I don't know that they are terrorists, but apparently someone is looking for Jessica and her daughter and they won't be able to find either of them here. The baby is all we have of the family."

We left it that she and Bob would meet me at the office parking lot. If the three of us could get Hamilton away from the park, there would be no one else for the growing crowds of strangers to be looking for here.

I set my cell phone to 9-1-1 and tucked it in my pocket for comfort and security. Advice my son, Kevin, gave me when he bought me the cell phone. "And if you don't feel comfort and security from it, at least I will, knowing you have it." I hadn't wanted it, but he insisted and even put me on his family account so I didn't have to pay for it. Personally, I found it annoying that any one of them could find me wherever I might be. Most of the time I kept it turned off or forgot to charge it.

At the moment, I was glad for the phone, though I didn't know how a cell phone works in an emergency. Without the landline, how do the police know where to find us?

Deciding there was no need to alert Violet and John as I hadn't told them about the new plan either, I skirted left from my front door, hoping they were busy wrapping presents or watching an old Lawrence Welk Christmas special on TV.

When I reached the central island, I walked on the grass, moving from tree to tree, keeping a careful eye out for strangers. Being Christmas Eve, many of the houses were illuminated with colored lights; all the palm trees lining the parkway were adorned with tiny white bulbs. When I reached Keegan Bay Court I saw two of the intruders ahead of me to the left near Ellen Egbert's house.

I ducked behind the next palm tree then edged my way further back and hid behind a more substantial live oak, watching the bushes across the way. The two men probably watched me. What we used to call a Mexican Standoff, though I'm not sure why a standoff was necessarily Mexican.

They stepped out onto the driveway in front of Ellen's with a casual nonchalance. The taller of the two looked at his watch, nodded to the other and they strode down the street in my direction. IDIOTS.

I pulled back out of sight and counted to thirty thinking that I'd give them time to get beyond my hiding spot. But when I stuck my head out, they were coming out from behind the next house on Keegan Bay Way into that front yard. The shorter one spoke into a walkie-talkie or a cell phone; it was hard to tell from this distance.

While they were peering in windows, looking for Jessica or her daughter, I imagined, I wondered if I ought to step out and pretend to meet them by chance. What could they do to me here on a sort-of public street?

Then I remembered Old Howard's story of the three men who

had carried Carol off and wondered if anyone else had seen that incident. I chose to remain in place for a few more minutes then I'd walk as fast as possible to meet Marilyn and Bob at the office.

New plan. I opened my cell phone and called Violet. She sounded as if she'd been sleeping; I could hear Lawrence Welk's distinctive voice in the background, "A-one and a-two..." followed by his orchestra playing White Christmas. "Vi, I've spotted two of the gray suited idiots in the park and Old Howard says there are more. Can you get John and head toward the clubhouse to see where the others might be?"

The clubhouse was in the opposite direction so they wouldn't be able to see me get Hamilton out of the park but she'd still be able to help keep track of all the IDIOTS. If Howard had seen four, there could be any number of them wandering around.

"No, I can't," Violet said, panic evident in her squeaking, tremulous voice. "They think I'm Jessica. Remember?"

She was right. So much for that idea. "Then call Michael on his cell phone and warn him. The park is crawling with them. He was heading to Carol's; I'm going in that direction now." Carol's house is near the office parking lot.

I dismissed Vi as I strode out onto the pavement and walked briskly down the center of the street toward Keegan Bay Way where the two men were about to turn into Keegan Bay Marina Way. They moved slowly as they scanned each house, looking for open blinds, undrawn shades and lights that indicated people in residence.

I caught up with them as they were about to skulk around Maggie Brown's house and cleared my throat loudly. That caught them off guard. They were obviously not expecting anyone to be out after the dinner hour. Smith and Jones or Chip and Dale, whatever they were calling themselves, were not the same two agents who had come to my house.

"Good evening," said Chip as he tipped an imaginary hat. Or did I imagine that he had? His stance was so formal, he might have.

"Nice evening for a stroll," added Dale, a mustachioed, shorter version of Chip. Only he extended it further when he held out his hand. "We haven't met. I'm Aaron Sanders and this is my colleague, Bart French."

"How do you do," I replied in a surly tone, unwilling to give them anything, including courtesy. They meant us no good and I wasn't about to help them. "What're you doing in the park? You don't live here. Visiting someone?"

"We came to talk with Jessica Robbins. We have news of her

daughter."

That stopped me. "You do?"

"But we can only tell Mrs. Robbins, and she's not home. Again."

"She's uh—she's on vacation. In Switzerland." That's the story we told Carol. I was guessing that if they ran into any other Blenders, that would be the story they used too.

"Really? I saw her only a little while ago walking down the street with a tall white haired man. She went into the house next door to you. Maybe you didn't realize she'd returned," Aaron said.

"But, the man who answered had no idea who we were talking about. He said his wife and he had just come home and that she was napping. She sure fit the description Smith and Jones provided," the tall, skinny one, Bart French, continued. "I thought Mrs. Robbins was a widow."

My skin prickled. I didn't like any of this.

"What description was that?" I asked stalling for time, wondering how to get rid of them before I met Bob and his friend.

"Short, heavy," Aaron began.

"White fluffy hair," Bart finished.

I chuckled. "That describes three quarters of the women in this park."

"But not everyone is short and fat," Aaron said.

I picked up the pace of my walk. They had seen Violet with John. Hopefully I would spot Michael before these two agents decided to take me someplace for questioning.

I tried to remember the name of their organization. I knew they called themselves IDIOTS, but what did that stand for? International and terrorist were the only two words I could recall, and certainly Jessica wouldn't fit into that category.

I reached the end of the street and turned left toward the office where security lights kept everything nice and bright.

I stopped so suddenly that Aaron bumped into me. No nice bright lights at the office. Carol had replaced the spotlights with a lawn light that projecting reindeer and Santa and I don't know what else onto the office wall. I tripped over the cord, pulling the plug out of the socket which sent the entire area into darkness.

Even if I didn't find Michael, there was always hope that the neighbors would see me. The men helped me to my feet and began to brush grass cuttings off of me.

"Stop that!" I scolded as I pushed them aside.

"I think you should go see the manager and let her know that you're here," I suggested, anxious to get rid of them. "All guests must register." I used the superior tone of voice that used to scare my boys, but these two weren't buying it.

"Isn't this the office?" Aaron asked.

"It's Christmas Eve," I pointed out. "She doesn't work on Christmas Eve, however she lives down that street, five houses in." I pointed toward Old Howard's house, knowing full well that he was safely sleeping at my house. Heaven knows where the other men took Carol, but I didn't think it would be wise to send these two to her home.

"Probably a good idea to speak to the manager, in any case," Aaron conceded.

"Are you going to be all right?" Bart asked. "Can we call someone for you? Your husband?"

"It would be nice if you could call my husband," I remarked with sarcasm, tinged with a little smugness. At least they didn't know *everything* about me.

"The number?" Bart whipped out his cell phone.

"He's lost in the Galapagos."

A car pulled in from the highway and stopped at the guard hut. Charlie was off for Christmas; the corporation must assume thieves and charlatans don't prey on senior citizens during the holidays, so visitors have to work out how to push a button to raise the gate. So much for security. Then a huge SUV pulled in and cruised slowly by. Someone's family, I could only hope.

Before the gate could close another car arrived. As it drew closer it rolled to a stop in front of us. Bob's Lexus. He left his headlights on when he stepped out. I eased myself forward, hoping he could read my expression. I was rolling my eyes and bobbing my head, trying to signal that these men were not friends.

Before he could say anything, I said, "Hello, Bobby. These two nice gentlemen from an international organization have just helped me. I tripped on an electrical cord, which explains why it's so dark here. Gentlemen, this is my son, Bob. He's a doctor."

"Hello, Doctor Reynolds. Bart French here. Pleased to meet Mrs. Reynold's son." He held out his hand which Bob accepted with only a slight look of puzzlement. I was surprised that Bart knew my name.

Aaron stood back, observing. "We're just heading over to the manager's house. Have a nice evening. Happy Holiday and all that." They turned and left, going toward Howard's place.

Bob stood outlined in the headlights. I couldn't see his face clearly, but I could tell he was confused.

"Sorry about that, Bob. It didn't seem the moment to correct him and go through explaining that you're Dr. Stewart. Then we could have pretended the name difference was from an earlier marriage. I do have a son named Robert, except in my first marriage my surname was..."

"This is Marilyn Anderson from Children's Services. We're here for Hamilton," he interrupted my explanation.

A woman wearing sensible shoes, about five foot four, weighing in at around two fifty, grayish brown hair, stepped out of the car.

I gasped. Children's Services! I couldn't see Mutt and Jeff, but I hoped they were out of hearing range. "You didn't say you were bringing in anyone official, Bob. We can't let Hamilton get lost in the system. Don't you read the newspapers?" I was referring to two notorious cases a few years back where children in the state's care were lost because of sloppy paperwork.

"It's no longer up to you, Mrs. Reynolds. Now, where is the child?" Ms. Anderson stepped into the light at an angle where I could see her face more clearly. I didn't like it. She had a mean mouth and sloppy eyebrows. How could Bob, our Doctor Bob who writes such great science fiction, betray us by sending Hamilton into the wretched state system?

"It is up to me. Violet has papers making her his guardian until his mother returns. You saw the paper, Bob." Bob took a step back as I moved toward him, fists clenched at my side, barely able to control my rage.

"Then we'll go to her house," Bob said. "Remember, you called me and asked for a safe place for him." Bob took Marilyn by the arm to escort her back to the car.

"He's not there. He's in *our* system and if you think I'm telling you where he is, you better think again. We don't have sloppy paperwork; we don't have *any* paperwork. Go home and have a nice Christmas!" I turned my back on them and moved away. Tears burning my eyes, I pulled out my cell phone. Betrayed by the one person I thought I could completely trust. I heard them driving away, probably to Violet's. That didn't matter; she wouldn't know where Hamilton was once I set the escape plan in motion. I opened the cell phone and pressed a button thinking it was the contact list. Through tear blurred eyes I watched it dial 9-1-1. When the emergency operator answered, I told her it in a trembling voice that the call was a mistake. Quickly closing it, I was more careful when I looked up Bea's number and said,

"There's a bee in her bonnet. We've got to rock and roll."

Bea said, "Is that you, Doll? Are you drinking anything?"

"No," I said. "There's a bee in her bonnet."

"What are you talking about? What bee in whose bonnet? Really, Doll. Pete, Scott and Alice are here. We're wrapping gifts for Hamilton. I bought him the most adorable Santa outfit to…"

I clenched my teeth and tried to speak. "Forget about it. We have to get him out of the park. There are agents and terrorists crawling all over the place. I had a plan, but it didn't work out. Now a social worker's on the prowl for him as well. Get him ready and I'll pick you up in half an hour. I've got to find Michael first."

"That is not in accordance with our plan, Doll. I can't do that. How do I know they aren't holding a gun to your head right now?"

"No one's holding a gun to my head."

"Yes, they are," a man's voice said from behind me. "Give to me the phone."

I shut it and passed it behind me. That didn't stop whoever was there from redialing.

Chapter Twenty-Six

They pulled the SUV into the entrance to find an empty guard house. A notice explained that after hours, guests should push the red button under the window and sign the register. A guest book on the window ledge stood open on with a pen dangling on a string. There was one name on the page dated five days ago.

Moira leaned forward so she could watch for the street signs. "My mother's house is on the right side of the park. You'll go over two traffic bumps and then Keegan Bay Central Court is the next right turn. She's immediately on the left but you have to go all the way around the circle. Wouldn't you think on Christmas Eve there'd be more activity? Not much going on here."

"Over there. In the parking lot," Vance pointed. "A group of people. Can you see anyone you recognize? Son of a bitch," he said before she could even focus on them. "IDIOTS! What are they doing here?"

"Hurry!" she urged David.

"Speed limit's ten," he responded. "Don't want to get caught out for a speeding violation."

"And just who the heck do you think is out checking speed limits on Christmas Eve in an old folks' trailer park? One more speed bump, and we're there."

Meanwhile Vance got on his cell phone and gave instructions to Fern and Vern to come into the park and scout around for IDIOTS and KARP people.

Fingers knotted under her chin, Moira leaned on the back of his seat watching for her mother's house, vaguely aware of Christmas lights. A woman hurried down the street going in the opposite direction. A quick glance told her it wasn't her mother. This was a large, determined looking woman.

Second traffic bump followed by a right turn. She leaned back prepared to leap from the car the moment it stopped.

The SUV pulled up behind Jessica's car and within seconds

Moira was at the kitchen door banging on it. "Mom! I'm here!"

David and Vance circled the house while she waited for her mother to open the door.

"Mom!" she shouted again, this time banging harder on the door.

She leaned forward and tried to see inside but the room was dark. She couldn't imagine that her mother was in bed already; it was only a little after eight o'clock. Could she have gone out with friends to church for Christmas Eve? With Hamilton? She didn't think that was likely. She ran out to the street where she met Vance and David just finishing their circuit of the premises.

"No sign of anyone around the house. No obvious evidence..."

Moira had barely finished speaking before she was headed to the house next door. She noted that Vance and David once again split up, leapfrogging to the next two houses. No one home right next door. She skipped past them and went to Number 6 where lights suggested people at home. The name over the doorbell read "John and Violet Hathaway." She pressed the bell while she also knocked breathlessly on the door, shifting from foot to foot waiting for someone to respond. It seemed forever, but was actually only moments before a portly man peeked anxiously between a slit in the doors' window curtains. He turned on the outside light, called to someone and then opened the door. As he did, Vance and David came up behind her. The man's eyes widened in fright as he tried to shut the door on them, but Vance shouldered his way past Moira and was inside before the poor, terrified fellow could stop them.

"Jessica Robbins. Is she here by any chance?" Vance asked, looming over him.

The man, presumably John Hathaway, looked at the three people now standing in his kitchen. "Jessica Robbins?" he asked with a weak voice.

"Jessica's in Switzerland!" a short, dumpy woman, Violet, Moira guessed, said as she entered from the living room wearing a fuzzy purple bathrobe. One look at the group standing in her kitchen entryway and she grabbed the top of her robe with one hand and pointed at them with her other. "Who are you?" Then, without looking at her husband she commanded, "John, call Michael,"

"Tell *Michael* Moira Robbins is here," Moira said. If she didn't see her son and her mother soon, she would scream.

"You're the mother? You're *Moira*? The one who's been missing all this time?" The old girl's face turned white and she looked like she was about to pass out.

"I'm not missing; I'm here. Where's my mother?"

"Oh boy," the old lady said and turned around to stagger into the living room where she collapsed onto an overstuffed, chintz covered chair.

Her husband remained in the kitchen using the telephone while they followed the woman into a dimly lit living room cluttered with overstuffed Victorian furniture and an incongruous large flat-screen television.

"I don't want to sit down; I want to know where my mother is."

"Can I get anyone a drink?" Violet asked. "You can move those newspapers and sit over there on that sofa." She pointed with a shaking finger.

"Hamilton Robbins is my son. Where is he? Why isn't my mother with him at the house?" Moira ignored the chair and stood, hovering over Violet.

"Hold on a minute. Who are these men?"

"What men?" Moira asked, turning to see who she was talking about. "Oh, you mean Vance and David? They're my bodyguards and if you don't tell me where I can find my mother, they'll be glad to help you remember where you last saw them."

Two more bodies in the room made it feel like a New York subway at rush hour. She inched around the chair as Vance entered.

Vance laughed, not really a pleasant sound, but at least Violet stopped looking like she was about to wet her pants. "Her Highness, the Princess al Wafiki, is making a joke. But, she is right about one thing, we do need to find the baby as quickly as possible. If the others find him first, his life will be in very serious jeopardy."

Violet's glance jumped erratically from Vance to David to the kitchen and back to Moira as she spoke. "I have no idea who you're talking about. My neighbor, Jessica, went to Switzerland to visit her daughter, who is married to a prince. They don't have any children."

"Jessica informed us that she told her friends here in the park about the baby," David said as he squatted down on one knee, in an effort to appear less threatening.

A sharp pain pierced Moira's right temple as everyone chattered politely. "Where's Hamilton?" she shouted over their voices.

"I've called Michael," John said as he, too, joined them in the small room. Moira thought she wouldn't be able to breathe.

"Who the hell is Michael?"

"He's working with Doll and she told us she'd be going out tonight, so he's technically the second-in-command," Violet explained. She'd recovered her composure as soon as her husband was beside her.

"Doll?" Moira asked, feeling defeated by the tiresome plodding of this senior citizen as she sank against the back of the chair she'd been leaning on.

"Doll Reynolds. She lives next door to us."

Reynolds. That was the last person who answered her mother's phone. Doll Reynolds. Moira's throat suddenly went dry. "Doll Reynolds? Doll Reynolds is the woman my mother told about Hamilton! You do know about him! What have you done with my son? Where is my mother?"

"I already told you. She… left for Switzerland." The poor old dear's eyes filled with tears and Moira feared she'd gone too far. But if she knew something about her son, well, too bad, old woman.

"And left Hamilton here?" She didn't believe what she'd heard. Couldn't believe it. She looked to Vance and David to see if they bought into the fact that her mother would abandon her grandson that way.

"Please don't ask us anything more," John said as he entered the living room. He moved behind his wife and placed his hand protectively on her shoulders.

Violet's eye welled with tears as she reached up and patted her husband's hand. "Frankly, you don't look anything like I imagined. I pictured more Grace Kelly or Princess Diana. You mother said you were elegant and graceful."

Moira looked down at herself and remembered how she was dressed. Certainly, she didn't look anything like a princess, nor did Vance and David come across as high class private security. She took a deep breath and tried to control her anxiety. "My mother told me that Doll Reynolds knows about my baby. Can you please tell me where to find Mrs. Reynolds?"

"She's out. It is Christmas Eve, after all. People don't sit around their houses waiting for a bunch of bikers to break in and terrorize them," John said. "Now, I think it's time you left. If you want to leave a message for Doll, I'd be happy to give it to her when we see her again."

Moira hesitated. Was this old woman playing a trick on her? Were there KARP people or IDIOTS hiding somewhere in the house preventing them from talking? She looked to Vance for a hint of how to proceed.

"You mentioned someone named Michael as being second in command. In command of what?"

Violet began to weep openly. John stood taller and straighter, appearing far stronger than he did when they entered the house. "I think it's time you left before we call the police. We've been courteous and given you no cause to abuse us."

"These people have to know where he is. Come on. Old or not, we'll get it out of them," David said as he stood and slammed a clenched fist against his open hand.

Before Moira could warn David to leave the old people alone, Violet blurted out, "Don't hurt me, please. John has a bad heart, he couldn't stand it."

"No one's going to beat you, Violet, but if you don't give us more information about my mother and son, I'm going to order some serious arm twisting." Moira made the statement half-heartedly, touched by the fact that Violet was more concerned for her husband than for herself.

"Find Doll. She'll tell you everything. I never wanted to be involved. Honest. I didn't," Violet wept as John handed her a tissue from a nearby table.

The telephone rang, stopping everyone. They all stared at the old instrument on the end table near the sofa.

"Answer that," Vance ordered.

John handed the receiver to Violet who listened without speaking for a moment and then she said, "There's a woman here claiming to be Jessica's daughter. I think she has a bee in her bonnet." She paused to listen again. "I'm sorry, I don't remember that part, but there's definitely a bee in her bonnet." Another pause. "Um-hmm." She passed the phone back to John who replaced the receiver.

Moira waited for an explanation. Something about Violet Hathaway had changed while she was on the phone; her demeanor was calmer. The tears had stopped flowing, and she brushed her husband's hand from her shoulders. Even John looked puzzled.

Moira tried a different tack. "You said Doll went out. Where? Did she tell you?"

Violet nodded. "She said she was meeting a friend in the parking lot at eight o'clock. I think she said eight o'clock. She went out around seven thirty. Michael was at her house but he left earlier. I don't know what's going on. No one ever tells me anything." This time her plea of ignorance didn't ring true.

Moira suspected that wasn't necessarily true, but she didn't have time to dwell on that now. "The office," she said to Vance. "David, why don't you keep these two company and if anything else occurs to them, call us."

Vance asked, "What does Doll Reynolds look like? What is she wearing?"

"She's tall, kind of slender, dark curly hair; she colors it, you know. Makes her stand out in this community, let me tell you. It's really quite white. She's around my age, though she never says exactly, I'd guess seventy," Violet said.

"Who knows what people wear? They wear clothes," her husband added.

"I know because she's lost so much weight recently she can fit into her old clothes. The things she wore when Barclay was alive. Barclay was her husband, you see. She's secretly convinced he's still alive, but everyone knows he died when he went scuba diving with those Lithuanians in Polynesia."

"They were Norwegians in the Galapagos," John corrected.

"I was close." Violet pouted.

Moira wanted to scream. In a tightly controlled voice she interrupted the couple. *"What is she wearing*? How will we know her when we see her?"

"She had on her beautiful old navy blue pant suit with a white blouse and a cute antique reindeer pin on the lapel. If it's more than fifty years old, it is an antique, isn't it? She was probably wearing her good walking shoes, but I didn't..."

Violet was still talking when Moira and Vance raced out to the car. "She described the woman we saw with the gray suits when we came in," Moira said. "I hope Fern and Vern got there in time."

Ten miles an hour, Moira thought as Vance sped at a good thirty miles or more through the park, bouncing over traffic bumps on the way to the office lot. When they arrived no one was in sight, but Vern and Fern's motorcycles were parked haphazardly, as if abandoned in a hurry.

He pulled up next to them. Moira and Vance stepped out and looked around. She hoped, by staring into the night, she'd see Doll Reynolds with Hamilton and Jessica.

"I'll check the office." Moira followed the brick path toward the main entrance. Vance caught up with her and passed her a small flashlight.

"Interesting how the entire park is lit up with Christmas lights, even the entrance and the guard shack, but nothing around the office," he said. "Keep off the path as you approach the door. I'll check the windows. Do I have to tell you to shout if you see anything? Meanwhile, I'll try to locate Fern."

"And Vern," she said as she stepped on something on the lawn.

She turned on the flashlight and cast the beam down close to the ground. A cell phone. She picked it up, flipped off the light and called softly, "Vance, I've got something."

When he didn't respond she stepped close to the hibiscus bushes and pressed a button on the phone to light up the screen, then pressed redial. As she held the phone to her ear, her heart pounded.

"Doll. Thank heavens, it's you. What was that all about? Are you all right?"

"This isn't Doll. Who are you?"

"Doll's friend. Where is the man who called earlier? Where's Doll? What have you done with her? I'll have you know that I've already notified the police that something is wrong. I told them you people are using my friend's cell phone. And-and I don't have Hamilton. Someone took him earlier. He wouldn't say where he'd be going next so there's—"

"—no point in coming over there and beating on you," Moira finished for her. "Nobody knows so you can't be tortured into telling," she repeated Violet's comment. "This is Moira Robbins, Hamilton's mother. I'm looking for Hamilton and my mother, Jessica Robbins. Can you please, please tell me what's going on?"

Moira figured the woman was lying to her, just as Violet had been. She suspected the muted voice in the background might be telling her what to say. Was she being held by KARP? IDIOTS?

"The truth is we've been keeping him safe for you. But, today, so many people have been prowling around that Michael and Doll said they would take care of the next move. It began when Carol got suspicious."

"Who's Carol?"

"The park manager. She lives in the house just inside the entrance. Facing the park it would be the first house on your left. Maybe she knows something." The connection was terminated.

"Thank you." Moira said into the dead air and then stuck the phone in her pocket before starting around the building to find Vance. She ran into him as he was trying to jimmy open the back door. "Forget this; I just spoke to someone who says the park manager knows what's going on. She told me where the manager lives. Let's go. I still don't understand why they're moving Mom and Hamilton all around the park. If there are people here looking for them, then why didn't Mom just leave and take Hamilton someplace safe and then let me know when I called? Or leave me a message."

She realized her argument was sounding lame and dropped it. Her mother couldn't leave her a message. Anyone would have found it. But all this Mata Hari stuff, everybody claiming to know nothing, pretending her mother's in Switzerland, struck her as far too complicated.

"Vern and Fern are already there. No one is answering the door there either. I told them to wait for us."

"Uh-oh," Moira said when she spotted two gray suited IDIOTS headed in their direction. "Now what? Aren't they the ones we saw with Mrs. Reynolds earlier?"

"Could be. Hold my hand. We're having a walk after dinner."

"We're too young to live here."

"We're visiting our family. I'm sure that's permitted." He grabbed her hand.

She knew his other one would be wrapped around the gun in his pocket. Gray Suits on South Beach and now gray suited IDIOTS in Keegan Bay. They're supposed to be in search of terrorists. "They can help us," she said.

"What are you talking about?" Vance said under his breath as the IDIOTS closed in on them.

"They're looking for the KARP who are looking for me. And Hamilton." She held out her other hand before Vance could stop her. "Hi! I'm Moira Robbins, widow of Hamid al Wafiki. I understand you've been looking for me."

Vance dropped her hand.

The IDIOTS stopped, mouths agape. The one on the left bore slightly Asian features, the other looked Nordic. Neither one appeared prepared to speak.

"I'm looking for my mother. So far all I've heard is that she's in Switzerland which I happen to know isn't true. Would either of you or your fellow agents have any idea where she might be?"

"Abhaya Singh, at your service, madam." The darker man bowed.

"Nils Gundesen here," the blond gave a weak salute as he, too, bowed.

"And I'm Vance Eberhardt, Chief of Security to Mrs. Wafiki's family, here to take care of Her Highness, so if you have anything to say, you say it to me. If you'll pardon us, Your Royal Highness."

Moira couldn't have been more surprised if Vance had stepped forward and kissed the two men before them. Caught completely off guard and unsure how to respond, she stood wide-eyed and mute as the three men went to one side and spoke in hushed voices.

In her year of running, she'd entirely missed the point that she was, in fact, not just a wealthy heiress, but a *royal*, wealthy, heiress. As she concerned herself about protecting her son from an alien family she feared would have him killed, she never considered that she could have a position of authority amongst Hamid's people, the Kushawans.

Life as a small town girl had certainly never prepared her for this; hadn't prepared her for marriage to Hamid either, but he'd been so capable of taking care of everything and she so willing to give over her life to him, she now realized, she'd never grown up at all. She was nearly as naïve and unworldly as she was the day she'd met him.

All she'd learned over the years is how to ski better, play tennis better and find her way around and order food in several languages. She had been good at languages. Hamid had been proud of her, and she'd drunk it all in, glowing in his praise and approval. Everything he wanted, she wanted. Except Hamilton.

When she tried to bring up the subject of children, he'd refused to discuss it. For the public, he made statements about looking forward to a large family of sons. In private he told her he didn't want any.

As time went on and the relationship became stale, she played the role, convincing herself that this was the life she wanted. Year after year of playing at being Peter Pan. She told herself she loved her husband and behaved obediently until she realized that soon it would be too late for a family and, in the end, she really wanted children. Without telling him, she had stopped her birth control pills. And then Hamid died.

The men's voice ebbed and flowed. She thought they might be speaking in Kushawan, but before she could focus and concentrate on the words their voices were drowned out by the sound of approaching sirens.

Chapter Twenty-Seven

Michael, Carol and I sat in a small circle facing one another on uncomfortable, straight-backed chairs in the center of the small kitchen off the manager's office. With no windows and the door closed, no one would know that we were in there. Two young men dressed completely in black with black ski masks over their faces paced nervously around us waving handguns, sometimes twirling them like cowboys, pretending to quick draw on one another like schoolboys at play. If one of us twitched, they reverted to a menacing mode, weapons pointed. The good news was that they hadn't tied our hands and feet.

Perspiration trickled from my scalp.

"Do either of you know what the hell's going on?" Carol whispered, trying to keep her lips from moving.

"I don't know why they haven't killed us all," Michael responded.

"Obviously not their orders," I said with a sideways glance to the twitchiest of the two. He checked his watch against the clock in the kitchen every few minutes.

"No talk, no movement!" the one leaning on the doorframe barked. That seemed to be their mantra.

As I watched them and waited for whatever would happen next, I recalled a time in the early seventies. Barclay and I were flying from Beirut to Paris when we made an unexpected landing at an unknown location in the middle of nowhere.

The plane bounced along a deserted runway and stopped before an enormous hangar. That was before hijackings had turned so horrific. So, while there was certainly plenty of concern, there weren't any visible signs of terror.

When the plane stopped before the hangar, the captain advised us in a calm voice to disembark. Men in paramilitary uniforms pushed a rusted set of steps up to the exit and we walked out into dreadful, suffocating heat.

Our hosts then pointed with weapons, indicating that we were to line ourselves up inside the perimeter of the abandoned building.

After a while with everyone growing hot and uncomfortable and nothing happening, even the adolescent guards appeared to be bored. They began joking amongst themselves, flipping their rifles, and then twirling them like batons, but clumsily. I prayed none of them would go off. No one informed us about what was going on.

After a couple of hours, with most of us whining and complaining, they allowed the flight attendants to bring us food and water from the aircraft.

Fruits, cheese and crackers, cakes and pastries—the good old days of flying—helped ease the tension. Some of the passengers even offered to share with our guards. I didn't feel that generous; it was late in the afternoon, I was hot and tired and wanted to get to Paris.

I whispered to Barclay that it would be nice to have a drink with the cheese and crackers and that's when we hatched our plan. Alcohol for terrorists—get them snockered.

"Teenaged hijackers with guns? You want to give them alcohol? What are you? Nuts? Not only do they have automatic weapons, now you want them *drunk* with automatic weapons?" was his initial reaction.

But after consulting with a few other male passengers we decided if we could get them drunk, the men could overcome them. Barclay, dressed in his most impeccable traveling clothes stepped forward, hands raised and, after working out a common language, French, they permitted him to send a flight attendant back onto the plane to collect drinks for everyone.

Barclay hadn't told the boy guards it would include hundreds of mini-bottles. When the alcohol and mixers arrived, another male passenger caught on to Barclay's scheme and between the two of them, they created a sweet tasting concoction and offered one to the group leader.

He sipped it suspiciously at first, then smiled broadly and finished it, holding out his empty glass for more and indicating that they should serve everyone a drink. Most of the passengers settled on colas and water, aware they would need their wits about them shortly. After one gin and tonic, I restrained myself as well.

Within an hour, our captors, whoever they were, couldn't tell up from down, guard from detainee. One particularly tall and skinny fellow began demonstrating how to march with his weapon slung over his shoulder. We all mimicked him, eventually marching right out to the aircraft, where the captain had remained with the chief perpetrator awaiting orders.

Our now thoroughly inebriated guards were either retching outside the steel building, or singing bawdy songs and sharing jokes amongst themselves.

When it was obvious that none of them knew American from Arab, Israeli from Congolese, the captain of our ship had words with his own private guard in the cockpit, who, upon seeing that his troops were out of control, quietly slipped away and we took off.

We flew on to Paris and never learned any more about that incident. Somewhere in the world there is a retired Pan Am employee who knows.

That incident continued to nag at me as I mentally inventoried the kitchen. I'd only been in there once when Carol had invited me to lunch to discuss working on a column for her community newsletter.

Afterward we had tidied up together—utensils in a drawer right behind me, tea pot on the burner on the stove, electric coffee maker on the counter, paper towels. Food and drink in the refrigerator. And bottles of alcohol in the cupboard above the sink.

Carol had served a nice white wine with lunch. Could there be more in the fridge? Could lightning strike twice? Would these two lads fall for it? Surely today's terrorists were far more sophisticated than they were forty years ago.

I cleared my throat and shot Michael a look that said, 'Pay attention.' "Water," I gasped, pointing to my mouth. "*Agua*. Water."

"No talk, no movement." After checking his watch, Twitchy raised his weapon.

I began panting, clasping my chest. "Water. Please. *Por favor. Si'l vous plait.*"

I closed my eyes and slid down in my chair, hoping someone would catch me before I hit the floor. Getting up is not so easy these days.

Hands grabbed me as I heard, "No talk, no movement!" followed by a string of foreign words.

Michael and Carol picked up my plea and begged on my behalf, miming for the guards. They got the picture and the taller one opened cabinet doors until he found a cup which he filled with water.

In my feigned stupor I moaned, "They obviously don't know a word of English. Mix a drink with the vodka and tomato juice. Act like it's medicine. Look worried!"

"I am worried, no problem there," Carol said under her breath. She pointed at Michael and said to the guards, "Doctor! Doctor fix medicine."

"No doctor. No move." But neither man made any attempt to

stop them from pouring the drinks.

Michael caught on quickly enough as he accepted the vodka from her and concocted a strong Bloody Mary. He held it out to Carol to pass to me, but pulled it back before she could take it and offered it to a guard.

The two of them eyed it suspiciously.

Michael smiled in encouragement. "Special water. Juice."

The first one lifted his mask far enough to take a sip, smiled and passed it to his partner who did the same. Michael made two more drinks, handing one to me, the other to the guards. He then ran water for himself and Carol.

Twitchy held his cup out for more. "No talk," he said as he waited.

"Damned right, no talk," Michael replied.

Having made the plan, I had to follow it, but personally would have preferred a Scotch or a gin and tonic. I sipped slowly, smiling my gratitude repeatedly at them, toasting with each sip. They drank and smiled in return. I'd guessed correctly that they were unaccustomed to strong drink; it didn't take them long to succumb. The first guard removed his mask so he could drink more easily.

Only it didn't go quite the way I had hoped. While they were happily drinking there was a noise from outside. They weren't so far gone that they couldn't be alarmed. They began arguing between themselves. I'm guessing trying to decide who should check out the noises.

Ugly drunks. They pushed and shoved at each other as the noise became a loud banging, which suddenly stopped. Twitchy inched open the door to a slit wide enough for him to peer through. He said something to the other and then they continued their argument.

"What now?" I mouthed to Michael.

"It was your idea. You figure it out," he said through clenched teeth.

"We have to get to Hamilton."

Carol, who has a strident voice when irritated, spoke up. "I still don't know what the hell is going on."

"No movement, no talk!" the now unmasked, smooth faced, well-tanned Twitchy slurred. He put his finger to his lips and hissed before pouring more tomato juice in his cup. As an afterthought he finished off the vodka before returning to his argument with his partner.

"Jessica Robbins's grandson is what's going on," I said, using a ventriloquist technique, trying not to move my lips and keeping my teeth clenched.

Guard Two raised his left hand to me in a rude gesture, which silenced me.

We would have to remain silent until they forgot about us. They continued bickering and drinking. Twitch had opened a bottle of bourbon. Now they were drinking bourbon with tomato juice. How much longer before they either passed out or started throwing up? I'd had the idea they were from a country where alcohol was forbidden; but maybe not. They sure seemed to be holding it well.

My faked anxiety was becoming all too real. I had to get Hamilton out of the park and away from these fools. According to Jessica's story we needed to keep him safe for about twenty-seven more hours. If they didn't find him before then, the theory was that they would give it all up and go home. Hard to believe, but Jessica had made it sound real enough.

Twitch propped himself against the doorjamb with his gun hand. Guard Two used his weapon to scratch his head while he argued a point. Whatever Two said, it sent Twitch into a fit of laughter.

Waving both of his hands over his head in a kind of triumphal wave, he managed to pull the trigger. The explosion of the gunshot was deafening in such close quarters. I watched as he appeared stunned and then slid gracefully and silently to the floor. Two looked at us, muttered something I couldn't hear, then bent to check on his buddy.

Taking advantage of the situation, heart in my throat, I picked up the emptied vodka bottle and whacked Two on the back of the head. Two fell on Twitch and we were out of there in a shake of a lamb's tail, slipping out the back door.

My arthritic hip caused me to lag behind Michael and Carol who rounded the corner to the front of the building ahead of me.

"If my message got through, then Hamilton ought to be…" I whispered breathlessly as a spotlight caught Michael and Carol in the middle of the lawn.

"Put your hands where we can see them!"

I fell back behind the bushes and slid into the darkness.

Chapter Twenty-Eight

As the sirens grew louder and it became obvious they were entering Keegan Bay Park, Vance and his new friends quickly escorted Moira down a side street and into the shadows of an empty lot. They sat huddled on a low, bench-height limb of an ancient live oak, trying to work out a plan. The two IDIOTS were all for making themselves known to the local police, assuming they would be helpful in a search for the missing heir to the throne of Kushawa. Vance knew otherwise.

It was all Moira could do to hold herself together. With no manager at the manager's house, she wanted to return to the old lady neighbor's house and begin again.

They were murmuring amongst themselves when a patrol car entered the street, its spotlight flitting across yards and over houses, lighting up every crevice.

"When's the last time you climbed a tree?" Vance asked Moira.

"Probably when I was twelve, why?"

"Well, here we go." He grabbed an overhead limb and hauled himself upward and then reached down to help her.

The IDIOTS quickly caught on and by the time the cruiser reached the lot, they were safely hidden in the foliage. The spotlight skirted around the base of the tree, never reaching higher than the first low, cradling limb.

"Let's sneak through the backyards and talk to the neighbor. She knows a lot more than she's telling." Moira slid down from her perch on the tree and skulked across the street, hoping she headed in the right direction. She didn't care if Vance came along or not.

She'd passed through a series of backyards, between houses and crossed three streets when she estimated that she should be level with her mother's house.

She moved toward the center island that divided the park in two. Her mother's house should be on the other side of the broad expanse. A wide street, the tree covered island, another street and then her mother's place. From there to the old lady. Sounds behind her suggested that Vance and possibly the other two followed. Checking left and right for traffic, she then made a mad dash for the center island and moved quickly into the shadows.

"Who the hell are you?" someone croaked from nearby.

Alert, nervous and now terrified, she stopped short and looked to where the voice came from. In the darkness she could just make out an elderly person sitting with a little white dog on a wooden lawn swing.

"Jesus!" she gasped.

"I doubt that, young woman. What are you doing sneaking around the park? I have my cell phone with me and can call the police, so don't try anything funny."

The person, she guessed from the wispy halo of white hair that it was a woman, raised a fisted hand. It could have been holding a cell phone or a bomb. The little dog leaped down from the swing, wagging its tail and jumped around Moira, begging for attention.

"I'm looking for my mother and son. Jessica Robbins? Do you know her?"

"You're her daughter? Humph. She stopped coming to Bingo ages ago. No one's seen hide nor hair of her in months. Heard she moved to Switzerland. But I don't know nothing about no grandchildren, dear. There were some young fellows looking for her earlier. For someone who doesn't play cards or Bingo anymore, she sure is popular all of a sudden."

Moira caught movement behind the old woman. Vance was signaling her to get moving. She thanked the woman, patted the dog on the head and charged on across the island, meeting Vance by the road, only to be toppled to the ground and rolled behind yet another tree.

"This is getting old!" she snapped at him.

He covered her mouth and whispered, "They're at your mother's house. Look."

Because of the streetlamp in the center island of the cul de sac, the fronts of all the houses were clearly visible. At first she didn't see anything and waited, annoyed at yet another delay. But in the end, she was glad she waited. A black clad form emerged from behind the house carrying a heavy object. As he crept toward the front of the house she could see that he was playing out a role of wire.

"Uh-oh," Vance's grip on her shoulder tightened. "Go tell that old lady to go home. As long as home isn't in any house nearby. I'll take care of him."

She hesitated. "It's not what it looks like. Tell me it isn't."

"Get the old woman out of here and clear out yourself. I'll take care of this!" he ordered, giving her a shove. "We've already ascertained that your mother and child aren't in there, now go!"

Moira scrambled to her feet and headed back toward the swing. She heard Vance talking to someone as she left him behind and approached the old woman. The dog saw her first and danced in circles, happy to see her.

While the dog bounced up she let it lick one hand while she made a shooing motion toward the woman. "You have to clear out of here. Right now," she whispered.

The old woman put a hand to her right ear. "What's that you said? You saw a deer in here?"

Moira raised her voice, "You have to get out of the way. Go home!"

"Didn't your mother teach you to speak up? Speak up, young woman!"

Afraid that the men at the house might hear, she took the old woman by the arm and tried to help her from the swing.

"What are you doing? And why are you dressed that way? You aren't one of those drug addicted people Carol's always warning us about, are you?"

Moira had her standing at least. She bent down and whispered as loudly as she dared. "You have to go home now. It isn't safe out here right now." She gave her a gentle nudge.

"You think I'm stupid, young woman? I take Betsy for a walk every night, Christmas Eve or not. Don't you be shouting at me like I'm deaf. I'll be leaving now, and don't you dare to follow me!"

Moira took her by the elbow as if to escort her, but the woman shrugged her off and dragged the reluctant dog away. Fortunately, she headed toward the opposite side of the park and, hopefully, would be safe.

Moira returned in time to see Vance wrapping wires around the wrists of the black clad man, while two other men crawled on hands and knees around the outside of the building.

Vance was telling David to evacuate the circle including the houses on the nearby streets. "Just in case he's set up explosives anyplace else around here. And keep a low profile. We'll take down the perps at the house. I've got two IDIOTS here to help me. Granger and Milkweed should be coming through the gates right about now."

Moira noted the two IDIOTS didn't appear any too thrilled to be helping tackle a group of foreigners intent on wiring a house with explosives.

More sirens from outside the park coming closer sent Moira

hurrying down the center of the island, moving in the shadows of the trees to avoid being seen by the men at her mother's house.

She met up with David as he helped load a golf cart for an elderly couple. David looked at her apologetically. "I tried to get the Hathaway's out quickly but they insisted on packing a few special things. They promised not to be more than a few minutes. I had to pry these two away from their television. It's as if the only thing that's happening in the world is inside that box. They can't seem to grasp that their lives may be in imminent danger. She wouldn't come out until she could gather up her purse and 'a few important papers.' She's got her whole life in that purse dangling from her arm, including her last will and testament. The duffel is loaded with photographs. As soon as they're off, I'm heading to the other houses. Send anyone you see to the clubhouse at the end of the park."

"I need to check these houses for Hamilton." Moira tried to push past him.

"Already done. Go to the clubhouse with these people."

"I can help with the evacuation," she started to offer but he raised a hand to stop her.

"You have to stay out of harm's way. Now go!" He turned his back on her as he headed for the next house.

Ignoring him, she ran to the next house with lights on and informed the residents they had to leave immediately, all the time praying that Jessica would be the one to answer the door, to assure her that she and Hamilton were alive and well.

With no time to spare, David went left and continued around to the next street. She continued to the end of the one she was on and met him at the intersection where he once again ordered her to the clubhouse. Instead of arguing, she skirted around a house as if to obey his order then doubled back toward the front of the park.

A patrol car zoomed down Keegan Park Way toward the clubhouse. It stopped when it reached the small group of homeowners who trudged in the same direction. When Moira had rousted the residents from their various Christmas Eve activities, rather than being frightened they were excited by something different happening in their lives, no matter that she just told them the neighborhood might blow up any second.

She couldn't hear what they told the police, but it didn't take long for the driver to put the car in reverse and back up to where Moira stood. She considered running, but knew it would be a fruitless effort.

"You'd better get back to your family, miss," a young woman called to her. "We've got a situation at the other end of the park. You can't go down that way. Want a ride?"

"A situation?" Her family. Her mother and son.

They must have found them. She looked frantically around for Vance or Fern and Vern. Even David would do. But none of them were in sight. Her mother's house, within view, appeared deserted as did the entire surrounding courtyard. Police stood at intervals along the street to keep people at bay. Vance had taken care of that situation as promised. She wondered briefly how much this officer knew about that particular problem.

"A disturbance with one of the residents. It'd be better if you move along in that direction." She pointed toward the clubhouse, opposite the way Moira wanted to be headed.

"Sure," she agreed.

The car moved away as Moira pretended to acquiesce. As soon as the patrol car caught up with the old folks, Moira sidestepped onto the grass and into the center of the median. Then she ran, tripping and stumbling over tree roots, toward the front of the park where there really was a *situation*.

Chapter Twenty-Nine

I overheard the officers asking names and requesting identifications. Carol and Michael answered without betraying my existence. Thank goodness for that; my heartbeat could slow down a bit.

I inched my way around the building and, under cover of darkness, sprinted as fast as my old legs could carry me across the street, my left hip giving me warning flashes of pain, and headed behind the row of houses facing Keegan Bay Court. Bea lived two houses from Hannah, at number five. Pete and Alice would be there.

Putting all our heads together, we should be able to devise a plan to get Hamilton safely away from the park and the police and all those other people looking for him.

As I tiptoed down the sidewalk that ran along the length of Bea's house, I thought about the people we'd run into recently. They were all looking for Moira Robbins or Jessica Robbins. Not one person asked us if we knew where Hamilton Robbins was. Could it be possible that no one knew of his existence?

Maybe we weren't in as much danger as we thought.

More sirens from outside the park. I wondered briefly where they were headed as I stepped into the carport and tapped on Bea's kitchen door.

I looked in through the top half of the window in the door. The interior struck me as awfully dim for four people playing cards. Not even her Christmas tree lights were on. I tapped a little more strongly.

Last I knew Bea had Pete and Alice with her. Her car was in the driveway but no sounds from the house. I knocked until my knuckles hurt, but even as I knocked, I had the sinking feeling they were gone.

I turned around, folded my arms and glowered, wondering where they might have taken the baby after that man with the gun called her with my phone.

That man who stopped me; he must have figured out where

Hamilton was when he used my cell phone. But, from the little bit of conversation I heard, no one told him anything. He had given up and tossed the phone into the bushes.

Now, I didn't even have that to call anyone. But, who would I call? Michael was with the police. Old Howard was passed out on my living room floor. Violet and John seemed to have quit on the project altogether. Justine was taken out of the loop. Bea, Scott, Pete and Alice weren't answering the door. Either they'd fled after the phone call or they were hiding in the secret room, afraid to answer the door.

I stalked around the outside of the house. The sirens grew louder and then stopped as the emergency vehicles approached the park entrance, bringing more people to crawl all over the park and Hamilton was out there somewhere.

When I reached the utility shed, which now encompassed part of one of Hamilton's new rooms, I stopped and pressed my ear to the siding, listening for sounds inside. With no windows, there was no way to tell if they were hiding in there. I tapped, just in case. Nothing.

"It's me, Doll," I whispered into a crevice where the secret door met the wall. Still nothing.

A car passed down the street, the beam of a spotlight flickering over the houses. I remained in place until it reached the end of the street and returned, passing back to Keegan Bay Way. It would head down the street behind me next.

I returned to the front of the house, completely perplexed by Bea's disappearance with Hamilton.

Maybe, I considered, Pete and Alice had taken everyone over to their boat in the marina. I could go check there. That made sense. That had been our plan of last resort.

If Hamilton was in immediate danger of being discovered, Pete and Alice would move him further north to their condo at Amelia Island. They weren't supposed to do that on their own without Michael and me approving; however, I could see how all this activity might have alarmed them. I decided to head for the marina when I heard a loud explosion.

Stunned I spun around trying to determine where the sound had come from. I wanted to collapse right there on the pavement and cry, but I couldn't. I'd made a promise to Jessica that I would keep her grandson safe and now I'd botched it all up and lost him. I had to find that baby and keep him safe only one more day. One more day and we could all get back to our normal lives.

I was on the back end of Keegan Bay Lane, which was six blocks from my place, the direction from which I'd determined the explosion had come. Without knowing for sure where Hamilton was, I chose to continue through backyards toward the marina.

As I picked my way through the darkness I heard footsteps behind me. In the distance, voices shouted and more sirens blared. The sky in the center of the park lit up, with flames and smoke rising rapidly.

Sick at what might be happening to my friends and neighbors, I nevertheless, crossed Keegan Alley and struggled through uneven yards and gardens to Keegan Bay Marina Way, where off to the right, lay the marina.

Hamilton had to be there.

As I scurried down the street in total darkness because the explosion apparently also wiped out the power to the park, I heard Maggie's voice.

"Doll, is that you? What can I do?" She caught my arm.

"Do you know where they took the baby?"

"I saw so many police and sheriff cars. Now your entire street is gone. I've been talking to Justine." She indicated her cell phone. "A man and a woman in an official city car rolled by a few minutes ago looking for you. They said they're from Children's Services here to collect a baby. Our baby?"

She had some nerve calling Hamilton "our" baby but at that point it didn't really matter. What mattered was that she had a cell phone and we could check with all the members to find out who had Hamilton.

"The police have Carol and Michael," I said as I tried to remember Scott's number.

Maggie hadn't learned how to store numbers in her phone, so now it would be a memory challenge to try to call people. I was huffing and puffing by the time we reached the gate to the marina. It stood open.

As we stepped out onto the wooden boardwalk that ran the length of the park along Keegan Bay, another spotlight flashed across the water as a police patrol boat sped into the bay. Maggie and I both scrambled behind the fence.

I headed for the bushes on one side of the street; Maggie disappeared behind Pete's house.

Chapter Thirty

A flash of light. A concussion. Moira had reached a street called Keegan Bay Marina Way and was nearly at the gates when the explosion came. Throwing herself to the ground, she rolled under the nearby bushes and covered her head with both her hands.

People screamed and shouted to one another in the distance, but as she held her breath and waited, there were no more explosions. Voices continued to shout in the distance, but more closely she heard footsteps and men's voices.

She peeked out from under her hiding place, but in the darkness, she couldn't make out the details of the speakers. All she knew was that they were men and they were looking for her. She struggled to make out the words. Kushawan! KARP!

"We know she is here in this development."

"If we fail to eliminate her child this time, we shall have to find new homes in South America."

Her scalp tingled with terror.

"You speak the truth, my brother. But, how to find her? The mother has completely disappeared. If we are to believe the man and woman we have captured, the mother is once again in Switzerland."

"That would be the grandmother, you fool. And we cannot believe these lying pigs."

"Please, do not say that word in my presence."

"I am a Christian; pigs are not a problem for me."

"I will be a problem for you if you continue to defy me. We must find the unnamed child of Hamid and the American woman."

So they haven't found Hamilton either. I can still get him out of the park and away from KARP. Only another twenty-four hours. Moira remained still as the men walked away.

Before she could make any decisions about what to do next, more footsteps approached from the opposite direction. These men spoke in English. IDIOTS. She slid noiselessly back until her spine bumped against the base of the foliage.

"Look, man, just think about it for a minute. We help Eberhardt find the kid, we get a cut."

"We're supposed to follow KARP and round them up. We're investigating terrorists, remember? Not kidnapping babies."

"Any of the others talk to Eberhardt?"

"Not that I know of, why?"

"So, let *them* round up the KARP."

"What's the deal with the kid anyway?"

Their voices were fading as they moved away.

"Who knows? There are sixteen different versions of why she might have run away with him. The one I heard is that the widow is supposed to be brought back to Kushawa and marry one of the other princes or sheiks. They want an heir born over there, not some American kid with a claim to citizenship here."

"I think they want to kill the kid to keep it from becoming another heir."

"It's more likely something to do with oil."

"Then what about the kid they're looking for?"

She couldn't hear the words but she did hear a chuckle as the two men continued down the street.

Her mind reeled. These IDIOTS had no idea why they were trying to rescue—or kidnap—Hamilton. She twisted around to get herself out from under the bush.

She heard a sudden intake of breath. Someone rustled close by. She stopped. Maybe an animal. Still holding her breath, she moved slightly, reaching behind where she felt a piece of fabric.

A whimper.

"Who's there?" she whispered and prayed no one would answer.

No response. She prodded the piece of fabric which covered a soft figure. The body moved out of her reach.

"Who're you?" a trembling voice whispered back.

"I asked first."

"I'm Doll."

"Doll."

"Hush! Someone else is coming."

Doll, Moira thought, the one who was supposed to have Hamilton.

A herd of footsteps ran down the street. As soon as they were gone she scrambled out from under the bush. The rustling continued as Doll managed to extricate herself.

Moira reached down to help her to her feet. "Aren't you

supposed to be taking care of my mother and son? Where are they?"

Doll stared up at Moira, with a wide-eyed incredulous expression.

Then Moira remembered that she looked like a very tall, tattooed biker. "My friends helped me with this disguise. Honestly, it's me, Moira Robbins. My son is Hamilton Robbins."

Doll hesitated for a minute as if to make up her mind and then reached into her jacket pocket and removed a tissue. She handed it to Moira. "You have blood on your face. Now, follow me."

She poked her head around the fence toward the marina then signaled Moira to follow her into a backyard where she led her through the darkness.

"Have you got Hamilton?" she begged as she dabbed at her forehead.

"No, but he's safe. Now you just follow me."

"Doll, is that you? Who's with you?" another woman called out.

Moira saw a sturdy no-nonsense woman emerge from a door she hadn't noticed.

"She says she's Hamilton's mother. I'm taking her to Michael."

"Hamilton's mother is here? What's going on? Why are all these people converging on the park all of a sudden?" she continued as she took Moira by the shoulders and turned her left and right, like a mother inspecting her child. Not looking entirely satisfied, she stepped back and folded her arms.

Moira fumed. "There are KARP and IDIOTS all over this park. We haven't got time to waste. I need at least another twenty-four hours and maybe a few minutes and then he'll be safe. What time is it now?" When neither old woman responded she shouted. "I've had enough of this. Where's my son? What have you done with my mother?"

Moira raised an arm in frustration before she realized she was about to attack a woman as old as her mother. She dropped her hand to her side as Doll pushed herself between them. "Now's not the time, Moira. We have to get to Hamilton. Then we can deal with traitors." She shot a warning glance at the other woman.

"And my mother?"

"You haven't told her?" Maggie said.

Doll seemed to shrink. "There's been no time. Not now, Maggie."

"What about my mother? Isn't she with Hamilton? What the hell's going on?" Her head felt like it was about to explode. She was ready to rip them both apart.

The solid woman squared her shoulders and opened her mouth just as Doll took a wide swing and slugged her on the jaw. Shocked, Moira reflexively caught her as she slowly sagged to the ground.

"What was that all about?"

"No time for that now. We have to find Hamilton! He's still got to be in the park. Maggie will be fine. She's from Vermont. Made of sturdy stuff." Doll held her right hand to her mouth like a puppy licking its wounds.

"I'm going back to my mother's house. It sounded like the explosion came from that direction."

"Good idea," Doll responded. When Moira didn't move immediately, she pointed. "That way."

"They'd better be all right," Moira muttered as she took off running.

Chapter Thirty-One

I hadn't expected the woman to take off quite so quickly. In fact, I'd hoped to lead her slowly back toward the clubhouse where I prayed Michael or the police might be so I could turn her in. How she expected me to believe she was the mother of that sweet child, I didn't know. As much as I could see of her in the glow of the headlights of all the emergency vehicles piling up in our small community, she appeared to be heading exactly where I'd directed her.

Maybe it would be all right. I'd catch up to her sooner or later and meanwhile Pete and Alice should have Hamilton on the boat by now and be ready to take off. I felt badly about hitting poor Maggie like that, but I couldn't have her telling the woman where Hamilton really was.

I was marching along the Keegan Bay Way as fast as I could when I heard the high pitched beep of a golf cart from behind. In the glare of its headlights I couldn't see the driver, but I signaled for whoever it was to stop.

"Merry Christmas, ho-ho-ho!" Jerry Carstairs roared.

Of all people. At least he had his wife with him. Joan, I think. The two of them were obviously feeling no pain. He wore a Santa hat, and she had fuzzy antlers.

"We were having a great time and then all the lights went out. Just like that." He tried to snap his fingers.

"How fast can this thing go?" I asked as I stepped around to the back and climbed onto the bench.

"Hold on to your hat, young lady!" He hooted the horn, roared again with a braying laugh and hit the pedal.

I grabbed the side rails to keep from tumbling out as he raced the cart down the street.

"What's going on?" Joan shouted over the sounds of the fire engines and police cars idling along the way. "Sounds like a fire, but there are way too many police for that. We thought someone's Christmas tree caught light. And we were having so much fun."

"I think it's a little worse than that!" I said as I twisted so I could watch for the fake Moira. She was ahead of us, still jogging up the road.

When we reached Keegan Bay Alley, two blocks away from my house, a policewoman directed Jerry to take a left. No traffic was going beyond that point. When I shouted that my house was up that way, she said, "Can you find some friends to stay with for the night, ma'am? If not, the Red Cross will be here shortly and can help you."

Not the Red Cross too! I jumped, gingerly, from the cart, thanked Jerry and headed through the crowd gathered on the corner. It was going to take some determined pushing and shoving to get through this bunch.

I found the policewoman and told her about Moira claiming to be the mother. "I think she's a fake, though. Her mother said she looks like Princess Grace, and frankly, this girl appears more like one of those biker-babes that comes around every October. A tall blonde with spiked hair dressed in black. She was headed to Number One Keegan Bay Central Court where Jessica Robbins used to live."

I pointed to the rapidly growing crowd of onlookers. Beyond them, Jessica's house was crumbling while firemen hosed down the house next door. Ken and Velma, the Canadians, would have quite a surprise when they came down after Christmas.

She spoke into her walkie-talkie or mobile phone as I went down Keegan Bay Alley which ran behind the houses and headed the back way toward my own house.

Chapter Thirty-Two

Moira approached the nearest uniformed officer, intending to get information. He was speaking on his cell phone.

"Holy crap!" the young man cried out as he slammed shut his phone and reached for his sidearm. "Don't move!"

The flames from her mother's house and the adjacent one cast a brilliant, Dante's Inferno glow on the scene as Moira watched the man move in slow motion, first removing a frighteningly serious looking gun from his holster and simultaneously speaking into his collar. "Officer needs assistance. Quick guys, this is Jeff, get your asses over here. I got one a them!"

It didn't make sense to her. He "got" one of what? She looked around to see what he was talking about, but it didn't take long for her to realize he was referring to her.

"I'm Moira Robbins! I need to find my mother. She lives in that house!" she screamed.

The gun came out of the holster in one hand as handcuffs appeared in the other. "Turn around and put your hands behind your back," he shouted above the commotion.

Moira panicked. Instead of putting her hands behind her back, she sprinted toward the center island, leaped over the police tape and dashed for the opposite side of the park.

She kept running, terrified of being caught. Although she'd been in Keegan Bay Park for a short period of time when she first brought Hamilton to her mother, she had no real sense of the layout.

During her stay here, she'd spent nearly all her time in the house with her mother and Hamilton. She headed once again toward where she thought the marina should be. With any luck she could make it there before anyone caught her. She could hide in a boat.

With a swarm of SWAT team members in pursuit of her, she managed to use the tree trick once again. Her palms were sweating as she grabbed a low branch. Her right hand slipped and for a brief moment she hung in the air, exposed. She reached up, willed her hand to stick and somehow managed to swing up out of sight seconds before two of them would have caught up to her. They continued running in the direction of the marina.

Hanging upside down, she checked for more pursuers and, seeing none, flipped herself upright onto the ground and headed back in the direction she'd come from, but this time she skirted around the crowd.

The entire community was out for the spectacle. Moira went beyond her mother's street, circled around until she figured she was in a position opposite the house. She looked out across the courtyard and saw the devastation. Her mother's house and the one next to it were already gone.

"Don't move. I've got you covered. Hands up."

She froze. "I'm just looking for my mother."

"Sure you are. Step back. Slowly. I got two more of you secured so don't think you can be calling for help."

Heart sinking, shoulders slumped, she moved backward until she felt the hard metal of the weapon at her back. The man guided her into the darkened shadows of the trailer. She turned to see who had stopped her. A tall, lanky man who looked a hundred years old, held a shiny silver gun pointed at her.

"I'm Moira Robbins, and I'm looking for my baby."

"Over there." He waved her toward a palm tree.

In the flickering light from the flames and the emergency vehicles, she saw two men sitting back to back, tied securely to the tree with extension cords. A string of Christmas lights was still attached to one of them.

"Who are they?" she said, pointing to the black clad men.

"Same as you, I'm guessing. Get moving."

"I'm telling you, my name is Moira Robbins. I'm the widow of Hamid al Wafiki and my son is named Hamilton. My mother is Jessica Robbins. She lives—lived—in that house over there." Moira's breath came in short gasps. There had to be a way to make this old fool understand that she wasn't one of the bad guys.

"Those men are trying to find my baby and kill him."

"These two aren't going to be killing anyone, Miss. Now, you just sit right there on the ground with your legs out straight and we'll wait for the others to arrive."

She held her hands out in a pleading gesture. "You don't understand. They're all over the park. You have to help me."

"You know the password?"

"Password?" Her heart sank.

"For The Blenders. You know the password?"

The way he waved the gun in all directions made her jumpy. "What the hell are The Blenders?" she shouted at him. "I want to know where my mother and baby are!"

"If you're really Jessica's daughter then you'd know she passed away over a month ago. Now get over by that tree before I shoot you."

Exhausted and frustrated, she refused to budge. "I'd know if my mother had died…"

Chapter Thirty-Three

I figured my heart rate must be over ninety as I hustled through the yards toward my house. With all the emergency vehicles and police littering the park, I couldn't tell exactly which street they were focusing on. Once I realized it was Keegan Bay Central Court, my street, I couldn't contain myself. I broke into a run.

"Wait up!" Maggie yelled over the din of the fire truck engines and crowd noises.

I thought I'd knocked her out. It didn't matter. The fake Moira ought to be in custody by now.

"Old Howard," I shouted breathlessly. "In my house!"

I heard a gasp from behind and then Maggie was beside me. She must have put herself into overdrive. "What'd you hit me for?" she gasped.

"I was afraid you'd tell that phony where we hid Hamilton."

"I don't *know* where he's hidden. That's what I was going to tell you."

We reached the police tape as the Canadians' house erupted in flames. The pumper turned its hose onto the house, but it was easy to see through the smoldering smoke that it wouldn't make it. At least they had a solid home in Canada.

I cast a worried look in the direction of my own home, the only one I owned. The house looked all right for the moment, but I caught movement at the side of the house; the fake Moira poked her head out for a second before something made her move back out of sight.

There didn't seem to be much hope of finding a police officer. The last I saw of them, they were running in the opposite direction. After the woman, I thought.

I took Maggie by the hand and led her toward the rear of my house. With our path blocked by so many onlookers, it was a good four or five minutes before we traversed the short distance.

Old Howard stood in the shadows, a gun in his hand, a body at his feet, and two men tied to a tree with Christmas tree lights and extension cords. They were shouting at him in some godawful guttural language.

"Howard!" I called to him above the din.

He turned toward me. Had he killed someone? I hoped not. As I moved closer to him I saw that the body was the fake Moira.

"Is she dead?"

"She fainted when I told her about her mother," he said. "Poor thing. She didn't look all that delicate."

I recognized the weapon in his hand as Maggie knelt beside the prone figure. "What are you doing with Barclay's old cigarette lighter?"

"It was all I could find. I had a snooze, and when I woke you and Michael were gone, so I decided to go home, except when I got to the front door I saw these two prowling around the neighborhood. Up to no good, as you can plainly tell by the conflagration out there. So, I went in search of a weapon. Caught these two. More got away, but I couldn't tell you how many. By the way, they don't speak English. Then this one shows up." He indicated the woman on the ground who appeared to be coming around.

"Let's get her up," I suggested. "We need to talk to her. And Howard, wait until we leave before you turn these two over to the police."

Moira, real or otherwise, groaned from her spot on the ground. "I'm Moira Robbins. Can you please tell me what's going on? What happened to my mother? Did they kill her?" Her voice quivered.

I looked down at the woman whose mother described her as "Princess Grace." This kid would make a great Sheena, Queen of the Jungle. I reached down to help her up. "If you had called, you would have known what happened to your mother. As Howard has already pointed out, she passed away several weeks ago. We've been taking care of your son for her. For *you*." I gave her the information bluntly, without feeling.

I couldn't help it; I was angry at her and not too sure I wanted to give Hamilton back to her. Like Howard, I wanted an explanation.

"I called. I called whenever I could but nobody ever answered. You're the last person I spoke to in Keegan Bay. Why didn't you say something?"

She had me there. "As I recall, I expected you to come here in person. It seemed like that would have been the kinder way to tell you."

Maggie tugged at my jacket sleeve. "We'd better go look for Hamilton."

"What do you mean, 'go look for?' You said you're taking care of him." Moira pushed herself upright and towered over us, putting me in mind of those warrior woman movies advertised on television.

"Your mother told us there were men from some group that sounds like a bunch of fish."

"KARP," she said.

"Right. She said they wanted to kill him before he entered his sixth month of age. I promised to keep him safe." I led her and Maggie through the yard behind mine into the next street. "Maggie and I were about to check on our last resort when a police boat arrived. Then the fire trucks came and I remembered Old Howard was sleeping in my house…" I stopped talking, being out of breath and feeling that any excuses I tried to make now would sound lame.

We continued in silence as we crisscrossed through the park toward Keegan Bay Marina Way and the entrance to the marina. Red, blue and orange lights, along with the flames lit the park as if it were Fourth of July. I led them one block beyond Marina Way in order to make a mad dash across Keegan Bay Way. When we reached the median, I had to stop for a rest.

"Lots of police cars in the office lot," Maggie pointed out.

"Lots of emergency vehicles all over the place," I commented. "I just hope Michael will keep his mouth shut and not try to show off about knowing what's going on," I said.

"Who's Michael?"

I looked at Moira. She had been the focus of our interest for so long, it seemed that she should know everything and everybody in our plot. "An ex-Marine who's been instrumental in keeping your son safe. Along with dozens of others here in Keegan Bay."

"But, you've lost him!"

"Temporarily misplaced." I brushed away the accusation with a wave of my hand.

Breath caught, we crossed the other side of Keegan Bay Way once again headed toward the marina. Pete and Alice lived right near the entrance so I stopped there on the off chance they'd taken everyone there. We'd reached the point now that whoever had Hamilton would probably be afraid to answer their door. "Use your cell to call them," I suggested to Maggie.

"I can't. I don't have their number."

"Oh, for Pete's sake." I headed to a bedroom window at the side of the house and then cupped my hands around my mouth and shouted, "There's a bee in her bonnet!"

We waited.

I thought I saw the curtain move.

"Vance!" Moira's voice squeaked, an unlikely sound coming from Warrior Woman.

I looked to see who she was talking to. A group of four men and one short woman, silhouetted in the moonlight, approached. "Moira?" the lead man said.

They ran into each other's arms like lovers in an old movie. "They've lost my baby," she sobbed.

He looked at me over her shoulder.

"Not really," I said weakly before composing myself. "Who are you?"

"Vance Eberhardt, chief of security for Mrs. Wafiki. These are my colleagues, Fern, Vern, Milkweed and Granger. There are a couple of IDIOTS coming along any minute. We've been looking for the KARP."

"Please, please, I need to find Hamilton! They can't get him now. We're so close to the deadline."

The secret panel in the back of Pete and Alice's house slid open as Bea stepped out. She was immediately overwhelmed by an onslaught of people demanding to know where she had Hamilton.

"You had him last." "He was supposed to be at your house!" "Where are the others?" "Who's got the baby?" "Isn't he with Violet and John?" "I brought his supper to Sally's house." "Sally's not even a Blender!"

"Stop shouting at me all at once," Bea screamed into the din. "Let me explain. When the man with the accent called my house earlier, we knew there was trouble so we all came here to Pete's. Then after the police boat passed by, we decided no one would be coming back to the marina, so Pete and Alice prepared to take him to Amelia Island. We couldn't find Michael!" she wailed.

"Last I saw him, he and Carol were occupied by the police. So far, I don't think anybody but us knows about Hamilton. Let's get Moira on the boat."

"Moira? The missing mother?" Bea said.

"I'm Moira, and I haven't been missing. I was leading everyone away from my baby. I didn't want the Kushawans to have him. KARP is after him. They want to kill him; and heaven knows what the IDIOTS are doing."

"IDIOTS are chasing down KARP," I heard Michael say before I saw him at the back of the group. "We have most of them in captivity right now. The police and I rounded up seven of them. Now it looks like with the help of Old Howard, we have nine in custody. They did know about the baby. We were right to make our plan exactly as we did. Well done, everyone." He pushed through the group.

"Now, let's get down to the boat before Pete takes off," I said leading my friends and neighbors onto the dock. "Vance," I asked as we clattered along the wooden boardwalk, "who was actually looking for Moira's baby? Jessica said we had to keep him safe from a variety of terrorists, but was never specific."

Vance stopped with the group behind running into him. "KARP and my security firm were the only ones who knew Hamilton even existed. The acronym stands for Kushawan Alliance of Royal Princes. With Prince Hamid dead, the boy has no official protection and if he dies before he reaches his sixth month, that's Christmas, he doesn't inherit his titles. As of December 26 no one can touch him. "

A baby's cry interrupted Vance's lecture. Moira pushed me aside as she scrambled into the boat, Pete's *Tee-d Off*, toward the sound of the squealing voice.

Alice looked out from the porthole, surprised to see our crowd. Her eyes were huge as she disappeared briefly only to reappear in the doorway, the baby swaddled in blankets in her arms.

A KARP leaped from the boat moored beside them. As he lunged for the baby, Michael shouted. "Quick, over here!"

Alice launched the baby over the heads of the crowd where Michael caught him, but by then the KARP fellow had knocked Alice to the deck, really pissing off Pete, who grabbed a buoy and pounded him on the head.

"Hamilton. My Hamilton..." Moira cried out. She turned to push her way toward Michael, but he was already headed down the road. Moira sprinted after him and as she caught up he whirled around and threw the baby like a football back over her head where the pass was intercepted by Fern. He tucked it under his arm, looked for a goal line and took off with Vern, Milksop and the ranger blocking for him.

"You'll kill him!" Moira screeched in hot pursuit.

They had all returned to us, huffing and puffing. Fern tossed the baby in the air, still clutching the blanket. What emerged was a plastic doll dressed in plastic swaddling, the baby Jesus from the crèche!

"Where is Hamilton?" I heard Moira over the clamor.

I pushed through the crowd and grabbed her hand. "Come with me."

She resisted, yanking her arm away which sent me toppling into the bay. An old lady fully dressed doesn't float well. I felt myself sinking even as I struggled to grab on to the nearest boat. A pair of strong hands grabbed my wrists and I rose from the water sputtering and spitting. After considerable struggle I managed to flop over the side of the boat, landing on the hip with the bursitis, of course. Michael helped me up and back onto the dock. My shoes squished.

"Where's Moira?"

"She was here a moment ago," he said. Now that the main event was over, the rest of the group were heading off the dock and back into the park.

"Do you know where the baby is?" I asked him.

"I thought you had the secret plans," he responded.

I remembered Bob and his social worker and felt ashamed. "I thought I did too. I made one up at the last minute but didn't have time to let anyone who could carry it out know." I frowned. "Except maybe Violet. In the beginning, we talked about ideas and things I'd read in mystery books. She's not very keen on them."

Chilled by the wet clothing, I considered going back to my house to change, but there was no time. We had to find the baby before any more KARP showed. "She isn't all that familiar with the park. Come with me. I'm guessing she'll be going back to our street."

Michael hijacked a golf cart from a couple who appeared oblivious to all the activity, and we raced along the roadway, bouncing over the traffic bumps.

Long before we reached the center of the park where my house was located we could both see that we'd never get through. I showed Michael the back way through the alleys and yards that would get us there and once again, hanging on for dear life, I bounced and skittered all over the bench seat as the golf cart raced through the night.

We reached my back yard where Christmas lights and extensions cords lay strewn about, the villains having been rounded up by the local authorities. Taking Michael's hand, I led him around the side, into my carport and pointed out where Jessica's house used to be. Oh dear. I guess I knew it had blown up, but actually seeing it gone was quite a trauma. I took a moment to catch my breath.

"She won't be around here, that's for sure. Violet's house is dark, too. The entire street is deserted." It only made sense, I supposed. That's why the streets had been cordoned off, to keep people out.

So, where was Hamilton? In the park, for sure. We returned to the cart and hauled off back to Keegan Bay Way and the clubhouse. My scalp suddenly crawled with a thought, a thought so outlandish that I wondered if I'd really thought it all. Surely, no one else in the part had as weird a brain as those two fools, Al and Larry.

We rushed to the pool but as we passed the clothesline, I grabbed Arlene Esteban's bedspread and wrapped it around my shoulders. I was beginning to shiver from the chill. Sure enough, I detected activity around the crèche. Instead of him being in the manger, the baby Jesus rested in Mary's arms. Joseph hovered protectively.

The level of the straw around the animals had risen considerably and the three wise men looked suspiciously like Howard, Scott and there was our Judy in robes with a staff in one hand and a gift of myrrh in the other. I don't suppose anyone would worry whether Melchior was a man or a woman. I nearly collapsed with relief.

Michael applauded. Small groups of residents sat at the tables surrounding the pool. A few leaned on the fence watching the activity, perhaps wondering what would happen next. It wasn't every Christmas Eve that a house blew up or three quarters of the city and county police and emergency vehicles arrived.

"Merry Christmas!" someone called from the crowd.

I looked down at my watch. It had stopped when I got dunked.

"Merry Christmas, Michael," I said, but thought, *Barclay.*

"Twenty-four hours and one minute," came a soft voice from the stable.

"Can you do it?" I spoke to the scene, trying not to look conspicuous in my soggy clothing and bedspread wrap.

"The people are supporting us. Take a look," Scott said. "I've been busy on the net and checking out your KARP and IDIOTS. They won't find any help in here. We can alternate during the night and day. Arrange food for the baby and we'll manage to keep him quiet. If anyone comes poking around, draw the crowd in tight. That should keep them at bay long enough to keep the kid safe."

"The kid" was contentedly sleeping in his mother's arms. The biker babe appearing like a true Madonna with her blue veil covering her head and draped over those horrific clothes. Her gentle smile was beatific. As her mother had said, "A beautiful and graceful young woman." Now I could imagine her as a princess.

Throughout the night, the crowd grew until Keegan Bay Park wound up on the local news for having the first all night Christmas vigil ever in the county. Police remained, maintaining their search for stray KARP and recalcitrant IDIOTS who were still determined to find the KARP themselves.

The clocked ticked through the night. When "Mary" needed to sleep, she snuggled in the back of the manger amongst the animals where, beneath the straw Michael and Vance, ever vigilant, had made themselves at home, ready and able to take on anyone who dared get too close to Hamilton.

Vance's colleagues moved throughout the crowds keeping an

eye out for stray KARP and any other miscreants they might come across.

The baby was delighted to be the center of so much attention and did his eating, sleeping and even suffered his public diaper changing in silence.

At sunrise a priest from the local parish arrived. "Maggie told me what you're all doing, and I think this is a miracle. Please allow me to bless all of you in your efforts to protect and save this infant." He took center stage.

By that time John stepped in to substitute for one of the wise men, and he didn't look happy to be forced aside, but did so grudgingly. Violet, now playing a somewhat aging Mary while Moira rested, smiled into the sunshine.

All moved along smoothly and the hours ticked by. From time to time voices spontaneously began a Christmas carol and others joined in. Noon. Fortunately not too hot. Two o'clock. The crowds grew.

Curiosity seekers, wondering what the big deal was all about, and pleasantly surprised at the generosity of an entire community to give up its traditional Christmas Day festivities to protect one small infant.

"Why not take him into protective custody?" one quick-witted youth suggested.

Michael, reached out from under his bed of straw, clutched the youth by the collar and said, "Listen, kid. We've been protecting this baby for months. You think now, at the last minute, we'll just hand him over to the authorities? You know what would happen if we did that?"

"No."

Michael rattled him.

"No, sir!"

"I'm a Marine. These are my people. See that old woman over there?" I looked around and then realized he was pointing at me. "She's tougher than you'll ever hope to be. We give this baby up and next thing you know it'll be in some government run social services office, and you think they'll give two—care enough to provide armed protection for him for another twenty-four hours?" He swore. "It'll take them three months to decide whether or not he needs protection."

The boy staggered away when Michel let him go. Puffed up and cocky, he strolled over to me. I had changed during the night and now sat comfortably with a hot chocolate and fresh buttered biscuit. Food had begun appearing during the night and kept arriving as the day wore on.

"Nearly midnight. Seven minutes and we're home free," he

said as he picked up a turkey sandwich from the platter. He reached over to the next table for a glass of iced tea.

"Home free," I repeated. "Isn't she beautiful?"

He looked at the stable scene. "Who? Violet?"

"No, Moira. When I first saw her I was prepared to choke her. I resented that she'd been so selfish as to leave Hamilton with Jessica. I wish Jessica could be here to see this. All these people who could have helped her right from the start."

Michael nodded. "You're right. Who'd a thought it?"

"If you don't shut me up, I'll go into a long patriotic, old age and Americans diatribe."

"Stop everything!" a woman's voice shouted from outside the fence. "You have to stop everything."

All eyes turned in the direction of the voice as Wilma Van Hess elbowed her way through the spectators followed by two more local police, a young man and woman, both looking uncomfortable. The woman carried a sheaf of papers.

"We have an injunction," Wilma's shrill voice penetrated the air.

I looked at Michael. Vance popped up from under the straw, his people materializing in front of the crèche as if by magic. Michael backed away from the table and joined the forces protecting Moira and Hamilton.

Two KARP in their black ninja outfits crept to the top of the stable and peered down at us. They looked equally puzzled by the disruption.

Smug, self-satisfied, weasel faced Wilma Van Hess pointed at me as she spoke to the red-faced officers. "She's the one in charge. Give it to her! And you people," she turned to the line of soldiers protecting the crèche and shrieked, "Take it down. Every last stick!"

I sat speechless. Stunned.

"Sorry, ma'am," the girl officer said as she put the papers in my hand. "It's an injunction against having religious displays on public grounds."

"It's Christmas!" I said as I gaped wide-eyed at her.

"Sorry, ma'am. You don't have to actually dismantle it right now, but if you'll just cover it so it doesn't continue to offend people…"

"Boo." A low rumble began in the crowd.

The sound was joined by hisses. The people gathered closer to the crèche, completely enveloping my table, the police officers, Wilma and the stable. Even the two KARP suddenly had no place to hide.

They had only minutes to complete their mission.

"Who is offended?" I shouted.

Sweat poured from my body, I was so angry. Wilma continued to look smug for about thirty seconds longer. The angry mob focused on her.

Without repeating the ugly names they called her, certainly none you'd find in a Christmas card, she realized she'd overstepped her bounds and began to seek a way out.

A trapped and frightened rat. *And so she should be.*

The two officers, changing tack, took her by the elbows and helped ease her around to the back of the stable where the crowds were the thinnest. Hands reached for her and she whined all the way to the police car.

I tossed the paper into the swimming pool. "Ooops," I said. "I wonder what that was about?"

More shouts and screams. I grabbed Vern's wrist and turned it to check her watch.

"Five minutes and thirty seconds," she said before leaping up to find out what the new noise was all about.

Before she could make her way around to the back of the stable, the police officers, having dumped Wilma out onto Keegan Park Way, returned with the two remaining KARP in custody.

Milkweed and Granger separated themselves from guard duty to follow the officers to their patrol car.

"Only a few minutes, and he'll be safe. I wonder what they'll do," I said.

"They," Moira's voice came from the shadows of the stable, "will most likely move to the American West. I think Hamilton will love Colorado or Oklahoma. Maybe even Arizona. No one need ever know he's a prince."

"You'd deny him his heritage?"

Her look shut me up. Those were issues she'd have to deal with through the royal family of Kushawa. If the KARP really did represent them, then maybe they wouldn't care if the boy went missing and grew up a regular American kid. An American kid billionaire.

At two minutes to twelve Larry and Al showed up with three shopping carts full of gifts for Hamilton. "People have been leaving them by the front gate. For some reason, they've adopted him as a Christmas miracle baby. We couldn't be more proud," Larry said.

Al nodded as the two of them began unloading the carts and placing gifts around the stable.

"Considering the amount of money Moira will now be able to

access, I think those can go to a homeless shelter," Vance's voice came from the interior of the stable.

"I'll thank you not to do my thinking for me," Moira said without moving from her kneeling position beside the baby. "That's exactly what I had in mind after I have a chance to open them and thank everyone for their kindness."

"I'll tell you what, Cinderella, how about thinking about this: I have a ranch in Colorado. I could protect you nicely there."

"Really?" I heard a flirtatious lilt to Moira's voice.

"Really. Fern and Vern can join us."

"Oh."

"There are several houses and cabins in the foothills and mountains that make up the property."

"Hmm. I'll have to think about that."

I wondered what Barclay would have thought of the events, especially the last few days. Most likely he would have come out of his office wondering why dinner was late one night. My Barclay. I sighed.

"What are you thinking?" Violet asked.

"Not much." I wiped a tear from my face.

Vance stepped out of the stable arm in arm with Moira. "One thing has puzzled me. When we first entered the park and were skulking about, not one dog barked to alert their owners."

"Look around; do you see any dogs?" I waited a second. "This is a senior citizen park, no dogs allowed. We follow the rules."

About the Author

Veronica was born in New York City, and raised in upstate New York, and Miami. She has lived in six states and spent several years in Iran. At age twelve she won first place for a play she wrote at Girl Scout Camp and thought she had found her niche, but thirty years would pass before she wrote again, selling her first fiction story to a Canadian religious magazine.

In 1994 she founded her own dinner theater company, writing and directing a repertoire of fourteen plays, including a musical, *Murder in Morocco,* which was awarded seven outstanding achievement awards by the New York State Theater Association.

Veronica loves to hear from her readers. You can find and connect with her at the links below.

Twitter: https://twitter.com/VeronicaHHart
Facebook: https://www.facebook.com/veronica.h.hart
Goodreads:
https://www.goodreads.com/author/show/4747858.Veronica_Helen_Hart

~~~

If you enjoyed *The Prince of Keegan Bay*, join Doll and the rest of The Blenders as they find themselves in the middle of another exciting adventure and a murder to solve.

MURDER.
MYSTERY.

JUST ANOTHER DAY FOR THE BLENDERS.

TURN THE PAGE
FOR A PEEK!

Chapter One

Keegan Bay Park, Florida

"I am not marrying Michael because I am still married to Barclay. Is that a good enough reason?" I shouted at my friend, Violet.

Violet only smiled. "Calm down, Doll. You know as well as I it's time to do something with your life. It's been over five years since Barclay went missing."

"You think I don't know that? I count the days, the minutes, hoping every second he'll walk through the door." I wiped an unwelcome tear from my eye, finished my drink and headed toward the liquor cabinet.

"Go ahead. Have another. And what will he find if he returns? You sitting here, feeling sorry for yourself. Drowning your sorrows in scotch." She pushed her stout body up from the chair near the bow window where we liked to have our afternoon "tea."

"You're not leaving already? You've barely touched your drink."

"I have my literacy group at the jail tonight, and I also need to feed John before he sets off for the theater."

"Oh, go ahead." I waved my glass at her, splashing some of the precious liquid onto the floor. "Rub it in how busy you two are. Fine. I'll sit here and enjoy my drink before I *feed* myself."

"You could join me tonight. The girls could use all the help we can give them. They're incarcerated for the poor choices they made in their lives. It's shocking how many of them are functionally illiterate. Imagine how thrilled they'd be to have a real published author to work with them."

I waved her off, sending more scotch to the floor. "If they're illiterate they won't know about me. Just go. I'll think of something. I had a new idea for a book, maybe I'll work on that."

"What happened to the last one you started?"

After sipping some of the drink, I returned to the chair opposite where Violet had been. She stood to the side of it, ready to escape. "It didn't gel."

"Maybe if you wrote first thing in the morning…"

"When I'm sober? Is that what you were about to say? Why don't you and your cronies leave me alone? Go be goody-two-shoes at the jail and tell the people here in the park to mind their own business. They can play bingo and watch their game shows." I turned my back on her, feeling lousy about the way I'd spoken.

She placed her hand gently on my shoulder. "Look, Doll, I'm your closest friend in the park."

"Only because you're the nearest year-round neighbor. Go away."

Her fingers tightened, but she didn't leave. I struggled to keep my face under control, fearing the tears would flow if she showed me any more kindness.

"People have been talking to me about you. I remind them about your missing husband and they all say the same thing."

"I know. It's time to get over it, declare him dead, and move on with my life." That word, *dead*, stuck in my throat. My eyes burned. She had to leave immediately or I would lose control altogether.

"That's right," she answered softly as she removed her hand. I listened to her footsteps as she headed for the front door.

At that moment the kitchen door burst open.

"Doll! You here?" Michael's voice boomed.

"Where else would I be?"

"Afternoon, Violet, just leaving?" His heavy footsteps crossed the living room. He scrubbed his hand over my hair then kissed me on the cheek. "Why are you crying?"

"Goodbye," Violet said. The door closed.

"Don't you ever knock before entering someone's trailer?"

"I did, and it's a manufactured home, not a trailer. Are you going to turn around and be hospitable or do I have to get my own drink?"

"Do what you like." I turned around.

He took Violet's place in the chair. Like a pair of rotating therapists, those two. "I'll skip it. New movie; want to go? It's about Iran. I know you and Barclay lived there once."

The man was far too cheerful for me. "The subject of Barclay is not open for discussion. And no, I do not want to go to the movies tonight."

"All right then, what *do* you want to do?"

"I want to be left alone."

"Can't do that, Doll. How about marrying me then we can be

alone together? You and me carousing the Florida waterways in my little boat." He leaned back in the chair, placed his right ankle on his left knee, looking like he was prepared to stay.

"You know I can't marry you. I'm already married. How many times have we been through this? Besides, I'd lose Barclay's social security."

A former Marine, Michael was by far the most fit and handsomest man in the entire community. He proposed on a regular basis. Why couldn't he turn those heavily lashed green eyes on some other woman, one desperate to have a man in her life?

"As if you need it after that huge inheritance."

Ignoring his reference to my newfound wealth, I said, "I might after I buy a house."

"What house?" His foot thumped to the floor, and he leaned forward.

"I've been thinking about it. This trailer is far too small. Always has been. When we first bought here we both agreed we didn't want to live in a trailer, but we couldn't find a house we could afford. Now that housing values are down and I have the means, it's time. Barclay will be so happy when he comes home to find we have a lovely new house that won't blow away with the first hurricane." The thought cheered me, and I didn't care what Michael had to say about it.

"That's a great idea, Doll. Where do you plan to look? Have you done anything about it yet? Called a real estate company? Will you sell this one or rent it out?"

Taken aback by his enthusiasm, I remained silent.

"Come on. I'll help. You need something to keep you occupied and searching for a house and then getting it all fixed up..."

"You mean instead of drinking alone every night?"

"I didn't say that."

"You didn't have to. Violet told me people are talking. I don't drink that much, you know. Only when people are around, so it seems like a lot."

"You might fool yourself, Doll, but you don't fool me. I'm here often enough to see those bottles replaced too often. I'd be happy to go to an AA meeting with you if you're worried about going alone."

"I don't need AA. I don't need you to go anywhere with me." I stood and stumbled into Michael as he stood at the same time. "I need to find a damned house!"

He grabbed me and held me in his arms. In spite of my anger, his warm embrace comforted me. Michael was the only man in the park taller than I, and one of the few still fit and active. All the widows in the park wanted to marry him except me. I wasn't a widow.

~ * ~

A week later Michael and I had visited sixteen houses which almost fit my criteria, and they were all in the right price range. Yet each one either had a significant drawback such as location, too small a garage, too large a yard or simply did not please me.

We sat at a donut shop drinking coffee. "I don't think you're serious about this house business, Doll. Looks to me that you're just filling your days."

"You don't have to come with me, you know, though I enjoy your company."

He made me laugh. At every house, as I looked for the good, he pointed out the negative with humor. At the most recent house, because it was so huge, he wondered how many roommates I wanted.

"Roommates?" I asked as I wandered through a modern, plastic looking living room.

"Evidence of rats in the kitchen," he called to me from that room. "And I saw two snakes in the back yard already, and we haven't even finished looking."

My scalp crawled at that. I'd thought he was referring to the size of the house. We scurried like the unseen rats from that one.

"I'll know it when I see it. You don't have to come with me." I picked up a cinnamon cruller and took a bite, feeling justified in eating it because of all the walking we'd done in our house hunt.

"In spite of your fears about the park, and your house being a mobile home, it has been there for twenty years and not moved an inch during any of the hurricanes that blew through. You have a nice layout there with the three bedrooms. A nice lot and even three new houses in your cul-de-sac. Why not stay?" He dunked his donut, leaving snowflakes of confectioner's sugar floating on top. "Plus," he held up a sticky finger, "we have the marina and my boat close by."

"I want a real house."

~ * ~

The instant I saw it, I knew my new address. My real estate agent, Rex, stopped in front of a house with an overgrown yard, majestic palm trees, and a welcoming, though leaf-strewn walkway leading to the front door.

Beaming, I floated through the four bedrooms, the oversized living room, the updated and modern kitchen, and most of all the enclosed pool deck, landscaped as a tropical garden, a waterfall at one end of the pool and even a hot tub-spa surrounded by tropical foliage. The house enclosed the pool on two sides. The third side had a high fence separating the property from the neighbors. The fourth side faced the Halifax River. A large screen room covered the entire pool and deck. The area would be very private.

"It's on the waterway too. You can motor across the river and be here in no time," I said.

Michael folded his arms and studied the area beyond the landscaped pool. "Maybe," he answered then followed me into the bedroom that opened off the deck.

"It looks like someone is still living here." I closed the door to a closet full of clothing.

"One of the heirs." Rex checked his clipboard. "Missandra Logan is living here temporarily to sell off the furniture and clear out the house," he said. "Come check out these bathrooms. Three of them, one nicer than the other."

We finished the tour. "What next? I like this place, everything about it except the furnishings. They're so wrong for such a Florida house."

He suggested an amount to offer, which I did. Then he explained the process. The seller's agent would present the offer to the owners and the agent would get back to me in a few days. Which he did, two days later. The family accepted my offer and a closing date would be set.

"This is an easy one," he said. "It's an estate sale, and there's no mortgage. The heirs want to get rid of it. They all have their own homes and have no need of another. They just want the money. We should be finished with the paperwork, title search, all that in less than a month. We'll set the closing for thirty days from now. How's that?"

I shrugged. None of that mattered. "Fine, as long as the heir empties it by then."

Barclay would love this house. I knew it in my heart. I wrote out a check for a significant down payment, leaving a relatively small balance.

"Come on." I took Michael by the arm. "We have to call a meeting of The Blenders and let them know."

He didn't seem as excited by the prospect as I did. The Blenders had become a close-knit group of friends last winter after we worked together for months to save the life of an infant who had been left in the park.

With incompetent ninja-like terrorists and government officials stalking around the park, blowing up several houses in the process, we Blenders, using skills compiled in our several lifetimes, managed to thwart them. Thank goodness no one was killed in the process.

~ * ~

Though my friends remained cool toward me, curiosity got the best of them so I drove them one at a time past my "new" house. During the first week, we saw no evidence of a pending yard sale. Maybe, I reasoned, Missandra donated everything to charity.

On Tuesday of the second week, three weeks before the closing, handwritten signs appeared along the streets leading to the house advertising a *giant estate sale*. It was scheduled for Saturday only. Maggie, my stalwart Vermont friend from the park, was my guest *du jour* as we drove past the house.

The grass stood at least a foot high. The shrubs looked scraggly. The hand printed sign belonged in a run-down neighborhood, not this one. I felt embarrassed to show my new home to Maggie.

"Don't worry. I'll bet it's beautiful inside," she said.

"It is," I insisted, now hardly remembering the location of all the bedrooms and bathrooms. The pool and deck area remained firmly imprinted on my mind.

Chapter Two

Costa Rica

Melvin Hobson strode through the front door, heedless of the sand he tracked into the living room. His glass needed refilling and the sun wouldn't last much longer. As he passed the large plate glass mirror, he averted his eyes, wanting to preserve his self-image of a svelte body and rich crop of dark brown hair. After his cataract surgery next month, he would be a completely new man.

He set his plastic glass on the counter, opened the fridge, grabbed a light beer, and then slammed the door shut quickly. Everything ran on a generator in the remote beach community.

His cell phone, which he had left on the counter to avoid getting it wet or damaged by the sand, indicated he had a message. Sighing he checked to see who called, dreading to know. Sure enough, Missy, otherwise known as Missandra Logan. With another deep sigh he played the message.

Melvin cringed when he heard the whining voice. "Mel, I miss you so. What did I do? Why do you hate me after all we meant to one another?" He closed his eyes and shuddered. "I have some good news for you. We sold the house. I'll have the money in less than thirty days. We can take that trip now. Oh, please call me, Mel. We have so much to talk about to plan—"

Her voice was cut off by the time limit on the service.

"Sold the house, huh?" He calculated what her take would be.

He forgot how many siblings had to share in the profits, but still, she'd collect at least a hundred grand. Depends on how much it went for in this crazy depressed market. He smiled. Maybe he could tolerate her a little longer.

"Hey, Melvin," a girl called from outside. "We need another player. You up for some volleyball?"

The phone dropped from his hand like a hot coal. "Be right out, sweetness!"

"Bring some beers, will ya?" Her voice faded as she continued to run toward the volleyball net one of the college groups set up four cottages down.

He beamed. This was what he loved about the place. No one cared that he was older than the rest of them. They liked him anyway. He pulled a full six-pack from the fridge, grabbed a towel and headed out. The kids warmed up, batting the ball back and forth over the net. He loved the way the girls' scantily covered breasts bobbled. And all those cute little asses. If only he could be twenty-one again.

"Here I am boys and girls and here's the beer. There's plenty more where this came from. Now, whose side am I on?"

Missy remained absent from his thoughts the rest of the day and far into the night until the phone sang to him. *The Girl from Ipanema.* Oh how he wished.

"Hello, Missy. Sorry I didn't return your call earlier. I've been horribly busy at work." He made his voice dull, depressed. She believed he was in Argentina working on a building project. He wasn't about to tell her otherwise.

"Oh, Mel. How I missed your voice, your touch. Just the sight of you would heal me. Did you get my message about the house?"

"Yes, it's very good news for you."

"I thought so, too. But it isn't, Mel. It's terrible. Camille says she wants Mommy's furs and her favorite chair. She wants most of the jewelry too. Charlie is sure to show up with his greedy bitch of a wife and they'll take whatever they want."

"I suppose they're entitled to some things." Melvin opened a top cupboard and brought out a bottle of rum. He mixed a generous portion with a cold Diet Coke.

"They're pillaging! This was *my* home. They were gone by the time Mommy and Daddy moved in here." Her voice broke. "They hate me because I didn't want to sell it and now they're all going to blame me because we didn't get as much as we should have for it."

"Don't cry." She had his attention. "So. How much did you get?"

"I can't tell you that until after the closing. There are so many expenses, you know."

He gritted his teeth and tried again. "Well, you mentioned a trip. I just wanted to know what kind of plans I should make."

"Oh, my darling, we can plan together. Just please see if you can take the time off and come be with me. I could use your help in selling all this furniture. Nobody wants to pay—they expect me to practically give it away."

"My pet, the furniture never really was yours. Why don't you sell to the first bidder and get rid of it? Whoever bought the place will want to put their own things in there. You haven't all that much time."

Just tell me the damned figure!

"Some old lady bought it."

"What does that mean?"

He pictured her skinny little shoulders shrugging. "I don't know. Just please come as soon as you can."

"I'll see what I can do."

What's next on your reading list?

Champagne Book Group promises to bring to readers fiction at its finest.

Discover your next
fine read at Champagne Book Group!
www.champagnebooks.com

We are delighted to invite you to receive exclusive rewards. Join our Facebook group for VIP savings, bonus content, early access to new ideas we've cooked up, learn about special events for our readers, and sneak peeks at our fabulous titles.

https://www.facebook.com/groups/ChampagneBookClub/

Made in the USA
Monee, IL
29 August 2021

76780036R00125